PRAISE FOR DHARMA KELLEHER

"Kelleher's characterizations and voice are fresh and new, the action comes fast and furious."

GREG HERREN, AUTHOR OF *BATON ROUGE BINGO*

"Dharma Kelleher has created one of the most unique characters in crime fiction. She takes readers on a thrilling ride that will have you turning pages into the wee hours of the morning!"

RENEE JAMES, AUTHOR OF *SEVEN SUSPECTS*

The action-packed scenarios don't quit, right up to the story's unexpected, satisfying resolution."

MIDWEST BOOK REVIEW

RED MARKET

RED MARKET

A JINX BALLOU CRIME THRILLER

DHARMA KELLEHER

RED MARKET: A JINX BALLOU CRIME THRILLER

Published by Dark Pariah Press, Phoenix, Arizona.

Cover design: JoAnna Kelleher

Ebook ISBN: 978-1-952128-27-1

Paperback ISBN: 978-1-952128-29-5

Hardcover ISBN: 978-1-952128-28-8

To my wonderful wife, Eileen. Even after more than twenty years, my heart skips a beat every time I see your lovely face.

I also dedicate this book to all of the loving, supportive parents of transgender kids. You are heroes.

CHAPTER 1

THE JAWS OF DEATH

"ANYBODY GOT eyes on the target? Over," I called into my radio.

"Negative, boss," replied Nathaniel "Rodeo" Kwan, my second-in-command. "No sign of him by the front of the house. Over."

I searched behind the line of overgrown shrubs that grew along the back windows. Our target enjoyed playing hide-and-seek, like many of the fugitives I was assigned to apprehend. And this one was a small guy, so he could hide in a lot of tight spaces. But he wasn't back there.

I leapt atop a cinder-block wall that separated the residential backyard from the business on the next street over. The added six-foot height gave me a better view of the surrounding properties. No fences separated them from one another, so the target could be anywhere.

I pulled my binoculars from my tactical belt and scanned the area. A cloud of smoke partially obscured my view. The next-door neighbor was grilling food. The aroma of mesquite and roasting sweet corn drifted in. My mouth watered.

It was five thirty on a Friday afternoon, and I hadn't eaten anything since breakfast. My team and I had spent the better part of the day chasing down a drug dealer who'd jumped bail. Now we had one more fugitive to catch before we called it a day.

When the smoke from the grill cleared, I spotted movement a hundred feet on the other side. "I see him. Behind the Davidsons' house. Who's over there? Over."

"The Davidsons'?" Caden Morrow asked, sounding out of breath. He had recently rejoined my crew after a serious gunshot wound sidelined him a few years earlier. "Which one's that? Over."

"Sage-green house." I leapt off the wall. "Second one west of the corner. Over."

"I'm across the street. Beige stucco with solar panels. Almost had him. Just too damn fast. Should we tase him if we get close? Over."

"No, it might kill him. Z? Where are you? Over."

"Three houses west of you, Jinxie. Over." Zahara Washington, the fourth member of our team, was a former MMA fighter turned bounty hunter.

"Shit."

"I can come around from the east side," Rodeo replied. "We can box him in. Over."

"Okay. Let's do it. Caden, join him. Z, back me up on the west side. Over."

She replied immediately, "Jinxie, we got bogies. Over."

"Bogies? What do you mean? Over."

"Coyotes. Three—no, four of them. Heading your direction. Over."

Living close to downtown Phoenix, I rarely saw coyotes in the neighborhood. But for the past few years, our usually wet monsoon seasons had been all but non-soon seasons. Only a few days of rain happened during the last summer, which further exacerbated our ongoing drought.

Desperate for water and food, coyotes, bobcats, and javelinas now wandered deeper into urban neighborhoods.

A day earlier, a security camera caught a puma padding down the streets of Old Town Scottsdale on the other side of the Valley, just as tourist season was beginning.

"Try to scare them off," I instructed Zahara. "The rest of us will zero in on the target. Over."

I strode east, keeping my eye on the quarry.

A man in a Hawaiian-style shirt approached the grill, holding a plate of raw steaks. He smiled nervously when he saw me, clearly not used to seeing me in my bounty-hunter gear. "Jinx? What's going on?"

I snatched a steak from his plate. "Need to borrow this, Harold."

"Hey!" he protested. "Jinx! What the hell?"

I ignored him, focusing instead on the target. When I was within fifty feet of him, I stopped by a flagstone path that led from a neighbor's porch to an empty birdbath.

"Oh, Teddy," I called and waved the steak in the air. "Look what I've got."

Teddy turned and met my eyes. For a moment, I thought he would bolt again. Instead, he started wagging his tail. A good sign.

Rather than continue toward him, I simply crouched down and whistled as I would to my golden retriever, Diana the Wonder Dog. Teddy trotted toward me, a wary look in his eyes. The golden light of sunset made his tan fur look like burnished bronze.

In the distance, Caden and Rodeo were closing in. I gestured for them to keep their distance. Didn't want to spook the little guy.

When Teddy was a few feet away, he stopped, clearly reassessing the situation. He knew me, but I wasn't sure if he'd seen me in all my gear—ballistic vest, tactical belt, boots.

"Hey, buddy," I crooned. "You hungry after all that running?"

Again, his tail wagged. He made the final approach. I resisted the urge to grab him right away and instead laid the raw steak on a flagstone. Teddy bit into it, tail wagging faster.

I picked him up along with the steak, allowing him to enjoy his reward. "Good boy."

"Jinx, you have any idea how much that steak cost?" Harold stood nearby with a pissed look on his face.

I glanced at the plate. Three more raw steaks glistened in the harsh rays of the dying day's sunlight. "Sorry, Harold. I'll pay you back. Just had to grab Teddy before the coyotes got him."

"Devon and I have guests over. Now we're one steak short."

"Sorry. Once I return Teddy here to Adelina, I'll run over to Fry's and grab you some more."

"These steaks are grain-fed beef from A.J.'s."

I sighed. A.J.'s Fine Foods was an upscale grocery store filled with gourmet items like Meyer lemons, five different colors of carrots, and sashimi-grade fish—the kind of ingredients featured on cooking shows but unavailable at standard chain supermarkets.

"Fine, I'll run up to A.J.'s and get you a few grain-fed steaks."

"Finally got him, I see." Z rubbed Teddy's head as he licked his lips, the steak nothing more than a fond memory. "He's a cute little guy."

Z reminded me of a much younger Grace Jones. Athletic build, close-cropped hair, intense eyes, and dark skin. But as tough as she was, she had a gentle heart, often reassuring our captured fugitives everything would be okay.

As the four of us trekked back to Teddy's home, I asked her, "What about the coyotes?"

"Chased them off for now, but they're still prowling the

neighborhood. Best we get him inside with his mommy before they return."

"We get steak, too?" Caden wasn't a tall guy, perhaps because he was trans. But in the past year, he had definitely bulked up and was looking ripped, either from the testosterone injections or a lot of time at the gym. Probably both.

After quitting the team a few years ago, Caden had worked an office job for a while. Less dangerous, no one shooting at him, better benefits. But eventually, he realized he missed the excitement. I, for one, was happy to have him back.

"You expect me to buy all y'all dinner?" I asked, half joking.

"We missed lunch, boss." Rodeo lowered his ever-present Stetson to shield his eyes from the glaring sunlight.

"Yeah, all right. Go grab us a table at Denver Steak House. I'll be along as soon as I drop off Teddy here and pick up some more meat for my neighbor."

I carried Teddy a couple of doors down to my next-door neighbor, Adelina Bosco.

Just as I stepped into Adelina's yard, my eyes registered movement in the hazy twilight. A coyote sauntered between the front door of the house and me. Another two crept up to the side of me, boxing me in.

Teddy got squirrelly in my arms and started whimpering. The coyotes barked and circled, looking for vulnerabilities. I counted four of them now, all in full predator mode, hackles up and teeth bared.

Coyotes were generally timid around humans. But a small dog like Teddy would make a nice dinner. I was sure the smell of raw meat didn't help. I remembered my mantra —WWWWD. What would Wonder Woman do? That didn't help much either. I couldn't outrun the critters.

"Get the hell outta here!" I yelled.

A coyote charged. I drove a steel-toed boot into its ribs

before it could lunge at Teddy. It squealed and veered off but remained too close for comfort. I didn't really want to hurt them, but they weren't giving me many options.

Teddy became increasingly frantic and harder to hold. I tightened my grip. He was a fierce little guy who might fend off one if he was lucky. But we were outnumbered. If he got loose again, he was coyote chow.

The door opened. Adelina stepped out, stunning as always. She wore a bright-orange sundress with matching sandals that complemented her deeply tanned skin. Adelina looked beautiful but vulnerable in this situation.

"Get back inside," I warned her.

Another coyote charged me and leapt. I countered with a roundhouse kick, nearly dropping Teddy into the waiting jaws of a coyote that had snuck alongside unseen. Teddy scratched my neck and tried to climb atop my shoulders, desperate to avoid the circling predators on the ground.

I held him with an iron grip in one arm, drew my Taser, and fired at the coyote at my feet. Tasing a human at this distance would have been ineffective. But both darts hit my small assailant.

When the juice flowed, the coyote let out a sharp cry and fell over, quivering. Its pack members closed in. There were six of them now. I could not possibly reload the Taser with one hand.

The report of a shotgun thundered, followed by a sharp, pitiful yelp from a coyote. No blood. It had been hit with a beanbag round. A second beanbag struck one of the coyote's pack members. The rest of them retreated to a safer distance.

Zahara appeared on my right. "Pup okay?"

Teddy was practically screaming in terror, even though the danger had largely passed. I could feel wetness on my neck.

"Dog's okay. Not sure about me."

The tased coyote was regaining control of its muscles.

Zahara stepped between us and ripped the wired darts from the wild canine's coat. It yelped and took off after its fellows.

"Thanks for the assist."

"Happy to."

By the time I got to the front door, Adelina was stepping back out. She smelled of hibiscus. "Are they gone?"

"For now." I handed over the pup. Teddy was happy to see her.

"Teadoro, perro malo!" She gave us both a worried smile and took him from my arms. "Oh my goodness, Jinx, your neck's bleeding."

I touched it, and my hand came away with a red smear. "I've survived worse."

"Hi, Adelina, I'm Zahara."

I blushed, embarrassed by my lack of social skills. "Sorry. Z here's a member of my team. She's the one who saved both the pooch and me."

"Thanks so much, both of you. Teddy normally doesn't run out when I open the door."

"After tonight, I doubt he will again," Zahara said, smirking.

"What do I owe you?"

"Owe us?" I laughed. "Nothing. I'm just glad Teddy's safe."

"You both have a good night."

When she went inside, I told Zahara I'd meet her at the restaurant.

As I jogged home, I pulled up the FamFinder app on my phone. My husband, Conor, and I used it sometimes to see where the other was. According to the app's geolocator, Conor was in downtown Glendale.

I called him.

"Hey, love! What's the craic?" he asked in his lovely Irish brogue.

"The craic is good, babe. The crew and I are headed to Denver Steak House. Care to join us?"

"Aye, love, save us a seat. We're just dropping one off at the Glendale City Jail. Should be along in an hour."

"See ya soon!"

I hung up and called Rodeo to let him know our party just grew from four to eight. Then I ran inside and quickly bandaged my neck, changed out of my gear, and drove to A.J.'s.

Harold and I would probably never be friends. He'd never said anything specific, but I didn't think he liked that I was transgender. I was sure the mob of hateful bigots that swarmed our street a year earlier didn't help.

Or maybe they didn't enjoy living a few doors down from a couple of professional bounty hunters.

Still, I tried to maintain at least a civil relationship with my neighbors. And his wife, Devon, was always nice to me.

I grabbed a bouquet of flowers and the package of the grain-fed sirloin steaks.

Devon answered the door when I arrived. "Sorry for stealing one of your steaks earlier. Hope I didn't ruin your dinner party."

She waved it off. "We managed. But thank you. These flowers are lovely. You shouldn't have."

I shrugged.

"Was that gunfire I heard earlier?" she asked.

"Beanbag rounds to fend off a pack of hungry coyotes that tried to eat Adelina's dog. No bullets. No drive-by. Nothing to be concerned about."

"Oh, okay." She didn't look convinced. "Well, have a good night."

I rushed back to my SUV and drove to meet the others at the steakhouse.

CHAPTER 2
LIBERTY FOR SOME

THE DENVER STEAK House lobby was standing room only when I arrived, with half of those waiting either my team or my husband's.

In addition to its usual cowboy theme, the place was decked out with autumn colors and Halloween decorations. The night of ghosts, ghoulies, and trick-or-treaters was a week and a half away.

"Hey, boss," Rodeo fist-pumped me when I joined everyone by the hostess stand. "Should be only a few more minutes for our table."

"Thanks."

"How's your neck?"

"I'll live." When I cleaned it, I noticed several long scratches, a few of them deep. None of them life-threatening. More irritatingly painful than anything.

"There's my girl!" My husband, Conor Doyle, stepped out of the men's room. His ruddy freckled face was damp where he had apparently tried to freshen up. He still smelled of sweat, but I didn't care. He was still the sexiest man alive, as far as I was concerned. I kissed him.

"Little bird told me ya branched out into the dog-fetching

business." He winked, and his emerald eyes turned my knees to pudding.

Suddenly, I was less hungry for steak and had more of an appetite for something else. "Just helping out a neighbor."

"Heard it got a wee tense."

"Nothing I can't handle. Well, provided Z's next to me with the shotgun."

"Aye, she's a good one to have around."

"We'll have to be careful taking Diana for a run, especially around dusk and early morning."

"Aye, been seeing more of them buggers of late. Lovely creatures, coyotes, but they don't play well with household pets."

"Jinx Ballou, party of eight," someone announced over the intercom. "Your table is ready."

We followed the young hostess to a long table near the back, who then disappeared after she took our drink orders.

Across from me sat a man with the build of Jack Reacher. His name was Paul Dzundza, but everyone called him Deez. He and Conor co-owned Viper Fugitive Recovery, where I'd worked for a few years before starting my own company.

"Hey, Jinxie!" Deez said. "What happened to your neck? Conor been giving you hickeys again?"

I blushed at his teasing. His question immediately drew my attention to the scar on his own neck, where he'd been shot six years earlier while taking down a fugitive.

Guilt still plagued me whenever I noticed it, because I should have spotted the guy before he got the jump on us.

"No, smartass. I was holding a neighbor's dog when a pack of hungry coyotes showed up."

"The pup all right?"

"Fine. Thanks to Z."

For an instant, I caught Z's glance down the table. She winked and went back to talking with Byrd, another member of Conor and Deez's team.

I was grateful to be in such good company. We were a strange mix of backgrounds—Black, Asian, white, straight, gay, pansexual, cisgender, and trans—but all professionals, working in an often misunderstood profession. Life was good.

"You hear about Womyn Born Womyn?" Caden, who was sitting to my left, asked after our server brought our drinks and took our dinner orders.

My happy thoughts evaporated in a flash of anger. The transphobic nonprofit organization known as Womyn Born Womyn had wrecked my wedding and nearly killed my father the previous year.

"I thought they disbanded after most of them went to prison."

Caden shook his head. "Elise Holbrook's running the show now. She got a suspended sentence, as did Leslie Reinhardt. They teamed up with the Patriots of Liberty Caucus to push new legislation targeting trans kids. Scuttlebutt is that this bill has legs. The Republicans are using it to win big in the November election."

"Shit. What's in the bill?"

"Banning trans kids from restrooms based on their gender identity. Banning them from all sports. Forbidding teachers from recognizing trans kids' new names or pronouns. But the real kicker is that it declares gender-affirming care to be child abuse. Prescribing hormone blockers and cross-gender hormones for anyone under twenty-one will be a class two felony."

"Are you kidding me? They can't do that!"

"Doesn't stop them from trying."

My appetite vanished. The whole thing was absurd. It was still rare enough for trans kids to have supportive parents. Those that didn't often took their own lives or ended up on the streets doing sex work or worse.

I'd been lucky. While my parents had been shocked when

I came out at age eleven, they accepted me wholeheartedly. They helped me get on hormone blockers and, eventually, estrogen under the care of my pediatrician. And soon after my eighteenth birthday, they paid for my gender confirmation surgery.

Now these fucking ignorant fascists wanted to make all of that illegal. How many kids would die just so that these politicians could attract more voters? The whole thing would be ironic if it wasn't so cruel.

The real irony was that while many members of Womyn Born Womyn identified as lesbian, they had allied themselves with the ultra-right lobbyists of the Patriots of Liberty Caucus despite their extreme misogyny and anti-LGBT stance. Fascism made for strange bedfellows.

I had done all I could. I had written my representatives. I had participated in rallies and public hearings. But it didn't matter. The majority of the politicians didn't care about the truth or medical science or protecting trans people. They relished cruelty, control, and power.

"Anything we can do to stop them?" I asked Caden.

He shrugged. "Lambda Legal and the ACLU have agreed to fight any anti-trans legislation in the courts. They've had some success in other states where bills like this got passed."

"Still, this is the last thing that trans kids and their families need right now."

"Agreed."

When my dinner came, I picked at it despite my body's need for nourishment. "I'm glad Lambda's finally fighting for our rights, but maybe it's time for another Stonewall. Sometimes, it takes throwing a few bricks to get people to wake the fuck up."

"Not sure violence is the answer, love," Conor clasped his strong hand around mine. "The Stonewall riots might've kicked off the queer rights movement in the States, but it's not what changed people's minds."

"No, but it galvanized our community. And it sent a message to the authorities that we wouldn't be bullied anymore. If they're going to use the law as a weapon against us, then let us be outlaws."

"Trust me, Jinxie, my people have been fighting the loyalists in Northern Ireland for the better part of a century. Cost my sister her life and my da his freedom. And for what? The Brits are still in charge. And the Protestants still hate the Catholics. Not bloody worth it."

"Then what's the answer? Stick our heads in the sand and hope it goes away on its own?"

He sighed and squeezed my hand. "I don't know, love. Protect the ones ya love however ya can. Beyond that, I haven't a clue."

I stared at my half-eaten dinner as the wheels in my mind turned. *What can I do to protect the ones I love? What can I do to protect trans kids fighting for their right to exist?* I didn't have a clue either.

CHAPTER 3

NEW ASSIGNMENTS

THE FOLLOWING MONDAY, I was sitting in the Assurity Bail Bonds office in downtown Phoenix. What was once owner Sadie Levinson's one-woman operation was a thriving business with a team of bail bond agents operating around the clock.

That made my life as a freelance bounty hunter easier because I didn't have to get jobs from so many other agencies. Of course, that also meant putting more of my eggs into one basket, something that had bitten me in the past a few times.

On the plus side, my relationship with Sadie had warmed considerably over the past year since my wedding.

I laid a couple of body receipts on her desk, proof of the bail jumpers I had apprehended on her behalf.

"How's your father doing, Jinx?" Sadie asked.

"He's doing well. Planning to return to work soon."

"Been a long recovery."

"Yeah." Before my dad was shot at my wedding, Sadie had never been much for small talk. "For a while, we weren't sure he'd ever be able to go back to work. At least not as a psychologist. But if his own therapist gives him the green light, he'll be able to rejoin his old clinic. It's funny—he says the experience, as brutal as it was, has given him new insights into helping trauma patients."

"I'm glad. You're lucky." She gave me a sad smile, clearly thinking about her own father, who had died several years earlier from emphysema.

"I am."

She picked up the body receipts. "Steven Thomas, good. Paul Velasquez, finally. Where's Tony Milano?"

Milano had been charged with multiple counts of breaking and entering, theft by taking, and possession of stolen property. He was your garden-variety junkie, desperate to feed his habit.

But he was smart for a dope fiend. He knew how to disable alarms, charm guard dogs, and could blend into a crowd remarkably well despite the ravages that his addiction had taken on his body.

Only reason the cops caught him in the first place was that he'd pissed off his girlfriend, who'd turned him in. Hell, if he wasn't a junkie with a proclivity for taking things that didn't belong to him, I might hire the guy.

"Old Tony's still in the wind. I've spoken with all of his associates and family, including his ex. Zahara, Caden, and Rodeo have been taking turns staking out his house, but he hasn't showed."

Her expression returned to that of the Sadie I knew and, well, didn't exactly love—a stern businesswoman. "Ms. Ballou, I need him back in custody now. He's already missed two court dates, and the cops are liking him for a few other burglaries in the area. I can't afford to pay the full bail on him."

"Relax, Sadie. I've got some leads." *More like a few unsubstantiated hunches.* "I'll bag him today or tomorrow. I promise."

"Sooner would be better. I'm expecting the judge to declare this bond forfeit any day now."

"I will arrest him today." *I hope.* "You got any new ones?"

"Unfortunately, yes. Two."

"What do we got?"

"Tod Cooper, thirty-seven, white, charged with criminal trespass, assault, aggravated domestic violence, and violating an order of protection." She handed me his file.

I flipped through it. Tod's name was spelled with just one *D*. How odd. Or should I say, how "od"?

He'd served a few years on a previous conviction that included assault and possession charges. The guy's mug shot depicted a face with dead eyes and a permanent scowl. "Looks a real charmer. If only I were single."

"Next up, Donnie Krueger, forty-three, white, charged with multiple counts of fraud, abuse of a corpse, assault, and illegal transportation of human remains."

"Abuse of a corpse?" I asked warily.

I'd seen a similar case a year earlier. A female technician at the county medical examiner's office had been charged with multiple counts of necrophilia.

When we caught her near the Payson airport, she tried to convince us that what she'd done wasn't wrong. In her mind, at least, no one was harmed. The whole thing creeped me out, which was not an easy thing to do.

"Not another necrophiliac, I hope." My breakfast was threatening to come up at the thought.

"No, not that. Mr. Krueger is a body broker. He sells human remains donated to science."

"That's really a thing?"

"Apparently."

"So what did he do that was illegal?"

"He allegedly assaulted a grieving family member after allegedly selling their loved one's body to a military contractor that designs armor for tanks."

"Armor for tanks? What's a military contractor need with a corpse?" And then it hit me. "They blew the woman's body up?"

"Technically, they blew up an armored vehicle with the cadaver inside in order to study how well their armor protected against life-threatening injury. Allegedly." Sadie was fond of "allegedly" when it came to her client's charges.

"The family claimed their contract with Krueger only allowed for the body to be used for medical research. Nothing military. They showed up at his office to complain. Apparently, things got physical. Again, allegedly."

"How'd the family find out about the military contractor?"

"Someone on the armored vehicle project was a friend of the family. They recognized her. That opened an investigation. Bottom line is that Mr. Krueger missed his latest court appearance. I need him returned to custody. Him and these other defendants. Milano is a priority." She wrote out a check and handed it to me. "Here's your fee for Thomas and Velasquez."

"Much obliged. Happy Halloween."

I saluted her other bail bond agents, who were all either meeting with defendants' family members or on the phone.

I stepped out into the beautiful October day. I loved this time of year. The sky was a deep sapphire blue, and the air was cool. Well, "cool" was a relative term. The triple-digit heat of summer and the stifling humidity of the monsoon season had abated finally. The high for the day was only going to be in the mid-eighties. Practically freezing in comparison.

I may have to grab a sweater, I thought.

I strode to the neighboring parking garage, catching a few stares from people in business suits coming out of BoSa Donuts. My body armor, emblazoned with the words Bail Enforcement Agent in big yellow letters, tended to turn heads. But I liked to think I was just *so* good-looking that people couldn't help taking a second glance. Okay, maybe not.

I HOPPED into my metallic forest-green Chevy Suburban, nicknamed the Green Dragon. It was one of three similar vehicles that my company Ballou Fugitive Recovery owned.

Zahara drove a black one she called the Darkness. Rodeo had dubbed his navy-blue one the Blue Bomber.

Caden had rejoined the team after I'd purchased the vehicles, so he still drove his personal Range Rover, which had earned the moniker the Flying Pumpkin because of its orange paint job.

On the outside, the Green Dragon looked like a thousand other soccer-mom SUVs, complete with a four-person, stick-figure family decal on the back window and a bumper sticker that read Proud Parent of a Central High School Soccer All-Star. All lies to help us blend in and make us virtually invisible on a stakeout or while tailing a fugitive.

The interior of our SUVs featured a barrier between the front and back, and plastic rear seats without carpeting that were easy to wash out.

From Arizona Center, I made a side trip to the Tres Leches Café, then on to the Hub, a coworking space at Grand Avenue and Roosevelt Street that served as the home for dozens of small businesses.

Someone had festooned the exposed vertical steel beams of the Hub's industrial-style interior with black and orange streamers. Fake spiders and bats hung from the horizontal beams. Ethereal dark wave music played on the sound system.

Carrying my computer bag and a tray of coffees, I navigated the maze of occupied folding tables to the one I shared with Becca Alvarez, my best friend. She had her own business as an IT security consultant and occasionally helped me skip trace fugitives.

Her workstation comprised three monitors and an ever-growing pile of papers, computer parts, cardboard boxes, and food wrappers. She was a brilliant IT person but even less of a neat freak than I was.

She had long dark hair and tan skin similar to mine. Over the years, people frequently mistook us for sisters, despite her being Latinx and my heritage comprising a mix of Cajun and Italian. As far as I was concerned, we *were* family.

I handed Becca the soy pumpkin spice latte she'd requested and sat down opposite her. "Morning."

She popped the lid off her drink and took a whiff. "Ay, mi Diosa!"

"I don't know how you drink that," I teased. "Too sweet."

She shrugged. "Call me bougie, but the cinnamon, nutmeg, and other spices are like a warm embrace to my soul this time of year. A reminder that we've survived another brutal summer and that the holidays are approaching."

"I get that. Still, I'll stick with a boring cup of joe." I set up my laptop and began studying the files on my new fugitives.

"Sadie give you some new jobs?" The casters on her office chair made a grinding sound on the bare concrete floor when she slid to my side of the table.

"Yes. Still gotta find this Tony Milano guy—cat burglar extraordinaire. Cops suspect he's robbed a few more houses since being released on bail."

"Last I checked, SkipTrakkr's not showing any recent phone calls. I could try locating his cell phone again."

"Don't bother. It's probably still on his nightstand, same as the last time you pinged it. Judging from the amount of mail we found in his mailbox, he hasn't been home in a while. If he's got a phone on him, it's a burner."

I sighed. "I swear, these fugitives are getting smarter. They jump bail and ditch their cell phones first chance they get. Hardly worth putting you at legal risk of an illegal trace. Besides, as Conor keeps reminding me, we're *supposed* to be the good guys."

An evil grin spread across Becca's face. "Yeah, but hacking the phone companies is so much more fun. Your choice, hermana. I could run Milano's call log and those of his personal references through an algorithm. Odds are he's still talking to his friends. His burner may show up as a new number their call logs have in common."

"That might work. Sadie's freaking out. If I don't catch him in the next day or so, the judge will force her to cough up the remainder of the bail."

"I can run it this afternoon."

"What? Bringing you a cup of sweet cinnamony goodness isn't enough to put me at the head of the line?"

"Lo siento, mi compa. I'm setting up a new network server for a client and am up against a hard deadline."

"Whatever you can do would be great. Thanks."

"Anything for my bestie. Who else did she give you?"

I showed her the files one by one. "Tod 'With One D' Cooper, an asshole who violated a restraining order and beat up his boyfriend again. And this guy, Krueger." I opened his folder.

"Krueger? As in Freddy Krueger?" She chuckled.

"Donnie Krueger, actually. But this one may very well be haunting my nightmares. He's a body broker. The dude sells corpses for a living."

"They never told us that was an option on Career Day at Aristotle Collegiate High."

"I know, right? I could have done something fun for a living."

"I heard about this cabrón on the news." Becca shook her head in obvious disgust. "The police found all kinds of chopped-up bodies at his place of business. ¡Muy horripilante!"

"And just in time for Halloween. Lucky me."

"What did they bust him for, anyway? The news story I read said something about assault and fraud but no details."

"Apparently, Creepy Krueger sold somebody's dead mother to a military contractor, who used said cadaver to test tank armor."

"Test it how?"

"They blew up a tank with dear old Mom's remains inside. The family showed up at Krueger's place all pissed off. Mayhem ensued."

"Oh my gourd! To do that to someone's dead mother? That's a special kind of low."

"No kidding."

"I'll run the algo on your cat burglar once I get this new server up and running." She slid back around to her side of the table.

I opened my laptop and ran the SkipTrakkr app to pull up what I could on my new fugitives, starting with Tod Cooper.

While he had only the one prior arrest, Cooper had been the subject of multiple police calls for domestic disturbances. Two with Lillian Moss, his ex-wife and mother of their son, Timmy. One with Sebastian Castro, his ex-boyfriend and the man who'd filed the order of protection.

His employment history showed that he worked construction and made decent money doing it. Earned his GED several years ago. No college.

He currently had a checking account with $23.17 in it. Recent bank transactions included charges at several bars and a twice-monthly paycheck from Arroyo Valley Developers, but only one was deposited so far in October. No paycheck in mid-October. Had they fired him? Didn't say so on his bail bond application. Maybe it slipped his mind.

He had deposited a personal check in the amount of two hundred bucks from Ken Milburn, who was listed as one of Cooper's references on his application. My guess was someone was borrowing money from a friend to pay the bills. Odds were good he'd be at home, so that was where I'd start with him.

Donnie Krueger was a different story. According to SkipTrakkr, he was the CEO and director of New Life Medical Resources and made beaucoup bucks doing it. Owned a three-thousand-square-foot house free and clear in the Vistancia neighborhood in the northwest Valley.

He had several thousand in checking, plus some money market accounts and a sizable stock portfolio. Apparently, selling dead bodies was a lucrative business to be in.

I checked his website. It was bright, featuring many stock photos of smiling doctors who were supposedly learning new techniques and saving lives thanks to the cadavers Krueger was peddling.

To my surprise, he had earned an MD from Johns Hopkins. How the hell did a medical doctor end up selling cadavers for a living?

An internet search turned up the answer. Several news articles from ten years earlier reported that he'd been a transplant surgeon. An investigation revealed that Krueger had burned his initials into a transplanted liver with an argon beam coagulator, whatever the hell that was.

Creepy Krueger must have thought it'd be clever to sign his work. The Arizona Medical Board saw things differently and stripped him of his license, though he faced no criminal charges at the time.

Well, he faced them now. And I intended to put him back behind bars to face the music.

After I had accumulated as much relevant information as I could on my cadre of fugitives, I decided Cooper was the most imminent threat to public safety, especially his boyfriend's. And his bounty was forty thousand, which was nearly double Krueger's. I'd go after Cooper first.

I called Cooper's number from a prepaid phone I used for a tip line. Naturally, the call rolled over to voicemail. "Hi, Mr. Cooper. This is Liz Windsor with Assurity Bail Bonds." It was an alias I often used. "We've run into a minor issue with your bond. I just need you to call me so we can get the matter cleared up. Shouldn't take long." I left my number and hung up.

Odds were one in three that he'd call me back. If he did, I'd arrange to meet, whereupon I'd slap on the cuffs and take Cooper back to jail. I left a similar message with a woman at Krueger's office.

I then reached out to my crew and instructed them to meet me at Tod Cooper's residence off Adams Street, just west of the I-17 freeway.

CHAPTER 5
SIDEWAYS

THE SINGLE-FAMILY HOMES in Cooper's south Phoenix neighborhood were small but well kept. Several had bars on the windows. The lots were large but barren except for an occasional tree or shrub. No lush lawns or fancy landscaping. Shoes hanging from power lines and strategically placed graffiti tags indicated gang activity, most likely the Westside Jaguars.

It looked like a place where good families tried to make a living despite a greedy, corrupt system and the all-too-present criminal element.

I parked the Green Dragon across the street from Cooper's house. The bright-red Dodge Ram pickup backed in under the freestanding carport matched the one listed on Cooper's bail bond application.

Ten minutes later, Rodeo pulled up behind me in the Blue Bomber. Zahara used the Darkness to block the driveway in case Cooper had any ideas of running. Caden arrived soon after in his Range Rover.

We huddled on the street side of Zahara's truck, everyone outfitted with body armor, radios, Tasers, cuffs, and other necessary gear. Zahara and Caden carried beanbag shotguns, recognizable by their fluorescent orange stocks and sliding forends. Rodeo and I carried backup semiauto pistols, but they were a last resort. We didn't get paid for dead fugitives.

"Morning, folks. Our dirtbag's name is Tod Cooper. History of violence and drug use. Likes to use his boyfriend as a punching bag despite a restraining order against him."

"Sounds delightful," Caden said.

"Caden, I want you parked around back in the alley that runs parallel to the street. Zahara, cover the side door by the carport. Rodeo, make entry at the back door on my signal. I'll take the front door."

"Why do I always get stuck waiting in the alley or by the street?" Caden whined. "When do I get to be part of the entry team? I feel like I'm on the bottom of the pecking order."

"There is no pecking order, Caden," I insisted. "You're part of the team."

"So when do I get to breach the front door? Or even the back door? Why do I always have to sit in the car?"

"Cause you're the new guy," Zahara teased, chucking him on the shoulder.

"I'm not the new guy. I was part of the team before you were."

"For the record, Z's been part of the team longer than you ever were," I replied. "You suffered a major injury, and I'm glad you're back. Keep doing your job well, and I'll rotate you to other positions. Besides, that back alley looks rough. Your Range Rover can probably handle it better than our Suburbans."

Caden rolled his eyes. "Whatever. You want me waiting in the alley? That's where I'll be."

Rodeo gave him a nod. "Hang in there, little guy. You'll be top dog around here in no time."

"And stop calling me little."

"Okay, if our whine festival is quite over," I said, glaring at the two men, "we need to bag this guy before he rabbits. Everyone to their position."

"Roger that," Rodeo replied.

Zahara loaded beanbag rounds into her shotgun. "Let's nail this son of a bitch."

We turned on our radios. I grabbed a battering ram out of the back of my Suburban then approached the front door.

Caden hopped into his Range Rover and disappeared down the street. Rodeo hustled through a gate that led to the backyard. Zahara stepped cautiously to the side door.

I monitored the windows as I approached the house, looking and listening for signs of life inside. So far, nothing. But that didn't necessarily mean anything.

I spoke into my radio. "Team check in. Coyote One in position. Over"

"Coyote Three in position. Over," Zahara said over the radio.

Rodeo followed up with "Coyote Two in position. Over."

After a few moments, Caden called in, "Coyote Four in position. Over."

I set down the ram next to the front door and drew my Taser. My pulse quickened. I loved this part of the job.

I pounded on the door the way they'd taught me at the police academy years earlier. Establish your authority immediately. The sounds of movement and whispering voices drifted from inside, but no one came to the door. I knocked again.

"Tod Cooper, come to the door now!"

A dead bolt clacked. I readied myself. Eyes and ears alert. Body relaxed. Mind loose.

The door opened. The person standing there was not Tod Cooper but a tow-haired boy roughly six years old. That complicated the situation.

"We got a kid," I murmured into my radio. I lowered the

Taser to my side and spoke in a gentle voice. "What's your name?"

"Timmy."

"Hi, Timmy. I'm Jinx. Is Tod your dad?"

The boy nodded.

"Is he here?"

He glanced back into the house, then shook his head vigorously. The yellowish shadow of a bruise marred his otherwise cherubic face. I wanted to pound his father into the ground. The fucker was a waste of space.

"Does your mom live here or somewhere nearby?" I wasn't sure what the situation was with the mother. But I was hoping she could take custody of the kid once we'd arrested Cooper.

Again, the boy shook his head. "She's in jail 'cause she uses drugs."

I'd have to put in a call to the Department of Child Safety once we had dear old Dad in cuffs. I felt sorry for the kid. An abusive dad and a junkie mom. And now he was going to end up in the system through no fault of his own.

"I'm sorry to hear that, Timmy. Look, I'm here to help your dad out. Would you ask him to come to the door?"

"You gonna shoot him?" Timmy stared at the Taser in my hand.

"Not if he's nice."

Shouting from Zahara's side of the house caught my attention.

"Outta my way, bitch!" a man yelled.

I ran to assist her.

"Sir, drop the gun and get on your knees," Zahara demanded. "Do it now!"

I was coming around to the carport when I heard the report of a handgun followed by the boom of the shotgun. Zahara was on the ground with a hand to her chest.

Cooper was already in his pickup with the door shut

before I could get a clear shot with my Taser. I drew the Ruger 40-cal from the small of my back and stepped in front of the vehicle.

"Tod Cooper, get out of the truck."

Despite the glare off the truck's windshield, I could see the fury in his eyes. He wasn't giving himself up. The engine bellowed to life.

I put one round in the truck's front end before leaping away to avoid becoming roadkill. The pickup almost clipped Zahara's Suburban as it swerved onto the street and drove away.

I ran to Zahara, but didn't see any blood.

"I'm okay," she hollered through gritted teeth. "Go after the bastard."

I raced to the Green Dragon while barking into my radio. "Coyote Three down. Everyone assist. I'm in pursuit of the target."

I floored my truck down the street in the direction I'd seen Cooper disappear. With the Green Dragon's high-performance engine, my chances of catching him were good.

After swerving north onto Twenty-Seventh Avenue, I spotted the red Dodge pickup a half mile ahead of me. My foot pressed hard on the accelerator, pushing me back into the seat.

Times like this, I missed being a cop in a patrol car with lights and sirens. While I had the legal authority to arrest this guy for being a violent felon, bail jumper, and all-around scumbag, I lacked the authority to engage in a high-speed pursuit. But did that stop me? Of course not.

At Van Buren, Cooper blew through a red light. Tires squealed from vehicles avoiding his. By the time I reached the intersection, the light was green, and I was gaining.

I half expected him to turn onto the Papago Freeway, but as I approached the overpass, I could see a line of cars creeping along at a snail's pace. If he had taken the on-ramp, he would've been caught in traffic. I would've nailed him. He was smarter than I thought. I hated smart fugitives.

At McDowell, he ran another red light, clipping a VW Beetle. Not that it slowed him down much. I considered pushing my luck and was about to run the red, too, when a woman pushing a shopping cart stepped into the crosswalk. I slammed on the brakes. The Green Dragon shuddered to a stop inches from the woman. She shouted something I couldn't hear over the roar of my pulse in my ears.

Cooper vanished in the distance. Pursuing him wasn't worth it.

"Catch you later, asshole," I whispered.

As I waited for the light to turn green, I put my phone on speaker and called Rodeo. "How's Zahara?"

I felt bad leaving her there, especially since Cooper got away.

"Her vest took the impact. Bruised ribs possible but no permanent damage. You apprehend our target?"

"No joy. How's the kid?"

"Confused and crying. Caden's with him. You notice the bruise on his face?"

"Yeah. Put a call in to DCS. I'll be there in a few."

"Roger that, boss."

By the time I reached Cooper's street, two Phoenix PD blue-and-whites sat parked in front of the house. I removed my body armor and duty belt with the Taser and locked it in the car. Cops got nervous when anyone but them was armed.

A uniformed officer approached, gesturing me to turn around and leave. Police business—move along. Then I recognized her from my year on the force. "Rachel Wasserman?"

Her gaze narrowed. "Jinx Ballou? Holy shit. It's been a minute."

"Yeah, like, what, ten years? Good to see you. Made sergeant, huh? Congrats." I shook her hand.

"Taking the lieutenant's exam next month. Fingers crossed."

"You'll pass, no doubt."

"Hope so. So, you're with the bounty hunters looking for the boy's father?"

"Yeah, they work for me."

"Running your own crew now? Nice."

"Thanks. Cooper failed to appear on charges of violating an order of protection and domestic violence. His bail bond agent hired us to pick him up. You see his son's face?"

"I did. Poor kid. DCS is sending a social worker."

I gave her a statement of the events, albeit one light on details regarding my questionably legal street pursuit up Twenty-Seventh Avenue.

When she was satisfied, I met up with Zahara, Caden, and Rodeo.

"How are you feeling?" I asked her.

She grimaced. "Hurts, but I'll live."

"You want us to take you to the hospital?"

She rubbed her chest. Her expression showed more annoyance than pain, but I could tell she was hurting.

I'd been shot a few times. Even with a vest, that much force at point-blank range was like getting hit with a sledgehammer.

"Nah, I'm good. Bitches in the UFC hit harder than that."

"You change your mind, let me know. Next case is a little less risky. But creepy." I pulled Krueger's file out of my truck and went over it with my team.

"A guy named Krueger selling body parts?" Caden asked. "Happy Halloween! We going after Count Dracula next?"

"The real question is, are we getting paid in cash or candy?" Rodeo adjusted his Stetson. "And if it's candy, is it the good stuff? Or the cheap leftovers like that orange-and-black-wrapped taffy?"

Caden added, "Or those peanut butter maple candies. What were they called?"

"Mary Janes?" I suggested.

"Yeah. That's them."

"Or worse, candy corn," Zahara made a disgusted face. "That garbage tastes like sugar mixed with ear wax."

"You'll all be relieved to know we'll be paid in real money, not candy. But we have to catch the guy first. I made a call first thing this morning to his place of business and asked to speak with him. The woman who answered said he wasn't available at the moment. But I got the impression he might be there."

"Let's grab him," Zahara said. "I need a win. Been a real mother of a Monday so far."

We climbed into our vehicles and drove west on the Papago Freeway.

CHAPTER 6
FRANKENSTEIN'S MONSTER

NEW LIFE MEDICAL Resources was a squat office building in Peoria just off Thunderbird Road and the Loop 101. On the outside, it looked like just another of the dozens of medical offices in the area that catered to the senior citizens living in nearby Sun City.

Our convoy of trucks pulled into the parking lot that stretched between New Life and a cardiologist's office.

After we geared up, I instructed Caden and Zahara to cover the back door while Rodeo and I would enter through the front.

Caden didn't say anything, but I could see the complaint in his eyes as he grabbed one of the shotguns. He'd just have to get over it. At least he wasn't sitting in his truck this time.

Rodeo took the other beanbag shotgun. I drew my Taser. "Time to rock and roll."

The front door opened to a small reception area. A white woman with straight, shoulder-length hair sat behind a plexiglass barrier. I recognized her immediately.

"No way" was all I could say. "Look, Rodeo. It's the necrophiliac we bagged last year. Hey, Nancy. How's tricks?"

"Nancy Turner?" Rodeo chuckled and lowered the barrel

of his beanbag shotgun to the floor. "Shouldn't you be in prison?"

The woman's face went from impassive to smugly defiant. "I'll have you know the jury found me not guilty."

"And Donald Krueger hired you as his secretary? Kind of a step down from the medical examiner's office, isn't it?"

"I'm Donnie's office manager, Mr. Smartypants. You two need to leave. This is still a place of business."

"Yeah, we know about the business you and your boss are into," I replied. "Chopping up dead bodies. Selling them to get blown up. Not exactly medical research. You fucking any of them, Nancy? Still getting off on the dearly departed?"

"Do I have to call the police? You have no business here."

"Au contraire, we do." I holstered my Taser and showed her a copy of the bench warrant. "Your boss failed to appear. Bail's been revoked. Sound familiar?"

"He's not here."

"No? Where is he, then?"

"I'm sure I don't know."

"I think you're lying. Rodeo, you think she's lying?"

"Definitely lying, boss."

"Let me break it down for you, Nancy pants. You are wearing pants behind that desk, aren't you? No, wait, don't answer that. Bottom line is you lying to us about dear old Donnie's whereabouts constitutes aiding and abetting. Doubt you'll get out of that one. So what's it gonna be?"

"I told you, I don't know where he is. I haven't... I haven't seen or heard from him in a couple of days. I assumed you people had already thrown him back in jail. I'm just trying to keep things running. Everyone else quit after Donnie was arrested."

She went from smug to whiny. I half-expected her to start crying. Maybe she was telling the truth, but I wasn't taking her word for it.

"Then you won't mind us looking around."

"What? No, you can't. This is a private business."

"Run by a guy who commits fraud, punches grieving family members, and skips his court date." I checked the door leading to the rest of the building. Locked. Most likely a magnetic lock.

"If you people don't leave, I'm calling the cops."

"Be my guest. I used to be a cop. Got a lot of friends on the force. And I have a warrant from a judge revoking Krueger's bail. Who do you think they're going to side with? A former colleague or a serial corpse molester?"

Her mouth twisted, and her cheeks reddened. "This is so disrespectful."

"That's rich coming from you." The door buzzed. I opened it and drew my Taser. "Rodeo, go down to the back entrance and let Caden and Z inside. Keep an eye out for our guy."

"Roger that."

While Rodeo followed a corridor to the back door, I ducked into Nancy's little cubbyhole of an office, looking for a hiding Krueger. "Clear!"

She glared at me but said nothing.

Next, I stepped into a large, tidy business office that had to be Krueger's. I searched under the desk and in wall cabinets for signs of our wayward body broker. Nada. "Clear!"

The next room resembled a surgical suite, redolent with the scent of disinfectant and a hint of decomp. Three stainless steel tables, each eight feet long, gleamed under bright overhead lights. The concrete floor sloped slightly to a drain. Surgical instruments covered a smaller table nearby.

I tried not to think of what went on here, but creepy images of partially dissected bodies flashed through my mind. My breakfast threatened to come up.

"Breathe. Just breathe," I reminded myself. "Happy thoughts. Blue skies. Mountains. Forests."

"Boss! You're gonna wanna see this," Rodeo yelled from down the hall, pulling me away from my happy place.

I left the dissection room and found Caden in the hallway outside a heavy steel door with a rubber seal. He stood hunched over, leaning on his shotgun and looking a little green around the gills. The room on the other side of the door was a refrigerated cooler, I guessed.

"You all right there, Caden?" I asked.

He inhaled deeply. "Yeah, I…they're in the cooler." Without warning, he puked onto the floor. "Ughhh… God."

"Easy, buddy. Keep breathing." I put a hand on his back, and the smell hit me. *What the hell did he eat for breakfast? Shit.*

"Sorry, Jinx." He wiped his mouth with a handkerchief from his pocket. "It's just…"

And he puked again, getting some on my boot this time.

"Look, dude. Why don't you step outside and get some fresh desert air?"

"Yeah. Okay. Sorry."

While he ambled off, I opened the cooler door with a whoosh. A blast of chilled air hit me, along with an aroma that further unsettled my own stomach. *Hold it together, girl,* I told myself.

The cooler was the size of my living room. Shelves lined the walls, filled with what I guessed to be body parts in thick black bags of various sizes, each one labeled. In one corner was a large bin filled with unbagged heads. Eyes open and lifeless. Another bin contained skulls and long bones. Several feet away sat a five-gallon bucket of something. I approached to get a better view.

"Don't want to look in there," Zahara cautioned. She was also looking a bit pale.

"Why?" I looked and cringed. The bucket was filled with severed penises. "Shit."

"That was when Caden lost it," Rodeo said. "Not that I blame him."

I noticed a puddle of puke nearby and nearly lost it myself. I refocused my mind on the job at hand.

On the far side of the cooler were several full-length body bags on shelves. I didn't want to open them. Partly to avoid being disrespectful to the deceased, as if that were really an issue at this point. But mostly for fear of what I might find.

"We have to check each of these bags," I said.

"You're kidding." Zahara shook her head warily. "Why?"

"Fugitives hide in the most unbelievable places."

"Sure, but in a body bag?" When I didn't answer, she added, "Fine."

Each body bag was on a tray that slid out from the wall. I unzipped the first one just enough to confirm it was a dead Latinx woman who appeared to be in her seventies. She was completely nude and rail thin, as if having suffered from a long illness before she passed. Not Krueger.

I moved on to the next one. Heavyset white guy. Dead. Again, not Krueger.

After checking three more body bags, I came to one that left me staring, dumbfounded. My stomach was ready to go full-on Vesuvius. "Uh, uh, uh." *Happy place. Blue sky. Mountains. Forests.*

"Jinx, you okay?" Zahara asked.

"That's just wrong." I pointed at the body in the open bag before me.

The body was nude like the others. But it wasn't a cadaver so much as a composite, like the Frankenstein monster. The head was from a man who appeared to be Southeast Asian or Pacific Islander. The hourglass-shaped torso was several skin tones lighter and had size-C breasts. Two mismatched legs extended from a dark-skinned abdomen. Whatever genitals it once possessed had been surgically removed, leaving a gaping wound.

"Fuck! I got to get outta here." I rushed toward the door.

It didn't open. I hit the release button several times. "What the fuck?!"

"We're locked in?" Panic rang in Zahara's voice.

"Caden! We're locked in the cooler," I called into my radio. "We need you to open the door. Over."

All I got in response were static and garbled words.

"Caden, let us out of the cooler."

Again, nothing but distortion and static.

"I'll get us out. Hold this." Rodeo handed me his shotgun and slammed the door with the bottom of his boot. It dented but didn't open. He then body-slammed it. "Fuck!"

The door didn't give, but from his expression, his shoulder did.

My pulse raced. I wasn't claustrophobic, but I didn't like being trapped, especially in a cooler full of dead bodies and assorted parts.

Not going to panic. Not going to panic. I will get us out of here. I took a deep breath, trying not to think about what I might be inhaling.

Raised voices came from outside. Probably Nancy and her boss arguing. Fucking assholes.

"Enough of this shit." I cycled the sliding forend of the shotgun until it was empty of the beanbag rounds, then loaded two standard 12-gauge shells from a pocket in my cargo pants. Putting standard rounds in a beanbag shotgun violated our safety protocols, but desperate times…

With the butt of the gun firm against my shoulder, I aimed at where the locking mechanism would be. My finger slid inside the trigger guard. "Fuck this bullshit."

The sound of a shotgun thundered, but not the one I was holding. More shouting came from outside the cooler.

"What was that?" Zahara asked.

The door opened. Caden stood there, still looking like a guy who'd swallowed a slug on a dare. He held his shotgun in one hand. Nancy Turner lay cuffed on the floor near a spent beanbag round.

"You folks all right?" he asked.

The three of us rushed out of the cooler.

"We are now," Rodeo said. "Thanks, buddy."

"Yeah, thanks, man," Z added.

I was still too weirded out to speak, but clapped my hand on his shoulder.

"I'd left the back door open a crack when I stepped outside. Came back in when I heard pounding. Found this bitch had stuck the pin in the cooler door handle. When she refused to open it, I gave her a little non-lethal encouragement."

That put a smile on my face. "Any sign of Krueger?"

"Nope."

I walked over to Turner. She glared up at me, tears ruining her makeup.

"Had to make things difficult, didn't you?" I asked her.

Zahara put a hand on my shoulder. "Jinx, ease up. We're okay."

I took a breath. "Still don't know where your boss is?" I pressed Turner.

"I invoke my Fifth Amendment rights."

I leaned down in Nancy's face. "Listen up, bitch. I could let this little incident slide if you give us the 411 on your boss's whereabouts. Or we could return the favor and lock you in the little human chop shop you got going in there."

"Look, I'm sorry I locked you in. It was just a joke."

"Real funny," Rodeo said. "Where's your boss?"

"I don't know where he is. Honest," she said between sobs. "I've tried and tried to get a hold of him. Called his daughter. She hasn't seen him either. I'm just trying to keep the office going. I need this job."

As much as I wanted to make her suffer, it wouldn't

bring us any closer to the bounty. My gut told me she was telling the truth.

I debated what to do. Option one was to lock her in the cooler with Frankenstein's monster. But as much as she deserved it, I knew that would come back to bite me later.

Option two was to call the cops and report her for kidnapping, assault, and possibly the mutilation of a corpse. Again, she deserved it, but then we'd spend another few hours not going after fugitives. We'd already spent enough time today talking to cops. I had a business to run.

"Caden, uncuff her."

"What?" Rodeo looked at me like I'd lost my mind. "After she locked us in there with that… that meat puzzle?"

Rodeo was usually unflappable, but I guessed everyone had their limits.

"You sure?" Caden asked.

"Yeah. She doesn't know anything. We've got other leads to pursue."

Caden did as instructed, and I led the team back outside to our trucks.

"Thanks for the save, Caden. You really showed your mettle."

"Sorry I puked on your boots."

"No worries. So, anybody hungry for lunch?"

I got a vigorous shaking of heads. Apparently, our trip through Krueger's house of horrors was enough to kill all our appetites.

"Fair enough. I really want to bag this guy." My attempt at humor got only glares. "Maybe 'bag' isn't the best metaphor. Let's check out his residence. See if the little toad is hiding there."

"Sounds good," Zahara replied. "Let's hope he doesn't have any more surprises there."

CHAPTER 7
A NIGHTMARE ON ELM STREET

WE DROVE north on Eighty-Third Avenue, which became Lake Pleasant Parkway after several miles. At Happy Valley Road, we turned west and arrived in the sprawling Vistancia development, a tony neighborhood of two-story mini mansions.

Several houses were decorated for Halloween with inflatable ghosts and ghoulies—currently deflated. Others featured fake tombstones with humorous epitaphs or ghosts composed of white sheets with comical faces. Some settled for a more elegant approach to the season, with autumn-style wreaths and elaborately carved pumpkins.

Donnie Krueger's won the prize for the gaudiest house. Fake giant spiders climbed his walls, with artificial spiderwebs everywhere. Bats hung from trees. Enormous vampire teeth draped from the front of the porch overhang. Crime-scene tape spanned the front door next to a life-size Freddy Krueger cutout. Zombies emerged from graves in the yard. I hoped the zombies were fake and not real cadavers, but I wasn't making any assumptions.

I double-checked the address against Krueger's file and met the team outside.

Rodeo looked at me incredulously. "You're joking, right?

Our guy Krueger lives on Elm Street? At 13137? That's seriously twisted."

"See for yourself." I showed him the folder.

Zahara let out a dark laugh. "Selling dead bodies must pay well."

"Apparently. Zahara and Rodeo, take the back. Caden, you're with me, making entry through the front."

Caden pumped his fist. "Yes! Finally!"

"Don't screw it up, little man," Rodeo taunted.

"Stop! You'll give him a complex." Zahara grabbed one of the battering rams from the back of the Green Dragon. "Don't listen to him, Caden. If you didn't have what it took, you wouldn't be on the team."

"Shitcan the teasing, Rodeo. We're a team. Act like it."

"Sorry, boss. Sorry, Caden."

"Whatever."

I handed one of the shotguns to Caden, the other to Z, and pulled out the other ram for myself. "All right, people. Let's get in position."

A few minutes later, Zahara's voice came over the radio. "Coyotes Two and Three in position. Over."

"Roger that. Let's see if he's home." I replied, then turned to Caden. "You ready?"

"Ready as I'll ever be." He aimed the beanbag shotgun at the door.

I pounded on Krueger's front door, then stabbed at the doorbell for good measure.

A blood-curdling screech rose from inside, as if someone was being slaughtered inside.

I jumped. Caden must've panicked because his shotgun thundered. But instead of a beanbag round, a hole exploded in the door.

The screeching from inside the house turned into demonic laughter. "Fuck."

"What the hell happened?" Caden said in a panicked voice. "That should've been a beanbag round."

"Shit, my bad," I confessed. "I put a couple of 12-gauge shells to force open the cooler door before you opened it. Guess I forgot to replace them with the beanbag rounds afterward."

"Coyote One. What the hell was that? Over," Zahara asked over the radio.

"Doorbell. Over."

"Sounded like someone getting murdered, followed by a shotgun blast. Over."

"Guy's got a twisted sense of humor. Over."

Caden was actually laughing—at me, no less. "You shoulda seen your face, Jinx, when that screaming started."

"Yuck it up, puke boy. We'll see who gets the last laugh. Least I didn't blow a hole in the guy's door."

I turned my attention to the house and shouted, "Donnie Krueger, if you're inside, come out now with your hands up!"

I waited, giving Caden the side eye as he continued chuckling.

"Coyote Three. Any sign of life by the back door? Over." I asked into the radio.

"Negative, Coyote One. Silent as the grave. Over."

I debated our next move. Did I have reason to believe he was in there? Probably. Did I want to go in there? Not really, considering what other unsavory surprises might be inside. Did I want to slap the cuffs on the bastard if he was in there? Abso-fucking-lutely.

"Coyote One making entry. Over."

"Roger, Coyote One. Coyotes Two and Three making entry at the rear."

Rather than using the ram, I reached through the hole in the solid oak door and unlocked it. About ten seconds after we stepped inside, we were treated to an earsplitting alarm for our trouble.

"Shit." If Krueger had set the alarm, odds were he wasn't home. But we needed to be sure and had only a few minutes before the cops showed up, looking for an explanation.

I popped in a couple of earplugs I kept on hand for just this occasion and handed a pair to Caden.

"Gotta move quickly," I yelled over the din when Rodeo and Zahara appeared. Everyone nodded, and we split up to systematically search the house.

The place was nice. Modern with a heavy touch of the macabre. It was if someone had opened a Halloween super-store inside some minor celebrity's crib. Despite the rush, we left no gravestone unturned, so to speak. We searched every cabinet and closet, under beds, behind drapes, anywhere a fugitive might hide.

We found skull-shaped bars of soap in the bathrooms, a closet full of leather and kink wear in a guest bedroom, and a collection of horror DVDs that covered an entire wall. Even a half-eaten meatloaf in the refrigerator shaped like a foot with onion slices for toenails. But no sign of our fugitive.

The four of us gathered in the front yard. "Anything?" I asked. At least it was quieter outside. The security alarm was getting on my nerves.

"The bar of soap in the master bath was damp," Rodeo said. "He's been here in the past twenty-four hours."

"Kitchen smelled like someone had been cooking recent-ly," Zahara added. "He may still be here."

"But where?" I asked.

"A safe room, maybe," Caden suggested. "A lotta rich folks have them."

"If that's where he's hiding, odds are slim we could force our way in even if we found it," I said. "We may have to take another approach."

My phone rang just as two Peoria PD black-and-white SUVs pulled up. The caller ID told me it was Becca.

"Not a good time, Becks. Cops just arrived."

"The cops? What happened?"

"I'll explain later."

"Okay, call me when you can. I got a lead on your cat burglar."

CHAPTER 8
THE EXTERMINATOR

"IT'S OKAY, Officers. We were bail enforcement agents executing a bench warrant for a defendant who failed to appear." We all had our hands in the air.

"Bail enforcement?" one officer asked. With his youthful face and gelled hair, he looked like he belonged in a boy band, not carrying a badge.

"Goddamn bounty hunters," the other snorted, lowering his weapon. He appeared to be in his mid-forties and carried himself like he was ex-military. "IDs and paperwork!"

We lowered our hands and pulled out our identification. From a pocket on the front of my vest, I pulled a copy of the warrant on Krueger and handed it to the older officer, whose nameplate read Shaw.

Shaw examined the paperwork, then asked, "So, where's this Krueger guy? In one of your vehicles?"

"Couldn't find him. He was here as recently as a few hours ago, judging by the kitchen."

"So you broke into his house for nothing?"

"Not for nothing," I insisted. "When we arrived, we heard screaming. We forced our way in, fearing someone was in danger."

"And...?"

"Turned out, it was his doorbell. Instead of the usual doorbell tones, it triggers a recording of someone screaming. Go see for yourself if you don't believe me."

Shaw didn't look convinced, so I continued. "Krueger sold a woman's body to be blown up by artillery. When the family showed up to complain, he got violent with them. And then he skipped his court date. How would you feel if he'd done something like that to your mother and then jumped bail?"

"Yeah, all right." Shaw handed the warrant back to me.

"What about the alarm?" the younger deputy asked. "And the front door?"

I shrugged. "Call Krueger. We left a voicemail for him earlier today, but he hasn't called back. Maybe if you tell him someone broke into his house, he'll show up. You can take him into custody. We get the bounty. The family gets justice. Everybody wins. Except Krueger, of course."

Shaw apparently considered it. "What's his number?"

I gave it to him. He called, left a message, and hung up. "Guess we'll see if he calls back."

I really didn't want to wait here, hoping for Krueger to call back or show. If he ever did. Not while Becca had a lead on Tony Milano. "I can leave a member of my team to wait."

"That won't be necessary," Shaw replied. "I think it best if you all move on."

"You sure?"

"Move on," he said in a sharp tone. "You've caused enough trouble for today."

On the off chance that Krueger showed up and no one on my crew was here, it was unlikely we'd get a body receipt for the bounty. But I wasn't pressing our luck with these guys.

"Come on, folks. You heard the man."

"Where we headed, boss?" Rodeo asked.

"Back to the Fry's shopping center we passed on the way. We'll decide our next move there."

Once we were on the road, I called Becca. "What've you got?"

"I ran that algorithm on the numbers in Milano's call log to find any numbers his frequent contacts called. I came up with three numbers that weren't assigned through a normal provider."

"Not through a normal provider? You mean burner phones?"

"Exactly. I pinged all three numbers."

"Becks, I'm not sure we should be pinging phones anymore. Too risky from a legal standpoint." I really was trying to live more on the straight and narrow.

"I know. But I figured what the hell. One last time, right? Do you want to know what I found?"

"Hit me."

"Got a location for two of them. The other is probably off and has its SIM card removed. Of the two, one is up in Flag on the NAU campus. The other is in the Valley, near Thirty-Sixth Street south of Indian School."

"Any clue which one our guy is using?"

"Unless Tony Milano's enrolled in college in the past month, I'm guessing his is the one that's local. Again, there's a chance this phone isn't even his. Could belong to another mutual acquaintance."

This information certainly narrowed things down. Or it could be another wild goose chase.

"Text me the address. We'll check it out."

"You find that creepy body broker guy?"

Before I could answer, my phone rang with an incoming call. I didn't recognize the number. Probably spam. Or it could be a lead. I'd put out flyers offering a reward for tips on Milano's whereabouts.

"Sorry, got another call. I'll fill you in later." I clicked over to the new call. "Ballou Fugitive Recovery. Jinx Ballou speaking."

"Jinx, it's Daphne."

"Daphne?" The voice and name were familiar, but I couldn't place either one.

"Daphne Dixon. Fiddler's ex-wife."

I remembered. When I worked for Conor's crew, Daphne was their receptionist. She was also married to Fiddler, a bounty-hunting legend in his time.

Daphne eventually retired and divorced Fiddler. I hired Fiddler for a time until he got involved with the wrong people and was killed a few years back.

"Wow. Daphne. It's been a while. How are you?"

"Fair to middlin'. Been meaning to reach out. Especially after what happened to Fiddler."

"I'm really sorry, Daph."

"I know, darlin'. That man could be fool-headed."

"A shame for him to go out that way."

"Well, he had the cancer. Not sure which woulda been worse. Wasting away in a hospital bed or a bullet to the brain. Death takes us all. How are you doing?"

After spending much of the day chasing after Krueger, I was happy she changed the subject. "I'm managing."

"I hate to trouble you, but..." Something in her tone worried me. "Would you mind terribly if I come by this evening? Assuming you're not on a stakeout."

"I should be there. What's going on?"

"Not something I wanna discuss over the phone. Is seven okay?"

"Seven's great. Listen, I hate to cut you short, but I have bad guys to catch."

"Of course you do, sugar. Good hunting. I'll see you tonight."

In the Fry's parking lot, I informed the team that we had a lead on Milano.

"'Bout time we caught a break on that one," Caden said. "Where is he?"

"Off Thirty-Sixth Street and Indian School." I showed them the address Becca had texted me. "Let's get over there, see if we can't put the cuffs on this guy. We need a win today."

It took us the better part of an hour to reach the neighborhood thanks to a multi-vehicle accident on the Loop 101.

I cruised to a stop in front of a nicely kept sage-green house. No cars in the open garage or driveway. The front door looked slightly ajar, but that could have been an illusion at the angle we were parked. My instincts told me to call Becca again.

"Ping that phone again. See if Milano's still where you said he was."

"I thought you didn't want to risk it," Becca replied in a teasing voice. "Hold on. Let me check."

A few minutes later, she added, "Nope, not there. Got a different location now a few blocks away." She gave me the address.

I punched it into my phone. "Do me a favor. Ping it every five minutes or so. Call me if he moves again."

"Will do."

I texted the details to the team, then drove off to the new location.

A white Ford Econoline sat in front of the house she'd mentioned. I parked right behind it.

The rear of the van read X-Treme X-Terminators. A giant cartoon rat lay underneath the words.

According to his bond application, Milano ran a pawn-shop on Thomas Avenue. And yet the plates on the van were a match for Milano. "Got it marked up to look like he's an exterminator. Clever."

I stepped out of the Green Dragon and gave my team the rundown. "Zahara, you're with me in the front. Caden and

Rodeo, take the back. Keep an eye on the windows, just in case he chooses an alternate exit. Let's get in position."

A moment later, Caden's voice came over the radio. "Coyote One, Coyote Four. There's a back bedroom window open. Over."

"Roger that, Coyote Four. You cover the window. Coyote Two, start banging on the back door, but don't make entry yet. I think this may be another home invasion. Over."

"Roger that, Coyote One."

I pounded on the front door. "Tony Milano, come out of the house with your hands up."

CHAPTER 9
CAUGHT IN THE ACT

AT FIRST, there was no response. I pounded again, shouting for him to come out, that we had the place surrounded. I thought I heard movement inside, but it was hard to tell because a leaf blower droned on a few houses down.

Movement to the side caught my attention. A leg emerged from one of the front windows. "There he is."

The leg quickly became a coverall-clad body that slipped to the ground with the grace of a ballet dancer. He held a canvas tote bag in one hand. Long black hair. Beady eyes. He was our guy, all right.

"Milano, stop right there. Get on the ground. Do it now."

Milano had other ideas. He ran. I took off after him.

Zahara's shotgun bellowed. I swear, I felt the breeze when the shot-filled beanbag whizzed past my ear and hit Milano in the upper back.

He stumbled, rolled, and was back on his feet and running in no time. Still, the beanbag slowed him enough for me to gain ground and nail him with my Taser. This time, he dropped and stayed down.

I snapped the cuffs on him and pulled his wallet out of his back pocket to confirm his identity. "Anthony Milano, you're under arrest for failing to appear at your court hearing. Assurity Bail Bonds and the State of Arizona have retained me to return you to custody."

"Get off me, bitch. You ain't taking me in."

"No? Okay."

Z walked up holding the bag Milano had dropped. "Looks like you dropped something, buddy. What have we got in here? An iPad, a few rings, necklaces, a prescription bottle of OxyContin, a pair of Bluetooth headphones. Nice haul."

"That's not mine! You're trying to frame me."

She squatted next to him. He turned and looked up at her.

I couldn't blame him. She was both breathtakingly beautiful and intimidating, especially in her gear. "Tony, we get it. We know about the time you served for possession. A drug habit makes people do crazy things."

"I don't have a drug habit. I've been clean for two years."

"Then why, Tony?" She sounded more like a concerned mother than a bounty hunter for hire. "Why risk your freedom for this junk?"

"I got medical bills. And lousy insurance. Then coming up with the money for bail."

"Poor thing. I know what that's like. Even with decent insurance, medical bills can hit you hard when something major happens. But Tony, as much as I can empathize, we both know that stealing other people's belongings isn't the answer. It eats at your soul."

"I know." Milano began to sob. "I just...I didn't know what else to do."

I watched in amazement as she got him to open up. With the warmth and compassion in her voice, she could've been a police detective. She had the touch.

Together, she and I lifted Milano to his feet and frog-marched him to the Green Dragon.

"I'm so sorry to hear that, Tony," Zahara continued. "What put you in the hospital? Were you sick? Or was it an injury?"

I opened the back door, and he sat on the seat of my truck.

"Appendicitis. Didn't realize what it was until it was almost too late. It burst just as they were trying to remove it. Spent over a week in the hospital."

"Well, Tony, I'm sorry you went through that. Unfortunately, you've only been making things worse for yourself. Especially with this." Zahara gave the bag a shake.

He hung his head in shame. "I know. Like I said, I didn't know what else to do."

"Tell you what. No one's called the cops yet. I'll just put this back inside the window you slipped out of. One less count of burglary you'll have to deal with. And we'll see what we can do about getting your bail reset."

The man's body racked with emotion. Damn, she was good.

"Thank you. What about my van?"

"Dude, you're charged with multiple counts of burglary and possession of stolen property," I replied. "We caught you breaking into another house. I'd say your van's the least of your worries."

"I could drop it off somewhere," Zahara offered.

I shot her a look. "No, you won't. Sorry, Mr. Milano, but your van is not our problem."

"But there's… stuff in there." The way he said that was suspicious.

"What stuff?" *Oh God, please tell me it's not a dead body.* After what we'd found looking for Krueger, all bets were off.

"Stuff that isn't exactly mine."

I exchanged a glance with Zahara that said, *See, this is why we don't get mixed up with our fugitives' drama.* "Then I'd advise you to call your lawyer after you get processed back in."

I locked him in the back. Caden and Rodeo approached. Zahara carried the tote bag back to the house.

"What's she doing?" Caden asked.

I shrugged. "Putting the stolen goods back in the house."

"We calling the cops?" Rodeo asked.

"Apparently not."

"Heart of gold, that one," Caden said.

With gloved hands, Zahara lowered the canvas bag of stolen property back into the window Milano had used for escape. She then closed it as best she could from the outside.

"Yeah. I'm just afraid it's going to bite her in the ass one of these days. You all can take off. I'll escort our guest back to the jail downtown. Good job, everyone."

On the drive to the Fourth Avenue Jail, Tony maintained his silence. I was glad, because my mind was occupied with why Daphne Dixon had reached out for the first time in years.

From her concerned tone, something serious was going on. But I couldn't imagine what it might be or why she needed my help. And why call me and not Conor? After all, she worked with him a lot longer than she did with me. Maybe it was a female thing.

CHAPTER 10
A FRIEND IN TROUBLE

AFTER DROPPING Milano off at the jail's intake desk, I checked in with Conor.

"Hello, love," he said over the phone. I never tired of listening to that Irish brogue. "Are ya home?"

"Heading there. Daphne Dixon's coming over around seven."

"Daphne? Haven't spoken to her in a while. Not since Fiddler's funeral. How's the old girl doing?"

"Something is bothering her, but she didn't want to talk about it on the phone."

"Well, bollocks. I'm in north Scottsdale at the moment. Just grabbed one of our guys. May be close to eight before I arrive home."

"Take your time. I'll see you when you get home. Love you."

"Aye, love ya too."

I ran through the drive-thru at Popeye's on the way, since I wouldn't have time to make dinner and Conor would get home late.

By the time I pulled the Green Dragon into our garage, it was nearly six thirty.

Diana greeted me when I walked in, tail wagging and

eager for a walk. "Hey, baby," I said. "No walk for now, but I can take you out back to do your business."

I didn't know if she understood, but she was happy to get outside and do her thing.

Once we were back inside, I fed her, then took a quick shower. Ever since my crew and I stepped inside the cooler at New Life Medical Resources, I couldn't get the smell of death out of my nose. I felt like it had gotten into my pores.

My hair was still damp when Daphne rang the doorbell. As I rushed past the kitchen, I caught Diana eating something on the floor by the table. The box of fried chicken. Shit!

"Diana! No! Go to your room!"

She turned to me and hung her head, tail between her legs. She'd chowed down on at least two fried chicken breasts and had probably slobbered over the other pieces in the box. Her bowl of kibble was barely touched. Could I blame her? Why eat dry dog food when there was hot fried chicken?

"Go on!" I repeated, and she slunk back to the bedroom to her bed. The doorbell rang a second time. "Coming!"

Daphne Dixon had filled out in the middle since I'd seen her last. Her hair was pure white. And her formerly ever-present smile seemed to have faded.

"I'm so happy to see you." I hugged her. "Come on in."

"Good to see you too, hon."

I led her to the kitchen and picked up the box of chicken and set it on the counter. I was starving but not hungry enough to eat Diana's leftovers. "Sorry. The dog got into the chicken, but if you're hungry, I could whip us up something."

She shook her head. "No, dear, I ate before I came."

"You don't mind if I eat?"

"Not at all. I remember the crazy schedule you all keep. Conor here?"

"Not yet. He's dropping off a fugitive at Scottsdale City

Jail." I opened the fridge, reached in, and grabbed some left-over pizza.

"Something to drink?" I asked, closing the door. "Water? Soda? Something with a little kick? We have an open bottle of Pinot Grigio."

"A small glass of wine would be lovely. Thank you. So sorry I didn't make it to your wedding last year. I'd just had cataract surgery."

"Probably better that you didn't." I poured a glass for each of us, still feeling a little guilty I was eating in front of her.

"Yes, I heard. The news said someone was shot?"

"My father."

"Oh dear. How horrible! And at your wedding, of all things. How's he doing?"

"Much better. Thank you," I replied between bites. "So, what's going on with you?"

"You heard about our poor excuse for a state legislature?"

"The anti-trans bill? I'm hoping it won't pass."

"Well, they passed it this morning. Governor Denton signed it this afternoon. Made a big to-do about it like she was so proud to be stripping trans kids of their rights to medical care."

As if my Monday could get any worse. "Sadly, that doesn't surprise me. Those assholes take a sadistic pleasure in hurting people in my community. Especially the kids."

"Jinx, it's why I called. I'm worried about my grandbaby."

I vaguely remembered her showing photos of her daughter's newborn, when I was working for Conor's team about a decade earlier. "I forgot you had a grandchild."

"Rayna's child. Her name's Leia, and she's eleven. Until a couple years ago, she went by... well, another name. Guess I'm not supposed to use it no more. A deadname, I think you call it." She took a deep breath and let it out slowly.

"Surprised the heck out of me when Rayna explained it, I gotta tell ya. He, or rather she, was always a little feminine for a boy. I figured she might be gay. Her coming out as transgender was a shock. But thanks to knowing you way back when, I know how to be supportive of her and Rayna both."

"They're lucky to have you."

"Unfortunately, Rayna's ex isn't so understanding. Mike refuses to use Leia's new name or her female pronouns. Berates her for being trans. Leia hates going over there. Always comes home crying. Rayna's been trying to get sole custody, but you know how that goes. Court system's slow as molasses and is reluctant to take rights away from a parent, no matter how abusive."

"Wow, that really sucks."

"Now with this new law, Rayna's terrified of losing custody altogether and fears Leia won't be able to get her hormone therapy anymore. Poor child is absolutely beside herself."

I pushed my plate aside and clasped her hands. "Daphne, I'm so sorry. Is there anything I can do?"

"I don't know. The new law categorizes gender-affirming care as child abuse, which is the most absurd thing I ever heard. How could loving and supporting a child be abuse?"

"That's the way it is with those bigots. Hate is love. Truth is a lie. Oppressing minorities is freedom."

"I'm just worried about what will happen. I don't have to tell you the suicide rate of trans kids who don't get family support and affirming care is through the roof."

"Has Rayna talked with a lawyer?"

"Her divorce lawyer is an idiot with no clue about trans issues. But he was all she could afford."

"Have Rayna call Kirsten Pasternak. She's trans and

specializes in criminal law. Her business partner is cisgender but specializes in civil litigation. Between the two of them, they could advise you on the best course of action."

"That would be great, but she ain't got the money. And I'm on a fixed income."

"I'll cover it. Kirsten and her partner helped me get a nice settlement against an asshole last year. And they work with Lambda Legal and the ACLU. They might even represent you pro bono." I gave her the number.

"Thank you, sweetie. I knew talking with you was the answer."

"I don't know about having the answer, but I'm happy to put you in touch with someone who might."

"You were always a good soul, Jinx. Unlike Fiddler."

"Fiddler was… complicated. He had his good qualities." I didn't like speaking ill of the dead, even if he had threatened to kill me shortly before he died.

"Oh, please. He was a sexist grump. I only stayed with him as long as I did for the kids. After my R.J. went to college, I moved out."

I recalled that R.J. or Robert Junior was their son, a few years younger than Rayna.

"Well, I'm happy to help your family however I can. What about Leia's medication?"

Daphne shook her head. "I don't know. Her pediatrician canceled her upcoming appointment and won't write any more hormone prescriptions until this legal issue is resolved. I can't blame her for not wanting to risk getting arrested, but still. We feel abandoned."

"Is Leia a member of the Phoenix Gender Alliance?" I asked.

"No, what's that?"

"It's a support group for trans people in the Valley. They have a separate group for minors called the Hatchlings. Safe environment. All the volunteer coordinators have been finger-printed and vetted. I'm sure Leia's not the only one dealing with the issues at hand. You might reach out to them. They may know of other resources to help her continue her medications."

"Thank you. I'll look into it."

"And if worse comes to worst, they're welcome to stay here until things get resolved."

I heard the front door opened. A flash of golden fur breezed past the kitchen. Diana's collar tags jingled as she rushed to greet Conor.

"I smell fried chicken," he called as the front door whooshed shut.

"We're in here," I called.

Conor appeared in the doorway. His eyes looked tired, clearly from having the same kind of Monday I had. But his smile brightened when he saw his former receptionist. "Evening, Daphne. Pleasure to see you."

"Hello, young man." She stood and hugged him, then looked him over. "Appears that married life agrees with you."

"I'd say so." He clasped my hand. "I'm a lucky man. Several times over."

"I cried when they said you died in that explosion a few years ago."

His smile faded. "Aye, that was some bad business. But it all worked out. To what do we owe the honor of your company?"

"It's my granddaughter." Daphne explained the situation.

"Oi! Those plonkers are a particular kind of evil, going after the kiddos. I'm sorry your family's going through it."

"I gave them Kirsten's contact info and offered to let Rayna and Leia stay with us if need be."

"Aye, we'd love to have them. And if Rayna's nasty

wanker of an ex-husband comes snooping around, we'll give him what for. Don't ya worry."

"Thank you both. I'm so happy for you. I missed you, Jinx, when you left Viper to start your own company."

I shrugged. "I was afraid it might have caused too much friction, me dating the boss."

"Maybe," Daphne replied. "But now that you're married, you two should join forces again. Make it a family business."

I caught a twinkle in Conor's emerald eyes. He had suggested the same idea a few months ago, but I had resisted it. I enjoyed being independent and running my own crew, and I liked working at the Hub. Joining Ballou Fugitive Security with his company, Viper, might make sense on paper, but I wasn't ready to make the leap.

"Definitely something to consider," I said.

"Well, I best be going. You two kids have better things to do than entertain an old woman."

After Conor excused himself to take a shower, I walked her to the door. "So good to see you again," I said.

"Just wish it were under better circumstances. I'm sorry it took something like this for me to reach out."

"I'm glad you did. Let us know if there's anything else we can do to help."

"Thank you."

CHAPTER 11

LIVING IN DYSTOPIA

AFTER DAPHNE LEFT, I was still hungry, probably because I hadn't eaten lunch. Neither had Conor. So I whipped up some scrambled eggs mixed with Boursin cheese, green onions, and bacon bits.

"What happened to the chicken?" Conor asked when I brought him his plate.

I nodded at Diana, who lay nearby. "A certain fur baby had a go at it. I could dig what's left out of the trash."

"Oi! No thanks." He turned to her. "Have you been a naughty girl, Diana?"

Diana wagged her tail at the sound of her name and Conor's endearing tone.

"I considered letting her have the rest of it, but I didn't want her choking on the bones, and I wasn't sure if the spices they put in it were bad for dogs."

"Aye, probably not the best thing for her."

"Conor, I'm really worried. SCOTUS overturning *Roe*. States banning books by queer authors. Attempts to ban same-sex marriage and criminalize queer sex. And now this new anti-trans law criminalizing gender-affirming care.

"There are political candidates with a better-than-decent chance of getting elected who are demanding that all queer people be rounded up and executed. Feels like what I imagine 1930s Berlin must have been like for Jews and gays there. Having to hide for fear of being arrested. It all feels just so…"

"Hopeless?" Conor put his hand on mine.

"Was gonna say dystopian, but yeah."

"When my family moved from Dublin to Belfast, it was a shock, I'll tell ya. Strangers hating us just for being Catholic. Armed paramilitary groups attacking Catholic neighborhoods, shooting innocent people, burning homes, and the law turning a blind eye to it all. It was why my da joined the IRA."

"And we both know how that turned out." My words came out harsher than I expected.

He got misty-eyed, no doubt remembering the bombing in Omagh that cost his sister Bernie her life. "Not suggesting we should go setting off bombs or committing any other acts of terrorism, love. I'm just saying, I understand what it's like to be a target of the hateful mobs. And when the government that's supposed to be protecting ya doesn't give two shites if ya live or die."

"I know you get it. I'm just on adrenaline burnout. Every time I think it can't get any worse, it does. The fascists have such a stranglehold over everything. If I thought that gunning the fuckers down would do any good, I'd consider it. But it wouldn't change a damn thing."

"Wish I had some answers for ya, love. If ya want, we could go live with my mum in Dublin."

I shook my head. "Siobhan's very sweet. And I enjoyed visiting her this past summer and seeing Ireland. But I can't run away from this fight. Not with people like Daphne's granddaughter in the crosshairs."

"Aye. You're right. This is the time to stand and fight."

I didn't sleep well that night, haunted by nightmares of a

crazed mob chasing me, fueled no doubt by the memories of a real mob swarming our home and crashing our wedding.

The one thing Conor and I had going for us was our nearly impregnable house. The walls were cinderblocks filled with cement and reinforced with steel. The windows were inch-thick, bullet-resistant plexiglass. This home, which I had affectionately named the Bunker, had a few other surprises for unwanted guests.

The next morning, I stared at my reflection in the mirror, remembering when I had first transitioned. I was so desperate to look like a girl. I wanted long hair, insisted on wearing dresses all the time, and cried when my parents wouldn't let me wear makeup until I was fifteen.

My hair was still long, though I usually put it up in a ponytail or a bun. I rarely wore dresses or makeup. I dressed for the job. Makeup would only melt off my face when I chased after fugitives in the heat.

The only jewelry I wore regularly was my wedding ring and a bracelet with a handcuff key. No earrings on the job after one got pulled out of my ear during a nasty scuffle.

After all these years, I simply didn't feel the need to try so hard. Maybe that was because I definitely had a woman's body now. Or maybe I was just too tired to bother anymore. I never got misgendered except by bigots who knew my history and were trying to get under my skin. But fuck them. Because I knew who I was too.

I arrived at the Hub at seven thirty, before most of the others who used the space. The place was peaceful and quiet, and I had a couple of fugitives to catch. Becca had sent me a text saying she'd be in at eight and would run by Tres Leches for coffee and conchas.

I'd already made a first attempt on Tod Cooper, the abusive boyfriend. That hadn't ended well, especially for Zahara. I'd made two attempts to locate Donnie Krueger, the creepy body broker. Looked like it was back to Cooper.

I created a flyer offering a reward for information leading to Cooper's arrest with the phone number to my tip line. With the standard template I used, I only had to fill in the blanks with Cooper's image and details. I designed a similar one for Krueger.

When it was complete, I upload the file to a printer's website. Z and Rodeo would need to pick up a stack to pass out around Cooper's neighborhood.

My first call was to Caden, instructing him to stake out Cooper's house in case he returned home.

"And what's everyone else going to do when I'm just sitting in my truck twiddling my thumbs?" Caden asked.

"If you must know, I'm reaching out to Cooper's contacts. Rodeo and Zahara will be canvassing the neighborhood and passing out reward flyers. Where is all this insecurity coming from, Caden?"

"Just feels like I get left out of the action a lot. Hell, I still have to drive my own truck."

"I will look into getting another company truck, okay? But dude, you're not being left out of the action. You were with me at the front door at Krueger's house. Blew a hole through his front door."

"I know, but that shotgun shouldn't have been loaded with live rounds."

"I'm not blaming you. Though you should know to keep your finger off the trigger until you're ready to shoot."

"I know."

"Also, you were on the back-door entry team when we brought down Milano. No one is leaving you out of anything."

"Yeah, but most of the time, I'm sitting in my truck somewhere while the rest of you take down the target. I'm afraid you think I can't handle the rough stuff."

"I don't know how many times I have to say it, Caden. If

I didn't think you could handle the job, you wouldn't be on the team. Period."

"And you're not pissed that I quit way back when?"

"Sure, I was pissed. More disappointed, to be honest. But I understood. And I was glad you came back. You bring your own unique set of skills to the team. If you'd rather canvass the neighborhood and hang up posters…"

"No. Maybe I just have this need to prove myself."

"Lighten up, dude. And trust me to make the right decisions."

"Yeah, okay. Sorry, Jinxie."

"Not a problem. And if you see Cooper or his truck, call, and we'll make a second attempt to bag him. Do not try to play hero. We are a team."

"Roger that."

My next calls were to Zahara and Rodeo, instructing them to pick up the flyers and canvass the neighbors on the unlikely chance somebody knew where he was hiding.

Then I called Cooper's associates, starting with the ex-boyfriend, Sebastian Castro, since he was the one who filed the order of protection against him. Figured he'd be motivated to tell us where Cooper usually hung out.

"Hello?" asked an androgynous voice with a slight accent.

"Is this Sebastian Castro?"

"Who is this?" The tone was angry, wary, and threatening. "If this is one of Tod's pinche buddies calling to har—"

"No, Mr. Castro, my name is Jinx Ballou. I'm calling to help you."

"With what, exactly?"

"Tod's bail bond agent hired me to put him back in jail so he can't hurt you anymore. Would it be okay if I came by to talk?"

After a long pause, Castro answered. "Why do you want to talk to me?"

"Figured you knew him as well as anyone, and considering you felt the need to get an order of protection against him, I thought you'd be more likely to talk with me than, say, the buddies he listed on his bond application."

"Order of protection. What a fucking joke!"

"I get it. I've been in an abusive relationship before. That's partly why I'm very motivated to get him off the street for good. So you no longer have to worry about him. Can I stop by?"

"Sure. What the hell. You can come by at ten. A morning person I am not." He gave me his address, a condominium in the Central Corridor.

"Great. I'll see you at ten."

After I hung up, I took a deeper dive into Cooper on the SkipTrakkr site. Just as the results popped up, my phone rang with a caller ID I didn't recognize.

CHAPTER 12
SHIT MEET FAN

"BALLOU FUGITIVE RECOVERY," I said when I answered.

"Is this Jinx Ballou?"

"Yeah, who's this?"

"Detective O'Reilly, Phoenix PD, property crimes." The name didn't ring a bell. Remaining focused on the search results, I pulled up Cooper's most recent bank transactions, looking for any clue where he might be—a bar or a motel. Not that he could afford either with only $11.23 in his account.

"What can I do for you, Detective? I'm kind of busy."

"You picked up Anthony Milano yesterday?"

That got my attention. How did he know that?

"Yeah, what about it?"

"Where did you find him?"

"What's it matter? We were hired to arrest him. We did that and dropped him off downtown. Should still be in jail, unless you folks let him out again."

"Still in custody. But we found his exterminator van parked in front of a house on Indianola, off Thirty-Fourth Street. The homeowner reported finding a bag of their belongings near a partially open bedroom window."

"And this has what to do with me?" Was I in trouble for not calling the cops?

"Neighbor reports seeing a group of people in military gear apprehend Mr. Milano and take him away. That would be you and your crew, I presume."

"So? We spotted him coming out of the house, arrested him, took him to jail. Same as you would do."

"How did you know to find him there?"

Aw, shit. I couldn't tell him we pinged Milano's phone, since that was slightly illegal. Or more than slightly. Fourth Amendment and all that. I sure as hell would not get Becca in trouble for hacking the phone company.

"We posted flyers in the area offering a reward for tips that led to his capture. Standard operating procedure. Someone called in a tip."

"Who is this someone?"

"Anonymous."

"Really?" O'Reilly clearly wasn't buying it.

"Detective, if you want to know if he broke into the house, I can tell you we spotted him just as he was leaving. We arrested him and took him to jail. What's your problem?"

"You were partnered with Luis Garza back when you were on the force. Is that right?"

Garza? How the hell did he know that? Had he run some background check on me? Then something tickled at the back of my brain. "Wait! You're Tommy O'Reilly? Worked patrol with Garza and me at the Maryvale precinct."

"Yeah, he and I were partnered up after you got suspended for groping a suspect."

"I did not grope a suspect, asshole. That murdering scumbag Phillip Nelson filed a bogus complaint after I arrested him for torching a dozen homes and killing several people. PSB found the complaint had no merit. End of story."

"And yet they fired you."

"Like hell they did. I quit after assholes in the department started harassing me. You know, for a detective, you really don't have a clue."

"So this anonymous tipster didn't want the reward you offered?"

I scoffed when I recognized what he was doing. Textbook interrogation technique. Keep the suspect off-balance and off-guard by repeatedly changing the subject. Make intentionally incorrect assertions so they feel the need to talk and set the record straight. Get them emotional, so they say something incriminating.

What I couldn't figure out was what he thought I was guilty of. Did he think I was conspiring with Milano? If so, O'Reilly was an idiot. Or maybe he was just pissed because he'd been assigned to investigate a burglary, only to find that a lowly bounty hunter had already solved his case for him. *Geez, dude. Just take the win already.*

"If a tipster isn't interested in a reward, it's no skin off my nose. And how I do my job is none of your business, so long as it's legal. You got any more questions, talk to Kirsten Pasternak, my attorney."

"Ms. Ballou, you need to—"

I ended the call and blocked the number. I'd already said more than I should.

I never should have spoken to him in the first place. Rule number one when dealing with cops—never talk to one without an attorney. Even if you'd done nothing wrong. Even if you were just trying to help. Too many cops were on an ego trip, and there were too many ways the shit could land back on you.

Becca arrived at the Hub around eight thirty, coffee and pastries in hand. Her eyes looked tired, and her skin was pale.

"Morning," I said, giving her a quick hug. "Chronic fatigue flare up?"

"Sí, almost didn't come in." She took a sip of her coffee.

"Why did you?"

She shrugged. "Promised you I would."

"Girl, you're your own boss. You don't have to come in just for me. Hell, I'm going to be heading out in a few hours, anyway."

"I know, but I would feel bad if you had to drink the swill that passes for coffee in the break room. And seeing you always makes me happy."

"That's odd. Most people start running when they see me."

"Well, you do chase bail jumpers for a living."

"I suppose there's that. How's Easton?"

"They're good. Just got a promotion. Won't have to travel anymore and can telecommute most days."

"Sweet. Guess you're liking that."

"Yeah." She paused, and her wan expression turned darker. "I suppose you heard about the legislation that our pinche governor signed yesterday?"

"I did. Fucking fascists. You remember Daphne Dixon?"

"Fiddler's ex? Used to work for Conor?"

"That's her. She's got an eleven-year-old granddaughter who's trans. And an ex-son-in-law who's a major transphobe. Deadnames and misgenders the kid whenever she's at his place. Daphne's daughter is afraid of losing custody under the new law."

"¡Hijo de puta! What the fuck is wrong with these people? Hating on their own kids. What are they going to do?"

"I referred her to Kirsten. I hope she can find a way to protect them."

"You making any progress on your current cases?"

"Nabbed Milano yesterday, thanks to you. But it may end up biting me in the ass." I told her about my exchange with Detective O'Reilly.

"What crawled up his ass and died?"

"My guess, he's pissed I didn't call the cops after we caught Milano breaking into a house. Honestly, I'd had enough encounters with cops yesterday. I just needed to turn Milano in and go home."

"Well, let me know if you need me to run anything. Ping phones. Run some algorithms. Hack into some databases." Her eye gleamed.

"I don't want to put you at risk anymore."

Becca shrugged. "What's life without a little risk, mi compa?"

I chuckled and went back to my research. Nothing of interest on Cooper's recent bank transactions. No phone calls on his cell. Maybe I'd have better luck when I talked with his boyfriend, Castro.

I switched gears and started calling Krueger's references. The first was his daughter, Amy. She had helped arrange his bail bond.

"Great Harvest. Amy Krueger speaking," she said in a pert, confident voice.

"Ms. Krueger, this is Jinx Ballou. I work with Assurity Bail Bonds. Seems there's a problem with your father's bond. I need to speak with him so we can get this issue resolved."

"I don't know where he is, if that's what you're calling about."

"It's very important I speak with him. Is there another number where we can reach him?"

"I'm sorry, but he doesn't confide in me."

From the tone of her voice, I got the impression that their relationship was strained. Not so much that she would refuse to help bail him out, but it didn't sound like they were close.

"I understand. I'd just hate to see this situation get worse. Don't want him to lose his home or his business." I honestly couldn't care less if the creepy guy ended up in a ditch somewhere. But establishing rapport required embellishing the truth a little and projecting a sense of empathy. "Does he have another family member or a friend he might stay with?"

"What did you say your name was?"

"Jinx. As I said, Assurity—"

"You're that bounty hunter. Nancy told me how you and your thugs assaulted her a year ago when they tried to frame her. And again yesterday in your attempt to railroad my father. You people are a menace."

So she and Nancy Turner were close. Interesting.

"Did Nancy the necrophiliac also tell you she locked my team and me in the cooler with the dead bodies?" The words just came out. I didn't normally lose my cool on the job like this. Maybe this new anti-trans law was getting to me.

"I'm sure she did nothing of the kind."

I took a breath and got my emotions under control. "Look, Ms. Krueger, your father missed his court date. I'm sure it was an honest mistake." Not. "All I want to do is help him get things sorted out. If he turns himself in to me, we can see about getting his bail reset until he and his lawyer can clear his name at the trial. But if he remains a fugitive, it makes him look more guilty. Worse, all kinds of bad things could happen. He could lose his home, his business, even his life. None of us want that to happen."

"Are you threatening my father?"

"No, I'm just..."

"To hell with you, lady! I won't help you frame my father."

The line went dead. Damn.

The next reference was a Dr. Matthew Stromberg.

After the first ring, a perky female voice asked, "Valley Transplant Specialists, how may I direct your call?"

"Yes, I need to speak with Dr. Stromberg about an urgent matter."

"Is this about an upcoming surgical appointment?"

"No, it's more of a personal nature. But it's vital he returns my call." I paused for effect. "A family emergency, I'm afraid."

"Oh my goodness. Has something happened to Judy?"

I had no idea who Judy was. His wife? His daughter? His pet Guinea pig? "Because of HIPAA restrictions, I can't really give any details."

"Unfortunately, he's in surgery until later this afternoon. But I can try to get a message for him to call you. Your name?"

"Liz Windsor," I lied and gave the number for my burner phone to the woman on the other end.

"Okay, I'll let him know it's urgent," she said. "Thank you for calling."

I called a couple more of Krueger's references, each of whom worked at mortuaries in the West Valley. Both were shocked that Krueger's bail application listed them as references.

One called him a lying son of a bitch. The other called his parents' marriage into question. Both hung up before I could use their animus against him to get any useful information. It was going to be another one of those mornings.

I looked at my watch and called Rodeo, asking him to meet me at Sebastian Castro's condo building. Caden would probably complain that I didn't choose him, but Rodeo was bisexual and could turn on the queer-guy charm that might encourage Castro to open up more.

"I'll see you later, Becks," I said, gathering my stuff. "Get some rest. And if you don't, I'll call Easton and have them drag your cute little brown ass back home."

She grinned tiredly. "Love you, too, bestie. Good hunting."

"Thanks."

CHAPTER 13
A THING FOR BAD BOYS

SEBASTIAN CASTRO LIVED in a pricy high-rise off Central Avenue. It left me wondering what a guy who could afford one of those condos was doing with a scumbag like Tod Cooper?

I parked the Green Dragon next to Rodeo's Blue Bomber in the condo's guest lot.

I wanted to convey to Mr. Castro that I intended to bring Cooper in and had the means to do it. But I didn't want to look so much like a cop that Castro would be scared silent. The queer community and cops have a long ugly history of conflict.

I removed my body armor and duty belt, but kept my badge hung on a chain around my neck.

"Any luck talking with Cooper's neighbors?" I asked Rodeo when I stepped out. He had similarly disarmed.

He shook his head. "The few who knew him didn't care for him much and had no idea where he might have gone."

"With any luck, his boyfriend has some answers. But just in case he's not immediately forthcoming, don't be afraid to turn on the gay-boy charm to help get him talking." I gave him a wink.

"Jinx Ballou! Are you suggesting I flirt with the man?" he

said in an over-the-top effeminate voice. "What would your brother think?"

"Knowing Jake, I'm sure he'd think it was hilarious. And I'm not asking you to sleep with the guy. Just be a bit of a cocktease."

He fanned his face in full-on Scarlett O'Hara mode. "I swear to the Lord, the things I do to make a living in this cruel world."

I punched him in the shoulder. "Puh-lease. Come on!"

The building's lobby was nice. Marble floors, decorative walls, security desk. Everything screamed money, privilege, and privacy. I knew the place catered to the upscale queer community, but I didn't know so many of us could afford such a fancy crib. These condos had to run in the high six figures or more.

I approached the security desk. A woman with deep-set eyes and a prominent nose eyed us warily. She looked like a cross between a Russian prison guard and Sister Mary Luke, who taught Sunday school at my mother's church when I was five.

"Can I help you?" Her affected accent was just a little too posh to be believable.

"We're here to see Sebastian Castro. He's expecting us. I'm Jinx Ballou. This is my associate, Nathaniel Kwan."

She gave us the suspicious side eye as she dialed the phone on her desk. "Mr. Castro, so sorry to trouble you. There are two guests in the lobby who claim you're expecting them. A Ms. Blue and a Mr. Kwang."

I wasn't sure if her mispronunciation of our names was deliberate or the result of incompetence, but I ignored it.

"Yes, sir. I'll send them your way." She hung up. "You may proceed."

"Told you," I said wryly.

If the building's lobby was impressive, Castro's condo was more so. From the original artwork on the walls to the furniture and accents, everything had an understated elegance, like the "after" from one of those home remodeling shows.

Castro himself looked to be in his early to mid-twenties. Slender and sexy, what some in the community called a twink.

His collarless button-down shirt and skinny jeans looked designer. He wore eyeliner and foundation, perhaps to cover the shiner on his swollen left eye. A finger on his left hand was encased in a metal splint.

How the hell could a guy his age afford this place? Maybe he came from money. Maybe he was a tech guru. Or maybe he made his money the old-fashioned way. Sex work.

"Can I get you two anything? A soda? Water? Maybe something with a kick?" He led us to a suede sofa. When I sat on it, it felt like I was resting on a cloud.

"I'm good." I assured him. "We're just here to learn more about your boyfriend, Tod Cooper, so we can return him to custody."

He strolled to a bar cart and poured himself a glass of whiskey.

"Not so much a boyfriend as a horrible mistake, I'm afraid." He sighed. "Tod the Bod. Tragedy that a man with a physique that fine had to be such a raging bitch. He was fun. Until he wasn't. Guess I've always had a thing for the bad boys." The ring finger of one of his hands gingerly touched the corner of his eye and wiped away a tear.

"We nearly caught him at home yesterday, but he managed to slip past us and took off. I'm guessing he's probably not going back there any time soon. Any idea where he might go?"

"Was Timothy with him?" Castro asked.

"He was. He's with DCS now."

"Pity. Cute kid." Castro tapped his lip as he considered my question. "Loved playing *Mario Kart* with me."

"Where might we find Tod the Bod, Sebastian?" Rodeo asked with a hint of seduction in his voice. He leaned forward, and the air crackled with gay masculine energy. I felt a bit like a voyeur.

Castro gave Rodeo the once-over, apparently liking what he saw. "You're cute. Don't really look like a Nathaniel to me, though. Maybe a Nate."

"Most people call me Rodeo."

"Ahhh, that definitely fits. Well, if you must know, I first met Tod at Stallions. Usually showed up around nine. Ever been there, Rodeo?"

I half expected Rodeo to blush. He didn't. He simply adjusted his Stetson and deepened his smile. "Maybe a time or two. Or many. Where might we find Tod during the day?"

"Normally, I'd expect him at work. Though with all that's going on, probably not. He liked to hang with some of his construction buddies after hours. Straight boys. Ugh. Don't even know Miss Thang is queer as a three-dollar bill."

"What are the names of his work buddies?"

"Chad or Steven or Doug or Ken. Buncha dumb meatheads, if you ask me. Not worth remembering their names. And did he ever introduce me to them? No, he did not." Castro rolled his eyes. "I was his dirty little secret. The boy toy he visited when he needed to get sucked and fucked. But that queen had the audacity to get mad if I dared spend time with anyone else. Hello! A girl's gotta make a living somehow."

"How do you make a living exactly?" I asked.

Castro narrowed his eyes at me, as if I were cockblocking him. "What do you care?"

I held up my hands in apology. "Just curious. A condo like this can't be cheap."

"My father bought this place for me. He's the founder of a large automotive manufacturing plant in Mexico City. So boring! He sent me to school at ASU, and after earning my bachelor's in business administration, I stayed. Honestly, I think Papi prefers it that way. Doesn't want his business associates to know his baby boy is a maricón. This place was a 'fuck you, goodbye' present."

"I'm sorry," I said.

"Don't be. The joke's on him. I make my own money now."

"Doing?" He was right, though. It was none of my business. And not relevant to finding Cooper.

"You think I'm a pinche puta, don't you? 'Prissy little queen, the only way he makes money is to fuck and suck for a buck.'"

"No judgment. I've had friends who were sex workers. No shame in it."

"Well, Miss Buttinsky, I'm a fucking game developer. I earn more in a month than my father makes in a year. Just so happens that the marketing director of the company I work for lives in Scottsdale. We hook up for drinks occasionally. Sometimes more than just drinks. I'm poly. The whole monogamy thing is so fucking patriarchal."

"So you don't know Tod's friends?" Rodeo asked, steering the subject back to the case.

"No, but I followed him one night after he smacked me around and called me a whore." Castro shot me a withering glance. "He met up with his buddy Ken for drinks at some shithole bar north of here."

"Ken got a last name?" I pressed.

"Melbourne, I think, like the city in Australia. I remember that because when the guy walked in, Tod got all über-butch and said, 'Ken Melbourne's in the house.'"

Ken Milburn had written Cooper a check for a few hundred dollars and was Cooper's first reference on his bail bond application. It must be him.

"What's the name of the bar?"

"Fuck if I can remember. It was in a shopping center on

the southeast corner of Northern and Nineteenth Avenue. I sat at the other end of the bar, glaring at him and making sure he could see me. Next day, he called, all apologies.

"That was his thing. Mr. Hot and Sexy one minute. Then, the moment after he shot his wad, he turned into a psycho bitch from hell. Next day, he would apologize. Total Jekyll and Hyde. And stupid me, I let him come over again. Big mistake. Big, big mistake. Soon as he stepped in…"

Castro shook his head and shivered. "Bitch damn near broke my eye socket. Broke my finger. Cost me a fortune in hospital bills. Then the cops had the nerve to ask what I'd done to make him angry. Fucking assholes. That was when I got the order of protection. Had him served at work, the little bitch. Not that it did me much good."

"Why? What happened?"

"I was coming out of Stallions the next night. He jumped me in the parking lot. Fortunately, there was a couple who'd just pulled in. I'd probably be dead now if they hadn't run him off."

"Did you call the cops?" I asked.

"You kidding? After what happened the last time? No thanks. Them boys in blue can kiss my tight brown ass."

"I'm so sorry that happened to you," Rodeo said, putting a hand on Castro's arm. "You think Tod's staying with Ken?"

Castro put his free hand on Rodeo's. "Don't know for sure, but that would be my guess, darling."

"Anywhere else he might stay if not with Ken? He have family in the area?"

"Far as I know, the rest of his family's in south Georgia. If he's staying someplace other than at home or with Ken, fuck if I know where."

"Well, thank you for your time." I stood up abruptly and nodded at Rodeo. We'd gotten as much as we could out of the guy, and watching him flirt with my brother's boyfriend was weirding me out.

"Yes." Rodeo squeezed Castro's hand, then stood. "We'll do everything we can to keep him from hurting you again. I promise. You've been most helpful, Sebastian."

"Come back anytime, cowboy. I'll bring the saddle and the chaps. Maybe even a whip. We'll go for a ride."

"Sorry, but I'm already seeing someone," Rodeo said with a stammer, breaking character at last. His face colored.

"Bring him. I'm sure the three of us could have loads of fun."

"I'll, uh, keep it in mind."

I couldn't help but chuckle. Rodeo didn't get his feathers ruffled very often. He was generally unflappable. So this was fucking hilarious.

When we returned to the parking lot, I asked, "Have fun talking with Sebastian?"

"This bar where Cooper met his buddy," Rodeo muttered, struggling to keep a straight face. "It sounds familiar."

"You didn't answer my question, cowboy."

"Stop it. Getting hit on with my boyfriend's sister right next to me was awkward."

"Oh, I'm the problem?" I said, taking mock offense. "Don't you know? Monogamy is so patriarchal. And hey, you were doing some serious flirting. Can you blame the guy for flirting back? Such a cocktease you are."

"I was playing the part you requested. And you were just enjoying that way too much."

"Damn right I was. Seeing you get embarrassed for once was priceless."

"Back to business. What's the plan now, boss?"

"Let me check in with Zahara and see if she and Caden have had any luck. Then maybe we can go check out this Ken Milburn guy. If we have no luck there, we can try that bar on Northern and Nineteenth." It sounded familiar to me too. Like I'd been there. Just couldn't recall the name.

"Copy that, boss."

I pulled out my phone and called Zahara. "Yo, Z. What's the word?"

"No sign of Cooper's truck. Passed out flyers around the neighborhood. Most of the neighbors didn't know him. The few who did said he was an asshole and did not know where he might be."

"Rodeo got the same reaction from the people he talked with. Good news—we may have a lead on him. Just need to have Becca check something for me, and I'll call you back."

"Sounds good, Jinx."

CHAPTER 14
BUSTED

I WASN'T sure if Becca had gone home to rest or not. But despite my earlier protestations, I sent her a text asking her to ping Cooper's phone. I then ran Ken Milburn's name and phone number through SkipTrakkr.

Milburn lived off Fortieth Street, just north of Thomas Road, close to where we caught Tony Milano the day before.

When Becca texted me back, confirming Cooper was at his buddy's house, I called Zahara and told her where to meet.

I saw no sign of Tod Cooper's truck, but Milburn's two-car garage door was shut. Could very well be in there.

We parked our four SUVs in a line, blocking off the driveway and entire front yard of Milburn's house. The only opening was the next-door neighbor's driveway. A twenty-foot saguaro and several barrel cactuses separated the two yards. Cooper risked getting crushed to death by the saguaro if he tried to use that driveway as an escape route.

I strapped on my body armor, and the four of us gathered on the street side of our vehicle barricade.

"Who lives here?" Caden asked.

"One of Cooper's buddies. A guy named Ken Milburn."

Zahara glanced at the house, then back at me. "You sure Cooper's here? I don't see his truck."

"Becca pinged his phone. He's here."

Caden raised an eyebrow. "I thought you weren't asking Becca to do that because of the legal risk and all."

"I prefer not to, but this guy beat up his boyfriend a few times. He violated an order of protection. And you saw what he did to his own kid. I don't want anyone else getting hurt. Since this isn't his residence, we can't force our way in and search the place unless we have proof he's here. We now have that proof." We just couldn't use it to justify our forced entry, unfortunately.

"Anyone else want to question my methods?" My question came out a little harsh, but I was eager to slap the cuffs on Cooper.

"You could call his number," Zahara suggested. "Just to be sure."

"We'd never hear it ring from here. We'd have to be up next to the house, and even then, there's no guarantee we'd hear it. He could have it muted or turned off."

They gave me questioning looks. Who the hell was running this show, anyway?

"Okay, fine. Before we make entry, I'll call the number. But even if we don't hear it ringing inside, I'm going in. He's here, okay?"

"Roger that, boss," Rodeo said. The others seemed content with that response.

"And don't forget who writes your paychecks." I added. Still, I had to remind myself that while I was in charge, I didn't need to put them in legal jeopardy unnecessarily. "Rodeo and Z, take the back. Caden, you cover the garage. I'll make entry through the front. Radios on. Let's do this."

Everyone checked in once they got into position. The muffled sound of what I guessed was a movie or TV show drifted from inside the house. I set my battering ram next to the front door, then pulled up Cooper's number on my burner, the same one I'd used to leave a message saying there was a problem with his bond application.

I thought I heard a phone ringing inside, but it was hard to tell over the sounds of the television.

After the second ring, a gruff voice said, "What?"

"Mr. Cooper, this is Ms. Windsor from Assurity again."

"Fuck you, bitch." The call went dead. But I was sure I'd heard him shout from inside. He was here. And we had him cornered.

I pounded on the door and rang the bell a few times. It was one of those fancy new ones with a video camera. Maybe Cooper could watch the video later showing how we nailed his ass.

"Bail enforcement! Come to the door now!"

A few minutes later, a white guy with the physique of an ogre opened the door. Six feet six at least. Somewhere north of three hundred pounds, all of it muscle. He matched the MVD photo of the Ken Milburn I pulled up on SkipTrakkr. Shit, he was big. Like he could pound railroad spikes with his fist.

"The fuck you want, lady?"

"I'm here for Tod Cooper. We know he's here."

"You don't know shit! Get lost."

He started to shut the door, but I blocked it with my boot. The man must've put his considerable weight into it because jolts of pain shot up my leg.

I pulled back before I lost my foot. The door slammed shut. A dead bolt clicked into place.

"Mr. Milburn!" I shouted. "Harboring a fugitive is a felony in this state. Don't make us haul your ass in along with Cooper's."

"Fuck you, bitch!" he replied.

"Okay, team," I called into my radio. "I called and heard the target answer. Resident refused me entry. Over."

"Roger that, Coyote One," Rodeo said. "We're ready when you are. Over."

"Let's rock and roll. Over and out."

I hefted the ram and smashed open the door with a couple of blows. I dropped it and drew my Taser.

"Son of a bitch!" Ken the ogre stood on the other side of his living room, talking to someone on the phone. "They're breaking into my house."

"Get on your knees! Hands behind your head. Do it now!"

He tossed the phone onto a couch and reached around his back with one hand, clearly going for a weapon.

I pulled the trigger on the Taser. Milburn's face contorted in pain. A camo-colored pistol dropped from his hand. He hit the floor next to it. I rushed in, cuffed him, and kicked the gun out of reach.

"All you had to do was give up Cooper, but you wouldn't listen. Where is he?"

"Fuck you, bitch," the ogre groaned.

"Not much of a vocabulary."

I replaced the cartridge on my Taser and called on my radio. "Front door breached. Coyote Two and Coyote Three, breach back door. Over."

A loud crack and the sound of shattering glass came from the other side of the house.

"Back door breached. Over," Rodeo replied.

"Coyote Four, keep your head on a swivel for any signs of our target in case he gets past us. Over."

"Wilco, Coyote One. Over."

I searched the living room while Milburn spewed a stream of profanity and threats.

Once I'd determined that Cooper wasn't under the furniture, I shouted, "Living room clear!" Then I moved on to the kitchen.

"Arizona room clear!" Zahara called.

I was checking the pantry when I heard the wail of distant sirens. *Someone's having a bad day*, I thought. Something my father used to say when we heard sirens when I was a kid.

"First bedroom clear!" Rodeo called.

Z followed with, "Guest bath clear!"

"Kitchen clear." I turned to check the laundry room.

"Coyote One, Coyote Four. We got company. Over."

The sirens were getting louder. Shit.

"Copy that, Coyote Four. Maintain your position. Over." I tried to remind myself that it would be fine once we had Cooper in cuffs. Until then, things might get a little awkward.

"Master bedroom clear," Rodeo called over the radio.

I ignored the sirens and searched the small laundry room, then opened the door to the garage.

The overhead light flickered on. I was tempted to open the exterior doors, but if Cooper was in here, I didn't want to give him an escape route, especially if cops had Caden distracted.

A Chevy pickup truck dominated one side of the space. The other side looked like a fucking arsenal. A wide range of weapons were mounted on the wall, including shotguns, assault rifles, hunting rifles, a couple of crossed cavalry swords, and a Japanese katana. A reloading press sat on a bench with a canister of powder and a large jar of spent brass cartridges. Flags hung from the ceiling, including the U.S. flag, a Don't Tread on Me flag, a USMC flag, and a Confederate flag. Guns, guts, and glory! Yee-haw!

"Tod Cooper, if you're in here, now is the time to surrender. I already have your buddy Ken in cuffs. Your son is with DCS. Let's not make things any worse."

The wail of sirens outside ceased. I searched the wall cabinets. Most were filled with assorted junk. Christmas decorations, tools, boxes of videos, and old stereo equipment.

"Boss," Caden said over the radio. Nothing but static followed.

"Say again, Coyote Four." Static. "Caden, you okay?" Shit.

"Guest bedroom clear," Zahara said over the radio.

"Master bath clear."

"Tod, come on out. I know you're in here." Honestly, I wasn't sure. A cord hung down from an access door to the attic. Could he be up there? I hoped not. If he was, sticking my head up there was likely to result in getting my damn head blown off.

"Ma'am, put down the weapon," called a male voice behind me. "Do it now!"

I turned toward the laundry room. A uniformed officer stood with his service weapon trained on me. Behind him, the ogre smirked.

"That's her. Bitch broke down my door and tased me."

I held up the Taser in a nonthreatening gesture, fingers far from the trigger guard. "Officer, this man is harboring Tod Cooper, a fugitive wanted for multiple counts of assault and violating an order of protection. My bail enforcement team had the right to enter and apprehend the fugitive. I can show you the bench warrant."

"Is this true, sir? Is the man she's looking for here?"

"Ain't no one here but me."

"Ma'am, did you find the man you're looking for?"

"Not yet. My guess is he's holed up there in the attic." But I suddenly had the sinking feeling he might not be.

Several years earlier, a different bounty-hunting team had received a tip that a fugitive was hiding out in a particular house. Only the tip turned out to be bogus.

The house they'd forced their way into belonged to the Phoenix PD chief of police. But if Becca had pinged the phone, Cooper had to be here. Hell, I'd heard it ring and talked to him, albeit briefly. Unless…

The cop once again raised his service pistol. "Ma'am, put down the weapon, get down on your knees, and lace your fingers behind your head. You're under arrest for breaking and entering and aggravated assault."

"Wait, wait! Stop!" I made a show of setting my Taser on the bench. "Cooper's here. You can't let him escape."

"What makes you think the man you're after is here?" the officer asked.

Obviously, I couldn't say Becca had pinged his phone. But I could call the number again and hope it rang.

"Officer, I'm going to reach for my phone. Please do not shoot me."

"Ma'am, you need to get on your knees."

"Officer, I used to be a cop too. Maryvale Precinct. Sergeant Szalkowski was my CO. I caught the Maryvale Arsonist."

His expression relaxed an iota. "You were a cop?"

"I was."

"But not now?"

"Long story. Point is, I can prove that Cooper is here. Just allow me to call his phone number. We'll probably hear it ringing up in the attic."

"She's lying," Milburn growled. "It's a trick."

"Not a trick," I insisted. "If I call his phone number, and we don't hear it ring, then by all means, take me in. But if it rings, then let me take my fugitive and leave. Deal?"

"This is bullshit!" Milburn stalked toward me like he intended to pound me into the concrete slab.

"Sir, step away from this woman. Ma'am, make the call."

My insides were shaking like Jell-O in an earthquake. What if I was wrong? What if Cooper was here when Becca pinged the number, but he left?

I called the number and listened. For what felt like an

hour, I heard nothing but the pounding of my pulse in my ears. And then the deedle-deedle of a default ringtone echoed in the garage.

The ogre's face turned crimson. "Bitch."

The phone, wherever it was, rang a second time. The officer turned to Milburn. "Sir, is that your phone ringing?"

I was confused. Why was his phone ringing? Had I dialed the wrong number? And then it hit me.

"Shit. They switched phones," I muttered.

"Ma'am, I'm afraid you'll have to come with me."

CHAPTER 15
JUMPING THE LINE

I HAD to give Tod Cooper credit. For a knuckle-dragging asshole, he'd bested me twice. And now I had to figure a way to get myself out of the situation.

I told my crew to keep their mouth shut, that I'd get us out of this mess, before they put us in the back of two squad cars and hauled us to Phoenix PD's MountainView Precinct.

They stuck me in an interview room and let me sweat for an hour.

A man in a suit walked in, grinning like the Cheshire Cat. "Well, well, didn't expect to see you so soon."

I didn't recognize him, but his voice was vaguely familiar. But then a while had passed since I'd been a patrol officer. Maybe he just had a better memory than I did.

"And you are?"

"Detective O'Reilly."

Then it clicked. The asshole who'd called me earlier that morning. O'Reilly was also the name of the former police chief whose home was invaded by another bounty hunter team several years ago. A relation, possibly?

"This whole thing is a big misunderstanding," I stated.

"Is it? Yesterday, you witnessed a residence being burgled but failed to report it. Today, we catch you breaking into a citizen's home yourself with some cockamamie story of the resident harboring a fugitive. And yet this alleged fugitive was nowhere to be seen."

"We didn't need to call you people when we caught Milano yesterday. We brought him to you."

"But you didn't report the crime."

"Nothing was stolen from that house. We made sure of that. No harm, no foul. The man's behind bars. As for today, we received a tip that Tod Cooper was hiding out at Mr. Milburn's house. And in fact, Mr. Milburn had Cooper's phone. So clearly, he had been there recently. Must've seen us pull up and escaped out the back. What's your problem, dude? Do I need to call my lawyer?"

"I don't know. Do you?"

"I'm not saying anything further. I want to call my lawyer now."

O'Reilly didn't move or say anything for several minutes. When he spoke, he said, "I don't appreciate vigilantes like you terrorizing my city. If you wanted to play cop, you shouldn't have turned in your badge. That mail-order bounty hunter badge is bullshit. I could get you for impersonating an officer."

Against my better judgment, I replied, "And I could get you for impersonating a human being. I am a sworn bail enforcement agent licensed by the State of Arizona. Those are the words printed on my body armor: bail enforcement. Nowhere does it say I'm a cop. At no time do I suggest I'm a cop."

He glared at me but said nothing.

"Assurity Bail Bonds hired me to return both Milano and Cooper to custody pursuant to a judge's order after they failed to appear. You guys are understaffed already. Do you really want to be chasing bail jumpers as well? We all have a job to do. We're both here to keep the city safe from violent criminals who need to be behind bars.

"Clearly, Milburn has been harboring Cooper. A man who not only likes to beat up other men but also his five-year-old kid. But you want to arrest me and leave Cooper roaming the streets? What's that say about Phoenix PD? I quit the force because of bullshit like this."

I let those words sink in.

Finally, O'Reilly stood. "I'm going to let you and your team go with a warning. That warning is this. Quit playing cop in my precinct. I find you breaking into someone else's house, I'm putting you and your team behind bars. I don't care who you're after."

I wanted to respond, but I didn't want to prolong things, or worse, get the asshole to change his mind.

By the time we'd all been released and had paid to have the SUVs released from the city's impound lot, it was two o'clock in the afternoon.

We were no closer to finding Cooper, and I was out several hundred dollars in towing and impound fees. A marvelous start to a week that was already lousy. All tricks and no treats.

"Okay, team," I said as we sat in a booth at Grumpy's Bar and Grill, close to my home. "After lunch, I want Rodeo to stake out Ken Milburn's house. Caden, watch Cooper's place. Zahara, keep eyes on New Life Medical Resources in case Krueger shows up. If any of you spot one of our fugitives, text the group for backup. Don't take him down by yourself. No heroes."

I eyed Caden. From his expression, he clearly got the message. As much as I understood his desire to prove himself to me, I didn't need anyone getting hurt or worse.

"I hear you," he said. "What're you going to be doing?"

"I'm going to focus on Krueger for the time being. Keeping tabs on all calls going into New Life Medical, calling his contacts, poring over his financials and phone logs. Looking for anything that might point to where he's hiding. Aside from the malpractice incident that lost him his license, this is the first real legal trouble he's been in. I don't think he has the street smarts that Cooper does. Once we apprehend him, we can focus all our resources on Cooper."

"New Life Medical Resources closes in a few hours," Zahara said. "What should I do then?"

"Tail his office manager, Nancy Turner, when she leaves. My gut tells me she's staying in touch with her boss. Hell, he may even be staying with her. Call me if you see anything suspicious."

"Will do."

When we went our separate ways, I drove to north Scottsdale.

Amy Krueger worked as the CFO of a nonprofit that operated a string of food banks throughout the Valley. I felt sure she knew where her father might be hiding. I just had to convince her it was in both her and her dad's best interest for him to turn himself in. Considering our short, tense phone conversation earlier, that was going to be a trick.

Along the way, I listened to KJZZ, the local NPR station. A news story came on about the new law criminalizing gender-affirming care for minors.

DCS had opened up investigations into seven families—four in Phoenix, two in Tucson, and one in Prescott. Meanwhile, pediatricians and endocrinologists throughout the state were now refusing to treat their trans youth patients for fear of being arrested and losing their medical licenses.

The whole thing made me sick. What the hell was this country turning into? The trans community's situation had seemed so hopeful. Better than when I had come out so many years ago. But then Donald Trump, or the Dick Tater as I preferred to call him, had turned the White House into a cesspool of willful ignorance, corruption, cruelty, and white nationalism.

The national midterm elections were only a week away. If they didn't go well, I dreaded to think what might happen. How soon before they started rounding us all up and putting us into concentration camps?

At the end of the segment, the station played Norah Jones's song "My Dear Country." Appropriate. Felt like half this damn country had become deranged. That every day felt darker than the one before. Much darker than any Halloween as Election Day approached.

I pulled into the parking lot of Great Harvest. The organization did a lot of good for the underprivileged and had helped more than a few of my friends over the years as they struggled through loss of jobs and homes after coming out as trans or otherwise queer. And with the rampant inflation, there was a lot more demand for Great Harvest's services.

The corporate office was in a four-story building just outside the Loop 101. They shared the second floor with a business that had a generic-sounding name and an equally generic logo. I often wondered how businesses like that survived.

"How can I help you?" the young man at the receptionist's desk asked with a smile that seemed genuine.

"I'm here to see Amy Krueger. I believe she's expecting me. It's about her father." I had taken off my gear, wearing a friendly blue polo shirt and nice jeans. I hoped I smelled better than the back of the patrol car I'd ridden in earlier.

The receptionist made a call, nodded, then hung up. "She'll be out soon."

I didn't have to wait long. A woman in a navy pantsuit stepped into the lobby. She had the same eyes and heart-shaped face as her father.

I offered my hand. "Hi, I'm Jinx Ballou."

"I told you to leave my family alone."

"Look, Ms. Krueger, I'm not here to cause you any

trouble or embarrassment. I have a lot of respect for your organization. They do a lot of good."

"But you're not here about what we do at Great Harvest."

"No. I'm here because your father failed to show up at court, violating his bail bond. I truly want to help him get past this so he can continue with his work and his life."

She studied me for a moment.

"Fine. Follow me."

She led me down a hallway to a sizable office and shut the heavy wooden door before sitting behind her wrap-around desk, arms folded, eyes defiant.

"My father didn't commit any crime. That guy hit him over a disagreement in the contract, not the other way around. He's not guilty of anything."

I held up my hands in a calming gesture. "I understand what it's like to be wrongly accused. But the only way to make the charges go away is to face them and show up to court. Failure to appear only makes him look guilty."

Her professional demeanor cracked, and her eyes watered. She dabbed them with a tissue. "It's not fair. He saved so many lives before he lost his license. He helped save my life."

"How so?"

"Many years ago, I had an infection that attacked my kidneys. By the time the doctors figured out what was going on, I was on dialysis three times a week. I couldn't work. Could barely function. Every day was a misery. And I was at the bottom of the recipient list. Through his contacts, he found a donor who was a match. It was a miracle."

"I'm sorry you got sick, but I'm glad you're better now."

"I realize my privilege in being able to jump the line, but now, I'm able to help other people in need as the CFO of Great Harvest."

I had many thoughts and feelings about all this, but I kept them to myself.

"He made one mistake several years ago, and now it just keeps haunting him. It was stupid what he did, burning his initials into someone's liver. He was just proud of his work, you know? Even now, he does a lot of good. I know that family was angry about how their mother's remains were used, but she's helping that company develop better armor. She's saving soldiers' lives. Isn't that a good thing?"

"The best way for him to get back to doing his good work," I said, trying to speak her language, "is to turn himself in to me. We can get his bail reset. He can face the charges, ideally get them dismissed or be found not guilty, and return to his life."

Neither of us spoke for several minutes. I let her process everything, hoping she'd realize I was right.

"I don't know where he is exactly."

"But you know how to reach him."

"Possibly."

I considered asking for the contact information, but I figured it might be better if she convinced him.

"Tell him to reach out to me." I handed her one of my business cards. "I won't even have to cuff him if he comes along quietly. We'll take him down to get processed. I'll call Sadie at Assurity to work on getting the bail reset."

"Yes, I think I can do that."

"Could you provide me with his phone number so I'll recognize it when he calls?"

"I swore to him I'd never give the number to anyone else."

"But these are special circumstances, Ms. Krueger. Amy. You and me, we're trying to help him put this whole mess in his rearview once and for all."

"I'm sorry. I will ask him to call you. But that's it. I won't betray him. Not after all he did to save me."

I realized I'd pushed her as far as I could. Any more and she'd turn on me. I needed to keep her as an ally.

"Thank you for your time, Amy." I stood. This time, she shook my hand.

I drove to the Hub, determined to track down Krueger with or without his daughter's help.

CHAPTER 16
FUN WITH CADAVERS

BECCA WASN'T at the Hub when I arrived, so I called her.

To my relief, she was at home, taking care of herself. She'd been pushing herself too much lately, and her chronic fatigue was seriously kicking her ass.

Before she and Easton moved in together, I often stopped by to help her with housework, bring her groceries, make her a meal, or just hang out.

She had been the first friend I'd made at my new school after coming out as trans in the sixth grade. We'd been besties ever since. A helluva pair, the two of us—the trans girl and the tired girl.

After my high school boyfriend's father nearly killed me at a graduation party, she'd been there for me. She'd supported me through breakups and when Conor was presumed dead from a terrorist's bomb. She was family.

"Is Easton there?" I asked her.

"No, they're at work. But I'm okay."

"You sure? Want me to bring you some fast food?"

"No. I'm good. Really."

My phone dinged, showing an incoming email. I ignored it.

"I've been digging into that creepy Krueger guy," she added.

"Becks, you shouldn't be working. You need rest."

"I couldn't help it. Something about that guy bugs me. Just sent you my findings."

"Anything interesting?" I felt guilty for asking. I should just let her go back to sleep and read her report on my own.

"Major crypto portfolio. Mostly Bitcoin but also some Ethereum, Dogecoin, and a few of the other currencies."

"A lot of people are into cryptocurrencies, especially creepy white guys with too much money."

"Yeah, but he's not your typical crypto bro. This cabrón's been receiving money via transactions on the dark web. Haven't yet been able to trace from where, but give me time, and I will. Also, I found an encrypted email account not listed on his bail bond application."

"Did you crack it?"

"No, not yet. You want me to?"

"Get some rest, girlie girl. I still have a few legal tricks up my sleeve. I spoke with his daughter. She's going to reach out to him, try to convince him to turn himself in to me. We'll see how that goes."

"You capture Cooper yet?"

I filled her in on our misadventures.

"Jinx, I'm so sorry. I led you into a trap."

"Just a minor inconvenience. No one was charged with anything. I spoke with Cooper's boyfriend and learned there was a bar where he liked to hang out. Got the team scoping out his place and Milburn's. Sooner or later, we'll nab him."

"Yeah, you will."

"I'll talk to you tomorrow."

"Mañana, hermana."

I hung up and opened the information she had sent. There were some high-dollar payments that he had received several times a month, ranging from ten grand to nearly six figures. The payments came from multiple sources, difficult to backtrack, according to Becca. But not impossible.

According to her, most people believed crypto transactions were anonymous. They were to an extent but not entirely. They were recorded using a technology called blockchain. This same technology also made them potentially traceable.

Clearly, Krueger was making money he didn't want others to know about. But who specifically was he hiding it from? The IRS? The cops or feds? The families of the deceased? All the above? The real question was, who was paying him? And what were they paying for?

I plunged down the rabbit hole of research and discovered that the cadaver industry was largely unregulated. Donating a body "to science" could mean many different things. The cadaver could go to a medical school for dissection or for researching cancer and other diseases. Parts of it could also be sold to medical equipment companies teaching doctors new techniques. Those outcomes were what most people expected.

But there were other, less savory uses. Body farms used them to study how the human body decomposed under various conditions. Human crash test dummies. Armor testing, as I had already discovered. The list went on. Some were seriously morbid.

One of my college roommates kept an actual human skull on her bookshelf. She was going through a serious Edgar Allan Poe fetish at the time and had his poem "The Raven" memorized.

That skull was once part of a living person. Someone's child who once had hopes and dreams. And now their skull was little more than a tchotchke on some goth's shelf. It had seemed cool and weird at the time. Now it just felt depressing. We were food for worms, as Robin Williams said in the movie *Dead Poets Society*. Sad but true. Even for Williams himself now. All that brilliance gone.

And then there was the whole organ transplant industry, which directly saved a lot of lives and was somewhat more regulated. It was illegal to sell a kidney or other organ for donation. And yet even with legit transplants, a lot of money changed hands for the medical services and other costs associated with the procedure. And the industry was shrouded under a blanket of so-called anonymity, opening up all kinds of potential for abuse.

I found the topic equally fascinating and gruesome. Situations like this, involving life and death, often led to unanswerable questions about mortality. I wasn't religious like my mother or even spiritual like my father, but this topic left me wondering about those deeper mysteries.

When I believed Conor had died, I had found myself wondering what life and death were. Did souls exist? Or were we merely complex chemical reactions that became self-aware through some quirk of chemistry? Were we the universe developing instances of consciousness?

My ringing phone pulled me out of the contemplative rabbit hole. I didn't recognize the number on the caller ID.

"Hello?" I said, hoping it was one of my fugitives. Or possibly someone with a tip looking to claim a reward.

"Is this Jinx Ballou?" asked a female voice.

"Yes, who is this?"

"Rayna Dixon. You know my mom, Daphne."

"Right. How are you holding up?"

"Not well. DCS is investigating my family, thanks to my asshole ex-husband who reported us. I'm afraid they'll try to take Leia away and force her to detransition. I don't know what to do."

"Shit. I'm sorry. Where are you right now?"

"At home. The social worker just left."

"Okay, I'll be there shortly. Do you know Kirsten Pasternak?"

"My mom said you mentioned her. Is she a member of the Phoenix Gender Alliance?"

"Yes. She's also an attorney. A good one. Call her now. I'll text you her number."

"I can't afford an attorney, Jinx. I'm barely making ends meet as it is."

"Don't worry about the money. Call her. If she won't represent you pro bono, I'll take care of her fees."

"Jinx, that could be tens of thousands of dollars. You don't even know me."

"Doesn't matter. I've known your folks for years. And with your daughter being trans, you're family. This is what family does."

"I don't know what to say, but thank you."

"Just call Kirsten. I'll be there soon. And don't open the door to anyone but me or her. Got it?"

"I will."

I gathered my stuff and rushed out of the building.

CHAPTER 17

GOING INTO HIDING

ALONG THE WAY, I called Conor and let him know what was going on. He agreed to meet me at Rayna's house.

She lived in Glendale near Olive Avenue and Fifty-Ninth Avenue in a modest, nicely maintained home.

Kirsten's silver-blue Mercedes sat parked on the street in front of the house when I arrived. I pulled in behind it and was getting out when Conor showed up. We met in the driveway and walked together up to the porch.

A smiling jack-o-lantern sat next to a doormat that read Welcome with a rainbow heart in place of the *O*. A younger, slimmer version of Daphne opened the door.

"Ms. Ballou?" Rayna asked warily.

"Call me Jinx. And this is my husband, Conor Doyle."

"Thank you both for coming. Please, come on in."

I followed her into the brightly lit kitchen. Daphne, Kirsten, and a preteen girl—Leia presumably—sat around a bleached wooden table. Rayna made introductions and offered Conor and me a drink. I took a bottle of water, Conor a beer.

"So, what's the situation?" I asked.

"A social worker showed up a couple of hours ago

asking all kinds of questions. Started out okay. What did I do for a living? How long have we lived here? Why did I divorce Leia's father? And then it got uncomfortable."

"Uncomfortable how?"

"Invasive." She pulled out her phone and read from it. "He asked if I have a boyfriend or girlfriend. If I ever let dates spend the night? Have any of my dates molested Leia? If there are any positive male role models in Leia's life. If I have sex toys or porn in the house. If I ever let Leia watch shows with sexual or gay content. Have I ever caught her masturbating? Then he started asking whether Leia was taking hormone blockers or estradiol and what her pediatrician's name was. And then he just got downright insulting."

"How so?"

"He asked what I might have said or done to make Leia want to be a girl, such as encouraging her to wear dresses or play with dolls or put on makeup. I tried to explain that I didn't initiate any of this. But he looked at me as if I were a liar. Started throwing around terms like *grooming, brainwashing,* and *coercion.* Then hinted that I had chased off Leia's father so I could have her all to myself, as if this was all some nefarious plan. It was all so humiliating."

"I'm sorry, Mom," Leia said, putting a hand on her shoulder.

"Oh, baby, this isn't your fault." Rayna wiped the tears from her face then met my gaze again. "I don't know what it was like when you came out, Jinx, but when Leia was eight, she started having trouble in school. She became withdrawn and openly defiant at times. At first, I assumed she was depressed over Mike and me arguing all the time. I know I struggled emotionally after my mom left my dad.

"But Leia insisted her behavioral changes had nothing to do with Mike and me. When I pressed her for an explanation, she'd insist nothing was wrong when it obviously was. I chalked it up to normal preteen rebellion."

"Yeah, I can relate," I said. "I did some of the same things."

"Finally, I got her to open up to me about feeling like a girl in a boy's body. I wasn't sure what to think at first. Was my child gay? Was this a phase? Some quirk of an overactive imagination? I researched the issue online and came across that story that *Phoenix Living* wrote about you."

My face grew hot. That story was supposed to have been about my work as a female bounty hunter. I hadn't known when I interviewed with the reporter that he would out me. I never mentioned being transgender once.

But when the issue came out that week, my face was splashed on the front page with the words *Tranny Bounty Hunter*.

Getting outed had cost me jobs. The reporter was later killed by the same Chechen mobster who murdered Fiddler Dixon.

"You read that article, huh?"

"Several times. It didn't say much about your journey, but it gave me the context and vocabulary I needed to find more information. It helped."

"I'm glad."

"Leia and I had a lot of heart-to-heart talks after that. For a while, I wondered what I had done to make her this way."

"Nothing," I insisted. "We're simply born this way."

"I realize that now. Eventually, I found a counselor who had training and experience with these issues. We agreed that allowing Leia to transition, socially at first, was the right thing to do. Mike was furious when I told him. Over the past few years, he's become a radicalized, diehard Trumper. It was why I left him. He tried to get my custody revoked, but he failed, fortunately."

"Sadly, I'm not surprised by his reaction."

"He stopped sending child support. He really went crazy when Leia went on hormone blockers and most recently on estradiol. Leia refuses to go to his house anymore because he deadnames and misgenders her. He once tried to break into our house and kidnap her. I called the police, but they didn't arrest him."

"I'm so sorry." I turned to Kirsten. "What can she do?"

"I'll be honest," Kirsten said. "I haven't handled a lot of domestic disturbance or abuse cases or other cases involving DCS. My official advice is to comply with the investigation, answer their questions as honestly as possible. But with the way the new law is written, Rayna, the truth could lead to you losing custody to your ex and Leia being forced to detransition. That could be extremely traumatizing."

Panic spread across Leia's face. "No, please. I don't want to go back to being a boy."

"I won't let that happen," Rayna said defiantly. "I will not let them take my child or deny her the care she needs to be comfortable in her own skin."

"I understand," Kirsten replied. "I transitioned much later in life. The thought of being forced to go back... just horrifying. So despite my being an officer of the court, my honest advice is to do whatever you must to keep Leia safe from those who would harm her. That includes her father and the state."

"You could stay with us for now," I said, glancing over at Conor, who nodded. "We've got a spare bedroom."

Rayna looked torn. "I don't want to impose. And we don't know how long this could last."

"You're not imposing," Conor replied. "We're offering. Stay as long as you like. We'll manage. No different from what families in Europe did during the Nazi occupation. Those bloody wankers at DCS won't be breaking down our door. I guarantee ya that. Not allergic to dogs, are ya, lass?"

Leia's face brightened for the first time. "You got a dog?"

"Aye. A big slobberin' golden-haired beast. And she loves kids."

"What's her name?" she asked.

"Diana," I said. "Named her after Diana Prince."

"Wonder Woman's secret identity," Leia exclaimed.

"Exactly," I said. "And she's a genuine superhero. Even saved my life a couple of times. She'll look out for you, even when Conor and I are at work. Speaking of which, Rayna, what about your job? Not to be intrusive."

"I'm a graphic designer. I work remotely for a company based in Portland, Oregon. So as long as you have a decent internet connection, I'll be fine. I have pulled Leia out of school for the time being."

Leia's enthusiasm over Diana the Wonder Dog vanished. "I miss my friends."

"Well, we hope it's only temporary," Kirsten added. "Just until we can get an injunction against this new law while the courts are getting it all worked out."

"Okay, then. It's settled," I said. "You'll be our guests. Just let us know about any dietary restrictions you may have. Also, Conor and I sometimes keep odd hours. But we'll provide you a key if you need to go anywhere, though you may have to avoid being in public for a while. Go grab whatever you need for the next day or so. And if you need to come back for something, we can escort you, make sure nothing bad happens."

Rayna led Leia back to the bedrooms.

Daphne reached across the table and put a hand on mine. "I can't thank you three enough for this. Leia's been so happy since she transitioned. And now this. I just don't understand what this world's coming to. Going after kids like that. I'd expected it from a waste of space like Leia's father. But for the state to pass a law criminalizing loving your own child? Never thought I'd see the day."

"Don't worry. We'll get through this together. Did you look into Leia joining the Hatchlings group?"

"Rayna did. They meet twice a month. According to their

website, they have a Halloween party coming up. Leia's looking forward to being there. It'll be nice for her to meet some other kids like her."

"It can make a difference."

CHAPTER 18
STAKEOUT AT COOPER'S

WHEN WE ALL arrived at the Bunker, I parked on the street to allow Rayna to pull her Honda Passport into the garage so it couldn't be visible from the street.

"Welcome to the Bunker." I checked my watch and saw the time was approaching six o'clock. "I'm due to relieve one of my team members on a stakeout. Probably won't be home until after midnight. But Conor can get you settled in."

"Why do you call it the Bunker?" Leia asked.

I smiled at Conor. "He'll tell you. Y'all have a good night."

Rush-hour traffic was still at a crawl as I drove south on Seventh Avenue. I called Caden to let him know I was running late. "Any sign of Cooper?"

The setting sun rested just above the horizon, nearly blinding me when I turned west on Van Buren.

"Not so far. I knocked on some more doors, but apparently, he doesn't really socialize with the neighbors. The few who know him aren't exactly fans."

"I'm heading your way to relieve you, but it may be a while. Traffic is moving slow."

"Take your time. Not much happening here."

"Talk to you soon."

I hung up and called Zahara. "Hey, Z, where are you?"

"Parked across the street from Nancy Turner's house."

"Any sign of Krueger?"

"Nope. Far as I can tell, she's alone in there."

"Okay, do you have any of the reward flyers for Krueger?"

"Got a whole stack of them. You think Turner's neighbors might have seen him?"

"Anything's possible. Canvass her neighbors and pass out flyers. Then do the same in his neighborhood. Then call it a night. I'm on my way to relieve Caden at Cooper's place."

"Roger that. I'll see you tomorrow."

By the time I pulled in behind Caden, it was nearly six-thirty. I strolled over to his driver's door, and he lowered the window. "Thank goodness you're here. My bladder's ready to burst. Peeing into a bottle doesn't work well when you don't have the right equipment."

"Trust me, I get it. That's the one thing I miss. Go on home. I'll see you later."

He raced down the street. I settled into my SUV.

The sun was down, and the streetlights were flickering on one by one. I pulled out a pair of binoculars and a bag of beef jerky. I would have preferred to eat whatever Conor was preparing for dinner. He was always a better cook than me. And when he was entertaining guests, he liked to go all out.

I called Rodeo to check in.

"Hey, boss. Any luck finding Krueger?"

"I had a good talk with the daughter. Hoping she can get through to him, convince him to turn himself in. For now, I'm staking out Cooper's place, having relieved Caden. Also, I have some new houseguests."

I filled him in on Rayna and Leia.

"It's a bad situation," Rodeo said. "If you need Jake and

me to put them up for a while or any other family with a trans kid, let us know."

"Thanks, Rodeo. I appreciate it. I'm guessing no signs of Cooper at Milburn's."

"All is quiet and dark."

"Okay, if he doesn't show by eight, call it a night."

"Will do, boss. Have a good night."

I settled in and watched the house. Naturally, my mind wandered. I turned on the radio only to hear another news story about the new anti-trans law followed by a few talking heads discussing what it could mean for trans kids and their families.

Then the host interviewed Josiah Faulkner, the right-wing nutjob whose lobbying organization, the Patriots of Liberty, was responsible for the new draconian law.

"We have nothing against people dressing however they like or calling themselves what they want," he lied. "We're simply trying to protect innocent children from being brainwashed by the radical transsexual agenda. Since transsexual women can't have babies, they have to recruit and groom children into thinking they're trans. It's the only way they can keep their sick cult going."

The snake continued to spew misinformation, bad science, and disproven conspiracy theories, portraying Evangelicals like him as the true victims in all of this. Not once did the host challenge any of these absurd statements.

I turned the radio off before my anger drove me to punch the dash.

I came out to my father at eleven years old, the same age as Leia. It was in the emergency room following a suicide attempt.

A few months earlier, I had been acting out in response to a growing sense of gender dysphoria. I didn't understand why I felt like a girl, but the feeling was insistent, persistent, and emotionally traumatizing. The word *transgender* wasn't even in my vocabulary.

At first, I thought I might be gay. But this unrelenting sense of being a girl had nothing to do with who I was attracted to. It centered on how uncomfortable I felt with a male body. Everything about it just felt wrong.

I skipped school, rarely talked to my family, and started hanging out with a bunch of kids who preferred to get drunk and high.

When the cops busted me for shoplifting a dress, my father enrolled me in a boys' military academy, hoping the school's strict discipline would force me to get my act together.

Instead, it put fuel on a fire. I spiraled the drain emotionally and broke into the commandant's office, looking for a gun I could use to kill myself. All I found was a bottle of Vicodin. I washed down two dozen pills with a bottle of twelve-year-old scotch.

Not that I really wanted to die. I just wanted to stop the soul-crushing pain and sense of worthlessness I'd been struggling with my entire life.

I woke hours later in the infirmary, my throat sore from having my stomach pumped. My father was at my bedside, tears in his eyes, begging me to explain why I wanted to hurt myself.

It was then, with my consciousness still altered by the booze and the drugs, that I told him I was transgender.

To my surprise, he understood. I guess it helped to have a therapist for a dad. He explained to my mother and brother what I was going through. It was awkward at first, but everyone rallied around me.

I was one of the lucky ones.

Most trans people weren't so fortunate. Many were kicked out of their houses by their families or sent to conversion therapy camps, where they were harassed, humiliated, and tortured into denying they were trans. Nearly half took their own lives.

And now the state was trying to criminalize transitioning. As if these kids weren't dealing with enough shit. And for what? For the Republicans to get more votes in the upcoming election by proclaiming that they were protecting innocent children from the scary transsexual menace?

The hours staring at Cooper's dark house dragged by while my brain went round and round. My father would've told me to calm my mind, to not let the fear, anger, and uncertainty rob me of my joy.

But at the moment, I wanted to feel angry and uncertain. I had reason to. And there wasn't shit I could do about the situation, other than provide temporary shelter for Leia and Rayna.

At eleven thirty, I called it a night and drove home.

CHAPTER 19
FBI AT THE DOOR

I DIDN'T SLEEP well that night and woke drearily when my alarm went off at six.

Once I'd turned off the alarm, Conor asked, "How ya holding up, love?"

"Worried."

"About?"

"Everything. *Roe* overturned. Voting districts gerrymandered and more onerous rules put in place to make voting harder. And now they're targeting trans kids. Won't be long before they try to invalidate our marriage and make Jake and Rodeo's relationship a felony."

He kissed me on the forehead. "Aye! Can't blame ya for feelin' that way. But don't give up hope just yet."

"I used to think these new laws would eventually get overturned when they reached the Supreme Court, but now most of those so-called justices are as bad as the bigoted congressmen."

"WWWWD," he whispered. "What would Wonder Woman do?"

It had been my personal motto for when things got rough. But lately, it didn't energize me much. "Wonder Woman was a demigod with superpowers."

"Who fought against bloody Nazis. And don't ya tell me ya don't have superpowers, love." A smile curled his lips. "Are ya not the woman who single-handedly caught the Maryvale Arsonist? Twice, no less! A woman who's captured countless fugitives, including one plonker on the FBI's Most Wanted list? No superpowers, huh? I don't believe it for a second. And might I add, ya look deadly in your Wonder Woman costume."

"None of that will change the laws these scumbags are passing. It's not like I can go assassinate them or stop the lobbyists paying the politicians to pass them. And what good would that do, anyway? If they die, someone just like them, or worse, will take their place."

"Aye, I'm not saying ya should kill anyone, love. Trust me, I've seen where that gets ya, and it isn't good. But you're bloody brilliant, tougher than any other woman I've met, and always willing to do what's right. And with all this bollocks going on, that's something. More than that, you're not alone. You've got me, your family, your team, my team, your friends, the Phoenix Gender Alliance."

"I know. Kirsten told me Lambda Legal and the ACLU are fighting to block these laws from being enforced."

"Ya see there? Those blokes will handle the legal end. You do what you can to protect the likes of Rayna and Leia."

"I love you, Conor Timothy Doyle." I kissed him.

"Love ya back, Jenna Christina Ballou-Doyle. Boy, that's a bloody mouthful, isn't it?"

I laughed despite my concerns. "A bit. Hey! Do you smell bacon?"

He sniffed the air. "Aye, I believe I do."

We shuffled into the kitchen and found Leia sitting at my antique table, eating pancakes and bacon. Rayna stood in front of the stove with a bowl of batter in one hand and a spatula in the other.

"I hope you don't mind," Rayna said, an apology evident in her voice.

"Not at all," I said. "I appreciate it. Did you find everything you need?"

"I believe so, yes. Please, have a seat."

"Don't have to tell me twice," Conor quipped.

I sat between Conor and Leia and helped myself to some pancakes.

"So, tell me, Leia," I said as I drizzled syrup on my stack. "How did you choose your name?"

"I really like *Star Wars*. General Leia Organa is my favorite."

"Yeah, she's pretty awesome," I agreed. "It's a good name."

"How about you?" Leia asked. "Why did you choose the name Jinx? Isn't a jinx a curse?"

"Leia," Rayna scolded. "Don't be rude."

"It's fine," I assured her. "Jinx is a nickname a friend gave me, a mash-up of my first and middle names, Jenna Christina."

"Oh, okay."

It felt nice to have guests in the house, especially when one of them was a young person full of laughter and questions. I thought of my mother, who was always harping on me about when I would have kids.

Rodeo and Jake were raising Gwyneth, Rodeo's daughter from a previous relationship. Being the cool aunt was enough for me. I wasn't sure I'd be a good mom, even if Conor and I were allowed to adopt, which, in this political climate, was doubtful.

The doorbell rang just as we were clearing the table. I caught the fear in Rayna's eyes.

"Relax. Probably just a landscaper looking for work," I assured her. "Stay put and stay quiet."

I exchanged a glance with Conor. After I shuffled into

bed last night, we'd agreed that if someone showed up looking for Rayna and Leia, Conor would lead them to the trapdoor in the coat closet.

I peeked through the peephole and saw a man and a woman, both in dark suits. I didn't get a DCS vibe from them, but it was hard to be sure through the distortion of the fisheye lens.

I opened the front door, leaving the security screen in place.

"Can I help you?" Now that I got a better look at them, I recognized them. "Well, well, Special Agents Deborah Velasco and Danny Gleeson. To what do I owe the honor of a visit from the FBI?"

"Ms. Ballou. May we come inside?" Velasco had the sharp eyes of a predator. I knew from my previous encounters with her that she was smart and had good instincts. I respected her, even though our given professions sometimes put us at odds.

"Not a good time. We're busy getting rid of a dead body."

They didn't so much as smirk. Tough crowd.

"Ah, Ms. Ballou, this isn't a social call," Gleeson said with a New England accent. Not Bostonian but somewhere up there. Maybe Maine or Vermont. Made him sound like an arrogant know-it-all.

He had shaved his head since the last time I'd seen him. That, combined with his fleshy face, made him look like a man-sized penis. Made sense. He was always a cocky little prick and not all that bright, in my opinion.

"We need to talk, missy."

"So talk."

Velasco looked annoyed. "We understand you're looking for a gentleman by the name of Donald Lawrence Krueger."

"I wouldn't call him a gentleman, but yes, I have been retained to return him to custody. You got any leads?"

"We need you to stop," Velasco said.

I stared at her. "Why? Do you have him in custody?"

"We're not at liberty to say. We're merely here to inform you that your services in this case are no longer required."

"Look, Agents, no offense, but I don't work for you. Sadie Levinson at Assurity Bail Bonds hired me to apprehend Krueger. So until she says the job is off, I'm still on."

"And I'm telling you, little lady," Gleeson replied, "that if you don't stand down, we will be within our rights to charge you with interfering in a federal investigation."

"What federal investigation?"

Neither of them answered. No surprise.

"If you want me off this case, call Levinson."

"We've left her a message," Velasco said.

"Fabulous. Then when I hear from her, I'll stand down. Until then, I think our little chat is done."

"Watch yourself, Ballou," Gleeson replied. "You've interfered in our investigations before and gotten a lot of people killed."

He was referring, no doubt, to the White Nation bombing incident. The terrorist organization had sent two trucks loaded with explosives into town. One blew up on the Piestewa Freeway. The other was stopped on the Loop 101 before it could destroy a sports arena full of people.

"As I recall, we were the ones who discovered where White Nation had their base of operations. Thanks to us, the Gila River Arena is not a smoking mass of rubble. And my husband risked his life to stop the one bound for City Hall. If we hadn't 'interfered,' there would've been considerably more loss of life."

That seemed to shut them up, at least for the moment.

Finally, Velasco said, "Just don't do anything until you hear from Ms. Levinson, all right?"

"Have a good day." I shut the door and returned to the kitchen.

"Everything all right?" Conor asked.

"Fine."

"Was that DCS?" Rayna looked concerned.

"No, nothing to do with you. You're safe here." I sighed. "I've got to get to work."

"Aye, me too," Conor added.

"You should be okay here while we're gone. Just don't open the door for anyone. And call me if you need anything. Okay?"

Rayna nodded. "Thank you both so much. I don't know what we'd do without you."

"You're most welcome," Conor said. "It'll all work out."

I excused myself and placed a call to Sadie.

When she picked up, I told her, "The feds are warning me off the Krueger case."

"They have him in custody?"

"Wouldn't say. Maybe they do, and maybe they don't."

"I got the message they left, but I haven't returned the call. I have heard nothing to suggest they have him. My advice is to keep looking for him. If they don't have him and the judge vacates his bond, I'm in deep trouble. Keep looking for him until you hear otherwise from me."

"Will do."

I was about to hang up when she said, "One other thing. What's this about you getting arrested for busting your way into someone's house, looking for Tod Cooper?"

"No one was arrested, just questioned. Cooper was at that house. Probably hiding in the attic. The resident had Cooper's phone on him. I'm not an idiot, Sadie. I don't force my way into a residence for the thrill." *Well, not just for the thrill. That was just a side benefit.*

"Stay out of trouble, Jinx. If it becomes a problem, I'll find someone else to handle these jobs."

"Like I said, Cooper was there, or he'd just left. And I

will find Krueger unless the feds have already snatched him up."

"See that you do."

The call ended. I finished getting ready and drove to the Hub. People had left messages on my tip line about both Cooper and Krueger. I needed to sort through them to find ones that might lead to my fugitives.

CHAPTER 20
STORMTROOPERS IN POLO SHIRTS

TO MY DELIGHT, Becca was at the Hub when I arrived. I wasn't expecting her, so I hadn't bothered to stop for coffee.

"How're you feeling?" I asked.

"Better. Functional. How's tricks?"

"Let's just say it hasn't been my best week."

"¡Pobrecita! It was my fault you and the team were arrested. I gave you bad intel."

I shook my head. "No, it wasn't your fault. His phone was there. He may have been there too. Probably hiding in the guy's attic like a roof rat. No charges were filed in any case."

"Have you heard any more from Daphne's daughter and granddaughter?"

"Rayna told me her ex filed a complaint with the Department of Child Safety. They're staying with us until the ACLU and Lambda Legal can stop the DCS stormtroopers from terrorizing families with trans kids."

"They're lucky to have you."

"Be better if they didn't have to hide in the first place."

"Amen, hermana."

I started listening to the messages on the tip line. There

were forty-seven, most about Tod Cooper. And most provided vague, useless tips.

"Cooper looks like a guy I saw at SaveMart."

"I saw a truck similar to his on the highway. I think it was on the 17. Or maybe the 10."

"My brother's girlfriend said her cousin's next-door neighbor thinks she saw Krueger somewhere in Peoria."

What these tips weren't light on was contact information and questions about how quickly they could collect the reward.

I was halfway through the messages when my regular phone rang. It was Rayna.

"Everything all right?"

"It's that DCS worker," she said in a hushed, frightened tone. "He's pounding on your front door."

"Okay, calm down. He's not getting in."

"How does he even know I'm here?"

"He probably doesn't. Just stay quiet. He'll go away. If he's still there in ten minutes, call me back. I'll come deal with him."

"Okay. Thank you, Jinx. Sorry to be so much trouble."

I managed to laugh. "You're no trouble. Not compared to the rest of my life. It will be okay."

I hung up and went back to work. From the large collection of tips, I made a list of the most viable ones. Six for Cooper, one for Krueger.

I called the first tipster, who was one of Cooper's female neighbors. She claimed to have spotted Cooper's truck in his driveway at four that morning and that he'd driven off an hour later. Probably to pick up a change of clothes or other necessities.

"When will I get the reward? And how much is it?"

"The reward's five hundred dollars. If this tip leads to his arrest, you should receive it in a few weeks."

"A few weeks? I got bills to pay now."

"And your tip doesn't give me a lot to go on," I explained. "Look, I'm not trying to stiff you. I will post a member of my team on the house. If we catch him there, you get the reward. Okay?"

"Whatever, bitch." She hung up.

Ah, the concerned citizen. Concerned about getting free money, not so much about helping me apprehend dangerous criminals.

The next few tipsters weren't much more useful. Light on actionable intel. Heavy on "gimme my money, bitch!"

Before I could return the last call, I noticed a guy walking into the Hub I hadn't seen before. Dumpy guy, conservative haircut, carrying a briefcase, and wearing a polo shirt with a logo embroidered on the front.

We got all types at the Hub, but something about him seemed out of place. He stopped and asked a question of someone near the front door. They pointed in my direction. The guy in the polo shirt made a beeline toward me.

"Shit," I muttered.

"What's wrong?" Becca said, looking up from her nest of three monitors.

"Trouble."

"Jenna Ballou?" the dumpy guy asked.

"Yeah. Who the hell are you?"

"Josh Cohen. I'm a social worker with the Arizona Department of Child Safety."

"Sorry, I don't have any kids for you to steal."

"We have a report that a Rayna Dixon and her son, Luke Ripley, are staying with you."

How the fuck did he know that? Had someone followed us when we led Rayna to our house? She had driven behind Conor and me, so it would have been impossible for me to spot a tail. But who would follow us? Didn't seem like DCS's style to conduct that level of surveillance.

And then it hit me. Rayna's ex. It had to be.

"You've got bad intel, my friend. Can't help you. Sorry."

"Your vehicle was seen at their house last night."

"So? Is that a crime?"

"No, but interfering with a DCS investigation and kidnapping are. We have a witness who reports Rayna and her son drove to your house last night."

"Kidnapping? Are you serious?" I stood up and got in his face. I towered over him by a few inches. "A little short for a stormtrooper, aren't you?"

"What?" Cohen looked confused. Clearly not a *Star Wars* fan.

"Who's your so-called witness?" I pressed.

"I'm not at liberty to say. But if you're harboring them…"

"Look, buddy, last time I checked, this is a free country. Even if you and our fascist governor are trying to turn this state into Nazi Berlin."

That comment hit the mark. His cheeks colored.

"I'm doing my job to protect children," he insisted, but some of the wind had gone out of his sails.

"Just doing your job, huh? More than a few Nazis said the same at Nuremberg."

"How dare you compare me to the Nazis! They murdered my great-grandfather at Dachau."

"If you don't like being compared to the Nazis, stop acting like them. Rayna's done nothing but love and care for her daughter."

"The complaint claims the child is being abused. Possibly brainwashed."

"Bullshit! Gender-affirming care isn't abuse. No one brainwashed Leia into thinking she's trans. Do you know what happens to trans kids who don't receive gender-affirming care? Depression. PTSD. Suicide. Providing care improves quality of life. Every major medical and psychological organization confirms this.

"But here you are treating them like criminals, like

vermin. So don't get all high and mighty over me calling you a Nazi. If the jackboots fit…"

The man was literally shaking with anger. I half expected him to either throw a punch or explode like an egg in a microwave. He pointed a trembling finger at my face. "If I find you're harboring them—"

"You'll what? Report me to der Führer? Get the fuck out of here, Cohen. Your grandfather would be ashamed of you."

The guy turned on his heel and stormed out of there. I was sorry about his grandfather but not about calling him out on his enforcement of this hateful law.

"You okay?" Becca asked.

I caught the eyes of everyone in the Hub staring at me.

"For now."

I went back to trying to track down my fugitives. I kept mentally replaying the conversation with Cohen over and over, thinking of more biting retorts.

I couldn't focus and was about to make a coffee run to Tres Leches when my phone rang. No caller ID. The voice on the other end was a hoarse whisper.

"This is Donnie Krueger. I hear you've been looking for me."

"Well, well. Donnie. Nice to finally hear from you. Ready to turn yourself in?"

"I'll be at New Life Medical Resources in fifteen minutes." His daughter must have talked him into coming to his senses.

Before I could respond, he hung up. The call struck me as odd. But then, creepy Donnie Krueger was an odd guy.

It would take me a half hour or more to get up to New Life. I sent out a group text to my team to meet me there.

CHAPTER 21

AMONG THE DEAD

A WHITE BMW SUV sat in the parking lot near the building's front door. The license plate matched the vehicle listed on his bond application. Decals on the car's rear made it look like an angry skull. Typical creepy Krueger. I tried not to take it as a bad sign.

I parked some distance away, and the rest of my crew pulled up nearby.

"He just called you, wanting to turn himself in?" Rodeo asked.

"And hung up before I could say much of anything. That's his Bimmer by the door. Caden, I want you to cover the back with a shotgun in case he has second thoughts about surrendering and rabbits. Oh, and make sure it has beanbag rounds."

He looked relieved. "Gladly. I really don't want to go back in there."

"Rodeo and Z, you're with me. Everybody ready?"

They all nodded.

"Let's get our man. Caden, call on the radio when you're in position."

"Will do."

As we approached the front door, I saw lights on inside the lobby. The three of us waited for Caden.

"Coyote Four in position. Over."

"Copy that, Coyote Four. Keep your head on a swivel. Over."

I pulled on the front door. It opened. "Making entry through the front. Over."

Zahara carried the second beanbag shotgun. Rodeo held his Taser. I held the door open for them as they stepped inside. Then I drew my own Taser and followed.

The lobby was empty. No one was behind the receptionist's desk. No sign of Krueger or Turner. I listened but heard no sounds of activity.

"Now what?" Zahara asked.

I tried the door that led from the lobby to the rest of the building. To my surprise, it, too, was unlocked. "We go inside."

"I don't like this, boss," Rodeo whispered. "Something's not right here."

"Keep your cool." He wasn't the only one sensing something was off, though. "We'll search the place. If he's here, we arrest him. If he puts up a fight, we take him down. If he's not here, we leave."

"Roger that."

We searched the offices, supply closets, and dissection rooms with no sign of anyone. My senses were on high alert. Something hinky was definitely going on. If Krueger's truck was here, where the hell was he?

The three of us huddled outside the cooler door. It was the only room of the building we had not searched this time around. I really didn't want to go back in there, and I sensed Rodeo and Zahara weren't too keen on it either.

"Z, stay out here and make sure no one locks us in. Poke your head inside if you see or hear anything. This shouldn't take long. Rodeo, let's take another walk among the dead."

Rodeo grunted in response.

The cold, death-scented air inside the cooler sent shivers down my spine that had nothing to do with the temperature. "Come out, come out, wherever you are," I muttered in a vain attempt to calm my nerves.

"Olly olly oxen free," replied Rodeo. Our shared bizarre sense of humor was one of the many reasons I liked him.

We swiftly moved past the dissected body parts and focused on the shelves of cadavers in body bags. And that's when we found him, sitting on the floor behind the last shelving unit in the back corner.

"Shit"

My radio squawked with static, and the cooler door opened.

"Jinx, Caden says two Peoria PD black-and-whites pulled up out back."

"Just a minute."

Donnie Krueger's pale body sat straight-legged on the floor with his back against a shelving unit. His sightless eyes stared up at me. A spray of blood and brain matter coated the left side of what remained of his face, as well as the shelf he was leaning against. A snub-nosed revolver lay near his right hand.

"Guess we're not getting paid for this one, huh, boss?"

"Looks that way."

The cooler door opened again. "Jinx, cops are inside."

"Fuck!"

Rodeo and I stepped out into the hallway.

"Police! Drop your weapons."

"We've been set up, Jinxie," Zahara whispered.

"No one says anything," I whispered to my crew. "I'll call Kirsten."

"No talking!" a cop said. "Get on the floor facedown. Do it now! Lace your fingers behind your head."

And suddenly, we were the ones being cuffed.

We were each relieved of our gear and weapons and spent a couple of hours in the back of the black-and-whites.

Finally, the door of the car I was in opened, and two familiar faces appeared. Special Agents Velasco and Gleeson. Of course.

"Ms. Ballou, we told you to back off this case," Velasco said.

I wanted dearly to engage in more witty banter. But discretion was the better part of valor, or whatever, so I simply uttered one word. "Attorney."

Two hours later, I was cooling my heels in a Peoria PD interview room when Kirsten appeared, wearing an orange blouse, a nearly black suit, and her usual yellow framed glasses. She seemed dressed for the Halloween season.

"Trick or treat," I said to her.

"Jinx, what the hell happened?"

I gave her the rundown.

"This is bad. They're charging you with first-degree murder and interfering with a federal investigation. They're working on getting a search warrant for your house." She gave me a look.

A chill ran through me. "Shit. Rayna and Leia."

"I called Conor. He's headed there now. But they're the least of your problems. Donnie Krueger was going to cooperate with the feds on some case they were working on."

"What case?"

"I don't know exactly. A bigger fish. Him being dead puts a wrench in their plans. They intend to make it your problem, since you defied their instructions to stand down."

"Looks to me like he offed himself. How is that my fault?"

"Maybe he did. But I get the impression they're going to hold you responsible."

"That's absurd. After Velasco and Gleeson told me to back off, I called Sadie. She told me to grab him. And then this morning, he called me to turn himself in. What was I supposed to do? Say, 'Not interested'? I don't think so."

"You sure it was Krueger who called you?"

I considered it. We'd never actually spoken to each other. It could have been anyone.

"The caller identified himself as Krueger. No caller ID on the phone, but I figured he was using a burner. How did the cops know we were at New Life, anyway? Or that Krueger's body was there? It's an obvious setup. Clearly, someone tipped them off too. Bet you good money it was the same person who called me. Unless, of course, the feds are tracking me."

"Let me bring them in here and see what we can do to get you out of this mess." She gave me a few pointers, then signaled to the cops that we were ready to talk.

A besuited man with a hawkish face and jet-black hair stepped inside, accompanied by Agents Velasco and Gleeson.

"Good morning, ladies. I am Detective Jamie Montana, homicide detective with the Peoria Police Department. I understand you're already acquainted with Special Agents Velasco and Gleeson of the FBI."

"Yeah," I said derisively. "We go way back."

"What can you tell us about the events leading up to the death of Donald Krueger?"

"Nothing," I replied.

"Nothing?" the detective asked. "Ms. Ballou, we're trying to help you out here. We understand things were, shall we say, tense between you and Mr. Krueger and his staff. Maybe you were just doing your job, trying to return Krueger to custody, and it didn't go as planned. But we can't help you if you don't tell us what happened."

"You want to know what happened? Krueger called me a

few hours ago, wanting to surrender. Said he'd be in the building."

"Did you record this call?" Montana asked.

"No. It was brief."

Velasco tilted her head inquisitively. "Why would he surrender to you? He'd already agreed to work with us. In fact, we were scheduled to meet later today."

"Maybe he changed his mind. Maybe he liked me better than he liked you."

"Jinx," Kirsten cautioned.

Gleeson got a disgusted look on his penis face. "You think this is a joke, girlie? A man is dead. And who knows how many others will be because of it?"

"Well, I sure as hell didn't kill him. I've got no motive. I don't get paid for dead fugitives."

"Ms. Ballou," Montana said, "take us through what happened, starting with your arrival at New Life."

"We spotted Krueger's BMW parked out front. I sent Caden Morrow, a member of my team, around to cover the back door. Zahara Washington, Nathaniel Kwan, and myself went in the front. The building was unlocked as if for business, but there was no one in the receptionist area, which was strange."

A thought occurred to me. *Where the hell was Nancy Turner? Shouldn't she have been manning the front desk?*

"Why was it strange?" Velasco asked. "Had you been there before?"

"Couple days ago. Krueger's office manager, Nancy Turner was there. She had let us search the place the day before." With a little encouragement.

"She just let you waltz in, huh?" replied Gleeson with a snort.

I ignored him. "When no one was at the receptionist's desk, I feared something unfortunate may have happened to either Mr. Krueger or Ms. Turner. Rightly, as it turned out in the case of Krueger."

"You sure it was Krueger who called you?" Velasco pressed.

"The caller identified himself as him," I said. "I've never spoken with Krueger previously, so I had no reason to believe it wasn't him. Said he'd be at New Life and hung up. That was the entirety of the conversation."

They still looked at me, stone-faced.

Montana asked, "What happened after you entered the building?"

"We searched the rooms and found his body in the cooler. That was when you people showed up."

"I think you left out the part where you shot him in the head," Gleeson growled.

"Again, what motive would I have?"

"Maybe you were involved with him in some other way. Perhaps connected to the case we're investigating."

"And what case would that be?" I glared at him. Damn, he really did look like a giant penis. And an ugly one at that. "You think I concocted some elaborate scheme to kill Krueger and cost my team the bounty? Are you really that dense, Gleeson?"

He glared back at me but didn't respond.

No one spoke for what felt like fifteen minutes. Cops liked to play the waiting game to give criminals and even innocent people enough time to say something incriminating. But I didn't bite. After all, I used to be a cop too.

"You didn't think this call was suspicious?" Montana asked eventually, breaking the silence.

"Why would I? Sometimes, fugitives realize that their best bet is to turn themselves in rather than spend the rest of their lives on the run. Or maybe he thought he could ambush me, which would explain why he had the gun. Only he might have realized he wouldn't have a chance and shot himself instead. Desperate people do crazy things. I'm sorry he's dead. Believe me, I'd rather have collected the bounty. Even if dickhead over here would rather believe some paranoid conspiracy theory."

Gleeson flushed with anger. Kirsten shot me a look that warned me to behave myself.

"Point is, I reasonably believed Krueger was ready to surrender. So we responded and found him dead from a suicide."

"Apparent suicide," Velasco corrected. "Manner of death has not yet been determined."

"You know what I'm curious about?" I asked. "How did Peoria PD know to show up there? My team didn't call it in. So who did?"

I studied their faces, but they gave nothing away. Another thought occurred to me, and I locked eyes with Velasco. "Or were you people tracking me?"

I hadn't noticed a tail on the way to meet Krueger, but the agents could have been tracking my phone.

"We asked you earlier this morning to stand down," Velasco replied coolly.

"I don't work for you, Velasco. I have a job to do, same as you. I spoke with Krueger's bail bond agent. She hadn't been informed of any changes in Krueger's fugitive status and confirmed that I needed to pick him up."

"We were negotiating a deal with Krueger's attorney," Velasco explained. "He was supposed to turn himself in to us this afternoon."

"So Krueger was going to flip on someone. Either Krueger had second thoughts or this someone else got to him first and made it look like a suicide. Sure as hell wasn't me. I wanted him alive."

"We think your motive was personal," Gleeson said smugly. "We've spoken with his associate, Nancy Turner. She says you have a grudge against her and, by extension, her boss. She mentioned that you accidentally locked your-self into the cooler the other day, blamed her, and threatened to kill both and her boss."

That last statement was a trap to get me to blame Turner for locking us in, thus adding to this supposed motive of a personal grudge. But I wasn't falling for it.

But Montana didn't let it go so easily. "Is there some history between you and the victim's office manager?"

"Turner's a perv with a necro fetish."

Montana raised an eyebrow. "A necro fetish?"

"She likes to have sex with dead bodies. Got fired from the M.E.'s office last year when she was caught and arrested. We apprehended her up in Payson after she jumped bail. No grudge. Just enforcing the law, same as you."

"And no grudge against Krueger?"

"Never even met the man until we found his body earlier today. And as for us getting locked in the cooler, we got out. No harm, no foul, no grudge. No motive." I enunciated the last two words. "I never threatened to kill either of them."

We went around and around. They were trying to twist my words to throw me off my game and get me emotional. But I'd been a cop. Maybe not a detective, but I knew how interrogations worked. Not like on TV, where they yell and scream at a suspect. Just mind games.

"Okay, that's enough," Kirsten finally announced. "You have no case against my client. She's been very forthcoming about her involvement in trying to apprehend a wanted fugitive. No laws have been broken by her or any member of her team. Now release Ms. Ballou and her team. We're done here."

"Very well," Detective Montana said. "You and your team are free to go, Ms. Ballou. For now."

"But this isn't the end of it," Gleeson warned. "You inter-fered in a federal investigation."

"Bullshit. For all we know, you people tipped off

whoever killed him. Wouldn't be the first time you stumbled over your own shoelaces, Gleeson. You got played, and I got set up. Clearly, this other thing you're investigating blew up in your face. Go after them. Not me. I've got fugitives to catch."

CHAPTER 22

A CALL FOR HELP

THE FIVE OF us crammed ourselves into Kirsten's Lexus, and she drove us back to the New Life Medical Resources parking lot, where we'd left our vehicles.

Along the way, I checked my voice mailbox and discovered a couple of messages. One was from Conor. Another was from Sebastian Castro. I called Conor back first, worried something had happened to Rayna and Leia.

"Everything all right?" I asked.

"Feds showed up earlier with a search warrant. Thanks to Kirsten's call, I arrived before they did and stashed Rayna and Leia in the tunnel while they searched the place. Leia got a little freaked out. Poor girl's not a fan of closed-in spaces. How did those wankers get a warrant for our house? What the bloody hell's going on, love?"

"One of my fugitives turned up dead. Cops thought I was involved."

"That Krueger bloke? This have to do with them showing up this morning?"

"Yes. I think he was going to flip on someone."

"Who?"

"No idea. Don't really care. They're just pissed because,

once again, their case went sideways, and I was in the middle of it."

"You're not under arrest, are ya, love?"

"Not so far. I'm more worried about Rayna and Leia."

"Aye. I'll stick around the rest of the day in case some other plonker shows up uninvited."

"Thanks, babe."

"They're good people in a bad situation. Happy to help. You all right?"

"More or less. One less fugitive to apprehend. Sadie'll be relieved she doesn't have to cough up the full bail amount, but she'll still probably complain that a dead client looks bad for her reputation. Somehow make it my fault. You know how she is."

"Aye, that I do, love. See ya for dinner? I'm making my ma's lamb stew for the four of us."

My mouth watered at the mention of it. "Count on me being there."

"Love ya, girl. Good hunting and be careful out there."

"Always."

I debated whether to call Sadie or listen to Castro's voicemail. Castro won. I was really in no mood to listen to Sadie gripe. She wasn't a bad person. Hell, she'd shown up to my wedding on the Jewish Sabbath, no less, which counted for something in my book.

But when things didn't go her way, she had a gift for guilting me over it. What she didn't realize was that her Jewish guilt was no match for my mother's Italian Catholic guilt. Sadie's just rolled off me like water on a duck's back.

"Ms. Ballou, help!" Castro said in a desperate voice on the message. "He's trying to break in! He's—"

I heard a crash, shouting, and what sounded like the phone getting bounced around. Then the message ended.

I called him back, but after three rings, it went to his voicemail. "Hey! It's me," he said in an especially effeminate tone. "Leave me your name and digits. And if you ain't no bitch, I may just call you back."

"Mr. Castro. Sebastian, it's Jinx Ballou, returning your call. Just making sure you're okay."

I hung up just as Kirsten pulled up beside our vehicles.

"Sebastian Castro?" asked Zahara. "Cooper's boyfriend?"

"Yeah. Something happened. I think Cooper forced his way into his apartment."

"Past the doorman and security?" Rodeo asked. "That would be a trick. That place was like Fort Knox."

"Yeah. I'm thinking maybe we should head over there. I'm worried about the little guy. That is, if you all are up for it?"

"Maybe you should call 911," Kirsten suggested. "If you think this guy's really in trouble, you don't need to be getting involved in someone's domestic dispute."

"No cops. I've dealt with enough of them for one day, and Castro's no fan. We'll go there ourselves."

"Jinx…" she pleaded. "If he's seriously hurt, the police can get there much faster than you can and could save his life. Don't risk getting in the middle of it."

"Thanks for everything, Kirsten." I opened the door. "I'll try to stay out of trouble."

"Yeah, thanks, Kirsten." Caden stepped out of the Lexus. "We got it covered."

Kirsten drove off with a wave.

Zahara met my gaze. "I hope Mr. Castro is okay. Maybe we should call 911 like Kirsten said."

"I'll consider it as we head over."

We climbed into our SUVs and arrived at Castro's apartment building in record time and raced into the lobby all geared up in case Cooper had gotten past security.

"Hey! Stop!" shouted the woman behind the security desk when we made a beeline for the elevators.

Two other security guards in the lobby approached cautiously, hands on their sidearms.

"Sebastian Castro is in trouble." I punched the elevator call button several times.

"What trouble?" asked the woman from the desk. She'd marched out and placed herself between the elevator doors and my team, her fists on her hips.

"Someone's breaking into his apartment. He called me begging for help."

"That's absurd. No one gets past us. And you can't just barge in here like this. You need the resident's permission to go up."

"Your resident could be dying as we speak. We're going up. You're welcome to come with." I played Castro's frantic voicemail message.

Concern etched the corners of the woman's eyes.She gestured to one of her fellow security guards. "Frank here will escort you."

"Fine."

On the ride up to Castro's floor, I swear I heard a Muzak version of a Joan Jett tune. What was this world coming to? The rise of fascism and domestic terrorism was bad enough, but to create an easy-listening version of "I Love Rock and Roll?" A sure sign of the approaching Armageddon.

When we reached Castro's door, Frank the security guard knocked on the door. "Mr. Castro, building security. We're conducting a safety check." When no immediate response came, he repeated his actions.

"We need to get in there," I snapped.

Frank inserted a keycard into the lock slot. A green light appeared, and the door buzzed.

I drew my Taser and followed Frank into the apartment. The glass inserts from the coffee table had been smashed to shards. A floor lamp was knocked over. A mirror on the wall was cracked. And there was blood on the floor.

"Rodeo, take the kitchen. Z and Caden, the guest bedrooms and bath. I'll take the master bedroom."

"Wait a minute," Frank said. "You have no authority here."

"Shut up, Frank," I said. "And stay out of our way."

I found the doorframe to the master bedroom shattered. The comforter was pulled askew and smeared with more blood. "Sebastian? You in here?"

A pair of feet stuck out from the other side of the bed. Sebastian lay on the floor, unmoving. Face swollen and bloody. I checked his pulse. He was alive.

"Found him! Call for an ambulance!" I searched the master bath to make sure Cooper wasn't still there, then holstered my Taser and rushed back to Sebastian.

"Hey, Sebastian? You okay, buddy?" I shook his shoulder gently.

He moaned, then cried out in pain and sobbed.

"Easy, easy. Help's on the way. Can you tell me what happened?"

"Tod."

"How'd he get in the apartment?"

"I let him in," he said and sobbed harder.

Seriously? I wasn't about to guilt-trip him, though. "It's okay. He's gone now."

I helped him onto the bed just as Zahara walked in.

"He okay?" The concern in her voice was so genuine, it broke your heart to hear it.

Frank marched in behind her, looking unsure what to do. He had his phone to his ear. "I've got 911 on the line. They're sending an ambulance."

"No," Sebastian shook his head. "I don't want to go to no damn hospital. I'm fine."

"You can tell them that when they get here," I said. "But you were out cold. Could have a concussion. Can you tell us what happened?"

I'd spent only a year as a cop, and in situations like this, my brain switched to rescue mode, making me ask questions to track down the bad guy. And Tod was already on my list of assholes I needed to snap the cuffs on.

"He called. Said he was sorry for everything. Coming out for a guy like him, it's hard, you know? Lotta internal homophobia to overcome. Afraid of losing his friends."

Listening to Sebastian making excuses for the guy made me want to shake him, but I just listened and nodded.

"He even brought flowers and wine. And not that cheap shit."

Zahara held his hand. "How did things go from apologies to violence?"

"Like they always do, I guess. We had drinks and were making out, and then, I don't know. It's like something switches in his brain. Same old of Jekyll-and-Hyde shit. Started calling me a fucking whore. No matter what I say, it's the wrong answer. Next thing I know, he's wailing on me. I got to the bedroom and tried to call you, but he broke in."

"Why didn't you call downstairs?" Frank asked.

Sebastian glared at the man. "I have, you asshole. All you people do is tell me to wait while you call the cops. At least Jinx and Rodeo came right away. Where is Rodeo?"

"I'm here," he said, holstering his Taser. "Cooper's in the wind again."

Sebastian tenderly touched his bloodied lip. "Fuck."

"Don't worry, we'll get him. I'm sorry this happened to you again." And I meant it.

Some people really knew how to fuck with your head and push all the right buttons. "You shouldn't let him in anymore. You've got a restraining order against him. He's not supposed to be here. Even if you want him here."

"I know. But I miss him. I know it's stupid."

"Just hang in there," I told him. "The EMTs will get you patched up, okay?"

Sebastian sobbed quietly for a moment. Then he said, "One-Eyed Jack's."

"What'd you say?" The name sent a chill down my spine.

"The straight bar where Tod hangs out with his buddies. I remembered the name. Real shithole. Even for a straight bar. Nineteenth Avenue and Dunlap."

"I know it," I said glumly. "A real bucket of blood."

Voices came from the living room. "Mr. Castro?"

"Cops are here," Rodeo said.

"Look, Sebastian. I know you like this guy when he's not in asshole mode, but he's not worth it."

I wrote down my father's name and work number on one of my cards, unsure about the ethics of referring business to my own father. But this kid needed help, and my father needed new clients since returning to work.

"This is my dad's information. He's a therapist specializing in trauma and abuse. He can help."

"Great, just what I need. A shrink poking around in my head."

"Up to you. But he's helped a lot of people. And he's queer friendly."

That last point registered with him, if his eyes were any indication. "Thanks."

"In the meantime, we will find Tod the Bod and put him behind bars where he can't hurt you anymore."

The cops walked in. We gave them a brief statement. I mentioned nothing about the bar where Cooper hung out, and to my surprise, neither did Sebastian.

CHAPTER 23

THE BOYFRIEND AT THE BAR

OUTSIDE IN THE condo parking lot, the western sky was an explosion of clouds and color, the kind that no sunset photo could do justice.

"Jinx, if you're thinking of going to One-Eyed Jack's and grabbing Cooper…" Rodeo started.

"Why not? We apprehended Freddie Colton there a few years back."

"And nearly got murdered by that angry mob."

"Only because Fiddler bailed on us in the middle of an operation, leaving the two of us to fend for ourselves. Now we've got twice the number. Odds are much more in our favor."

"What is this place?" Zahara asked.

"A hellhole," Rodeo answered. "When a fight breaks out, they don't bother calling the cops. They just mop up what's left."

"Doesn't scare me," Caden said. "I'm in."

"It should scare you, little man. These people are monsters. They'd chew you up like a bowl of beer pretzels."

"Hello, I worked as a corrections officer for four years. I can handle myself."

"You worked at Tonopah's women's prison. Nothing like these guys, trust me."

"Yeah, yeah, big scary dudes," I replied derisively. "We took on those psycho gun nuts in White Nation and came out okay."

"I seem to recall someone didn't fare so well." Rodeo shot a look at Caden. "As I recall, someone nearly died from a gunshot wound. How long were you in rehab, Caden?"

"I survived. But if you don't feel you're up to the challenge, dude, feel free to bail."

"I'm not bailing. Just concerned," Rodeo said. "Smart move would be to tail him when he leaves and grab him when he arrives wherever he's going. And that's assuming he's even at this bar in the first place."

I looked over at Zahara. "You care to weigh in?"

"Sorry, Jinx, but I'm with Rodeo on this one. If he's at this bar, we grab him when he's alone after he leaves. Better odds."

Two in favor, two against. Of course, being the boss, I got the deciding vote. "This guy drives like a maniac when he's being chased. It was how I lost him the first time."

Rodeo shrugged. "So we don't tip him off that he's being followed."

"Four nearly identical SUVs?" I asked. "He might get suspicious."

"Not if he's already half in the bag," Z added.

"Well, if that's the case, we owe it to public safety not to allow him to drive home."

No one spoke for several minutes.

Finally, I said, "Compromise. We don't grab him inside. We wait for him to come out. Grab him when he's getting into his truck."

My team members exchanged glances. "Fine. I can live with that," Rodeo agreed.

"Z?" I asked, turning to her.

"Seems prudent. Don't need any deaths from a drunk driver."

"And Caden?"

"Not as much fun as going in guns blazing, but I can live with it."

"Sounds like we have a plan. Let's just hope he's there. Otherwise, this whole discussion is academic."

We drove north a few miles, then turned west onto Dunlap and finally into the small parking lot at Nineteenth Avenue. Besides the bar, the L-shaped shopping center was home to a check-cashing business, a massage parlor, a gun store, and a shuttered doughnut shop.

A bald man with a linebacker's physique sat on a stool by the bar's entrance, focusing on his phone.

I immediately spotted Cooper's pickup truck in the second aisle of spaces and parked next to it. I could still see the bar's front door. The others parked at strategic locations across the lot to be ready when he emerged from the bar.

I turned on my radio. "Here's the plan. Coyote Four, I want you to wait near the bus stop on Nineteenth. When the target comes out of the bar, move in and follow. Make sure the target can't run back inside. And keep an eye out for the bouncer. Make sure he doesn't interfere. Over."

"Copy that, Coyote One. Over," Caden replied.

"Coyote Two, when the target passes the first row of cars, close in behind him. Coyote Three and I will intercept him from in front. We take him down quickly and quietly so as not to draw any undue attention. Got it? Over."

"Roger wilco. Over," Rodeo replied. Zahara also acknowledged the plan. And the waiting began.

At a quarter after seven, Conor called. Shit, I'd totally forgotten.

"Hey, love. Ya coming home? Stew's all ready. Leia helped me make some soda bread to go with it."

My stomach growled. Had I eaten lunch? I couldn't remember. "Sorry, babe. I'm staking out a fugitive at a bar."

"Just grab the wanker outta there and call it a night."

"It's One-Eyed Jack's."

"Ah. Perhaps a wait-and-see strategy might be the most prudent approach. How long's the bloke been in there?"

"At least two hours."

"Shite! Okay, well, the longer he's in there, the easier he'll be to grab."

"Hope so. I'll be home when I can."

A few long hours later, movement caught my eye, but it wasn't at the door of the bar. "Target's in sight," I said into my radio. "Everyone move in. Over."

"Where?" Caden replied. "No one walked out of the bar. Over."

I slipped out of my truck and quietly shut the door. "Massage parlor two doors down. Looks like he's headed toward the bar. Coyotes Two and Four, move in to intercept. Watch the bouncer. Over."

"Shit, I got him."

Zahara and I approached his truck from opposite ends of the row on the side nearest the intersection.

"Hey, Tod!" Rodeo called in a seductive voice. He'd ditched his vest and his tactical belt and now strolled toward Cooper. The bouncer was on the far side of them, with Caden approaching cautiously from behind.

"Can't believe you let me fuck you last night, but then you leave before the crack of dawn. Didn't take you for a love-'em-and-leave-'em kinda guy."

"Who the hell are you?" Cooper yelled back with a threat of violence in his voice.

The bouncer looked toward Rodeo and Cooper but stayed put for the moment. Caden had his Taser in hand, gradually closing the distance.

Rodeo approached. "Don't tell me you've forgotten my

name already? It's Lance. We met at Stallions, remember? I suppose you were kinda drunk. By the way, you owe me a new comforter after you threw up all over the old one."

"Stay the fuck away from me, you goddamn faggot!"

"What the hell's going on here?" The bouncer stood up from his stool.

"Stay put," Caden told him from fifteen feet away. "And stay quiet."

The bouncer turned to stare at Caden, who had clearly surprised him. He raised his hands in surrender. Was that a pistol in his waistband? "It's cool, man."

"What the fuck's going on?" Cooper looked back and forth between Rodeo and Caden.

"Let's move," I told Zahara. "Keep your eyes on the bouncer. Make sure he doesn't pull that weapon in his belt."

"Copy that."

Zahara leveled her shotgun at the bouncer. "Sit your ass back down, Tiny. Keep your hands in the air. You reach for that piece and you'll wish you hadn't."

I focused on Cooper, my Taser pointed at his chest. "Tod Cooper, your bail bond has been revoked for failure to app—"

He charged me like an enraged bull. I hit him with the Taser. The juice flowed, but he was already hurtling toward me like a planet-killer asteroid.

Drawing on my police training, I stepped to the side, grabbed his shirt with my free hand, and used his momentum to drive him face-first into the tailgate of a Ford pickup. He hit with a sickening thud then dropped to the pavement.

Distant voices echoes through the lot, but I tuned them out while I flipped Cooper onto his stomach and cuffed him. He groaned, letting me know he was still alive.

"Tod Cooper, your bail bond has been revoked for failure to appear. I am returning you to the custody of the Maricopa

County Jail. Any attempt to resist may result in additional charges and jail time."

I didn't know if he could hear me, much less understand. I was just glad to have him finally.

"Rodeo, help me get him up."

"Bitch," Cooper muttered groggily.

"What the hell do you people think you're doing?" the bouncer asked.

"Sir! Sit back down," Zahara ordered. "This is a legal matter that doesn't concern you."

Rodeo grabbed Cooper's other arm, and we hefted him to his feet. He managed to stand. Barely.

When we were within ten feet of my truck, I heard the thunder of a shotgun, followed by a baritone howling.

"I told you to stay put."

"Get off me. You people ain't cops." Cooper tried to shake us. "Fucking kill you, bitches."

"Shut the hell up, Cooper, or I'll tase you again."

"Jinx!" Zahara called. "We got company."

I opened the back door of my SUV and glanced back toward the bar. A couple of guys must have heard the shotgun and come out to investigate. I shoved Cooper inside the truck and shut the door.

"Come on!" I shouted to Z and Caden. "Time to go."

"You need me to follow you to the jail?" Rodeo asked.

"No, get on outta here. Make sure Z and Caden get away okay."

"Roger that, boss."

I hopped into the driver's seat. "Comfy back there, Cooper?"

"Fuck you, bitch."

"Same to ya."

I hadn't had time to buckle him in. Oh well. If he got bounced around a little, he sure as hell had it coming.

CHAPTER 24
WHERE'S MY SON?

I DROVE Cooper to the Fourth Avenue Jail and got him checked in. When I arrived home, it was nearly ten thirty. With Rayna's car in our garage, I parked in the driveway and walked around to the front door.

Just as I stepped onto the porch, movement caught my attention. A man I didn't recognize stumbled from the shadows. His clothes were disheveled, and he sported a few days' worth of stubble.

"Where the hell's my son?" he shouted.

"Excuse me?" I rested a hand on my Taser.

"My son! Luke Ripley. You took him, you stupid bitch."

It clicked. Ripley. Asshole was talking about Leia. This guy must be Rayna's ex, Mike Ripley.

"I didn't take anyone's son, buddy. I'd advise you to go home and sleep it off."

"I saw you, you perv. You and my woke bitch of a wife are grooming him, brainwashing him into thinking he's a girl."

"Sir, you are trespassing. If you do not leave right now, I will have you arrested. You will not enjoy it, I promise."

Instead of walking away, he started shouting. "Luke!

Luke! You get your pansy ass out here this minute! This is your father."

"Suit yourself."

Since he was so close, I used the Taser as a stun gun. Ripley's body stiffened and shuddered, then dropped onto the concrete. I cuffed him as he lay there. The guy's breath reeked like a brewery.

The front door opened, and Conor stepped out. "What the bloody hell's going on?"

"Leia's dad."

"Shite! Ya need me to call the police?"

I contemplated the idea. Calling the cops might put Rayna and Leia in further danger if they searched the house. But I couldn't just let this guy go.

For starters, he was too inebriated to drive. And who knew what else he might try? Unless I somehow convinced him that Rayna and Leia weren't here.

"Luke," Ripley grunted. "His name's Luke."

I put my knee into his back, just in case he got any ideas. "Listen up, asshole. Luke is not here. So we can play this one of two ways. Either I call the cops and have you arrested for trespassing. Or I call you a taxi, and you go home and sleep it off. So what'll it be?"

"I want my son."

I dug my knee harder into his back. "Your family is not here, asshole. They left. Gone. Do you understand?"

He cried out in pain. "Yes, yes, I understand."

"Excellent. So what's it going to be? Police or taxi?"

"Taxi."

"Good answer." I jerked him to his feet. "Here's the deal, Ripley. I'm going to call the taxi. When it shows up, I'll uncuff you."

"Don't need no taxi. I can drive."

The man smelled like he'd been swimming in a pool of cheap whiskey, and his speech was slurred.

"That's not the deal. You're too drunk to drive. So I'll ask you once more, taxi or police?"

"Fuck. Call me a damn taxi."

I ran a web search for taxi services and called one for a pickup. When they asked for the destination, I asked, "Mr. Ripley, where do you live?"

He mumbled an address, which I repeated for the taxi company. They replied they'd be there in about half an hour.

"Where are you parked?" I asked while we waited.

"Couple doors down."

In the gloom, I could make out the shape of a vehicle halfway between two streetlamps.

"Tomorrow, after you've sobered up, you come get your car. If I see you here again, you will get worse. I promise you. If I hear you've harmed Rayna or your kid, I will rain fire down on you the likes of which you won't believe. Are we clear?"

"Bitch."

I punched him in the kidney. He yelped.

"Are. We. Clear?"

"Yeah, yeah, we're clear…" he wheezed.

I wasn't entirely convinced.

When the taxi pulled up, I uncuffed him. He rubbed his wrists and then at his chest where the darts had made contact. "Bitch."

"More than you know."

He marched across the yard, got into the cab, and disappeared into the night.

Conor and I stepped inside, and I shut the front door behind us.

"Well, that was fun," I said to him.

"Aye. So, did ya get the bloke you were staking out at One-Eyed Jack's?"

I kissed him hard before answering. Exciting takedowns

always made me horny. A side effect of the adrenaline rush, perhaps.

"Yeah, we got him," I whispered when I finally came up for air.

The house was still redolent with the aroma of delicious food, a nice improvement over Ripley's odor of stale whiskey. My stomach felt as empty as a poor man's pocket. "Any leftovers? I'm starving."

"Aye. Plenty."

I followed him into the kitchen, where I popped a bowl of leftover stew in the microwave. "Rayna and Leia still up?" I asked.

"Leia's asleep," Rayna said as she walked in, looking like she'd aged a few years since I saw her that morning. "So, you met my ex."

"Yeah, charming guy. Can't understand why'd you leave him."

She sighed. "He was a nice guy once. But over the years, he started developing an attitude, like it's all got to be about him. Reminds me a bit of my dad."

I gave her a hug. "You know what they say, women tend to marry men like their fathers."

"I've been thinking maybe Leia and I should find other accommodations. I don't want to be a bother."

"You're not a bother," I insisted. "You're welcome to stay here as long as you like."

"Between the DCS social worker, the FBI, and now Mike…"

"Is there someplace else you'd rather stay?"

"That's the thing. I don't know where we could go. We could stay at my mom's, but DCS and Mike would show up there sooner rather than later."

"They could stay at Mariposa House," Conor suggested.

Mariposa House was a house I owned that served as a home for trans people with nowhere else to go.

"They're full up, last I checked," I replied.

My phone buzzed, alerting me to our security system detecting movement in front of the house. I pulled up the camera feed on my phone. The view showed not only our front yard but extended a few houses down along the street.

On the video feed, the taxi was back and parked next to Ripley's car. He emerged from the backseat, shouted something I couldn't make out. The taxi driver flipped him off through an open window, then sped off.

Ripley stumbled around to the driver's side of his car and disappeared inside.

"Damn," I muttered.

"What's wrong?" Panic spread across Rayna's face.

"He's back. Taxi must have circled the block and returned for some reason."

Conor snorted. "Driver probably didn't want the bastard stinking up his cab."

I watched, expecting Ripley to drive off. Instead, he sat in his car. At least he wasn't driving drunk. "Persistent little pissant, I'll give him that. Looks like he's watching the house. Or sleeping it off. Hard to tell from the video."

"So no matter where we go, Mike and DCS are bound to follow," Rayna said.

"The bugger won't follow you anywhere if he thinks you're still here," Conor said with a devious smile.

She cocked an eyebrow. "What do you mean?"

"The tunnel Conor hid you in earlier today leads to Prowling Tiger Tattoo Studio on McDowell," I explained.

The mention of the studio got me thinking about another tattoo artist I knew. I checked my watch.

"They should be open for another half hour. Let me make a call. I think I can find a place for you to stay where they won't bother to look for you."

I pulled up a number from my contact list and placed a call. "Avery, hey! You working tonight?"

"Just finished my last client. Why? You want to grab a drink somewhere?"

"Actually, I need your help. Got a friend with a trans daughter. DCS is looking for them."

"Right, that new law. Goddamn fascist fuckers."

"They've been staying with Conor and me for the past day, but the kid's father is onto us. DCS too. They need new accommodations. Think you could put them up for a little bit?"

"I just have a one-bedroom apartment. I suppose I could sleep on my couch, and they could share my bed. It's queen-size."

"Shit. No, I don't want to put you out like that."

"Bobby J.'s got two free rooms since I moved out." Bobby Jeong was the owner of the tattoo studio in Glendale, where they both worked and had been Avery's foster father when she was younger.

"That would be perfect. You think he'd be okay with it?"

"Are you kidding? He took me in after he caught me breaking into his shop downtown. With all the craziness going on these days, he'd be happy to help."

"Could he meet us at Prowling Tiger in, say, half an hour?"

"Bobby's still working on a client, but I can pick them up."

"That would be great. Thanks, Avery." I ended the call.

"You found someone who'll take us in?" Rayna asked.

"My friend Avery will be over shortly. She's a friend of mine from Phoenix Gender Alliance. You'll be staying with her father, who's a big-time *Star Wars* geek. We need to hurry and get you packed before Prowling Tiger closes."

Relief washed over Rayna's face. "Leia will love that."

I helped them gather their things, then led them back down into the tunnel.

Leia's eyes grew wide and wary. She was definitely not a fan of confined spaces, even though the tunnel was well lit.

"Just think of it like you're aboard a spaceship," I encouraged her.

"Spaceships don't go underground," she pointed out.

"True." I couldn't think of what else to say.

At the other end, we reached a ladder that led up through another trapdoor. Rayna handed me up their bags one by one then switched off the tunnel lights and climbed the ladder.

"Welcome to the back storage room of Prowling Tiger Tattoo. Follow me."

I walked through a thin wooden door into the main part of the studio. Most of the stations were closed for the night, but my friend Weevil was working on a back piece for a male client.

"Evening, Weevil."

He always looked like something the cat dragged in. Scruffy face and a hairstyle that made Boris Johnson looked well-groomed. He wore a leather vest and no shirt with matching leather pants braided along each leg.

"Hey! I don't allow kids in the shop."

"Relax, man, they're just passing through. The kid's abusive father is watching our house. We're trying to keep them safe."

"Oh." His expression softened. "In that case, come on through. Just don't touch nothing. Or sneeze on anything. Or..."

"Chill, Weevil. She will not cause any problems. And she's not contagious. She's just a kid."

"Fine."

"Let's go outside," I told Rayna and Leia. "Before Weevil has a stroke."

Ten minutes later, a black fifties-era Caddy with tailfins the size of surfboards rumbled into the parking lot.

The woman who got out was in her early twenties with raven-black hair cut in a Bettie Page style. She wore a low-cut blood-red blouse and a black lace skirt. Her makeup had a distinct goth style to it. Elaborate tattoos covered the top of her chest and both arms.

"Rayna and Leia, meet my dear friend, Avery Byrne."

Avery smiled. Something about her teeth reminded me of a vampire's, like her canines were just a little longer than they should be. "Nice to meet you."

Leia stepped back, looking more frightened than she did in the tunnel.

"It's okay, Leia," I assured her. "She's just goth. Not a vampire."

"So far as you know," Avery teased and gave Leia a wink. "But I don't eat kids. Only bullies. Did you say your name was Leia? Like Princess Leia?"

"General Leia," the girl corrected, rather sternly.

"Of course. My bad. Well, you are going to love my dad. He's the biggest *Star Wars* nerd I know. He even has a full-size remote-control R2-D2 in his living room. You want to meet him?"

Leia nodded vigorously.

"Then hop in the Gothmobile. I'll drive you to him."

Rayna turned to me. "Thank you so much. And I'm sorry for whatever trouble my ex caused."

"Not for you to apologize. I can handle punks like him. Just keep Leia and yourself safe."

I handed her a prepaid cell phone I'd grabbed from my house before we left. "Take this. Call me if you need anything. It's got about four hours of phone time left on it. Neither DCS nor your ex will be able to trace it."

"Jinx, this is too much."

"Relax, I got about a dozen of them. I mostly use them to lure in unsuspecting fugitives. Return it whenever. No hurry."

"Thank you again. You're an absolute lifesaver."

"My pleasure. I'll talk to you soon."

I watched them drive off, then hurried back through the tunnel.

CHAPTER 25
NANCY BEGS FOR HELP

THE REST OF THE NIGHT, the house felt empty, though our houseguests had been with us for only a day. Even though I'd hardly been home while they were here, I'd looked forward to getting to know them.

Meeting Leia brought back memories of my transition. The good and the bad. The elation of finally fitting into my own skin and my place in the world, combined with the trepidation that a lot of folks didn't want people like me to exist.

A part of me connected with Rayna too. She was such a devoted mom. I felt a desire to nurture and love someone the way Rayna loved Leia, leaving me wondering what I would be like as a mother.

Conor would be a great dad. How could he not be? He was funny, encouraging, tough, protective. I was less sure of my own parenting skills. And with our crazy work schedules, would we have the time to give a child the attention and care they needed?

How would we even have a child? Obviously, I couldn't get pregnant. Adoption? Hire a surrogate? I'd heard so many horror stories from my friends, queer and straight alike. Was any of it worth considering?

"Morning, love." Conor kissed me, pulling me out of my head as sunrise painted the bedroom in tones of apricot.

I gazed into his mesmerizing emerald eyes. "Good morning."

"Ya look worried. Something on your mind?"

"Just thinking."

"About?" He cradled my face in his hands.

"Stuff."

"Oh? Stuff, is it? Fascinating topic, stuff."

"About this Krueger case," I fibbed. "I hate finding a fugitive dead."

"You're a bloody liar, Jenna Christina Ballou. I can see it in your eyes. You're not thinking about the creepy bloke in the cooler. Something else is going on in that adorable head of yours."

My face went hot. How did he read me so well? "Fine, I was thinking about Rayna and Leia."

"And what were ya thinking about them?"

"How much I liked having them here."

"Miss them already? Ya hardly spent any time with them."

"I know. Still, I was wondering what it must be like for Rayna. All that she goes through to support Leia."

"She's a good mum."

"Yeah…"

"Something else. Considering becoming a mum, too, are ya?"

Geez, does he know me that well?

"You ever think about it?"

"Being a mum? Not that often. Though I think you'd make an excellent one."

Now my face heated up even more. "You think so?"

"I do, love. You're nurturing, bold, sensitive."

"Selfish, nutty, confused."

"Aye. Like every person on this planet."

"And you'd make an amazing father."

"Don't know about that. I can be quite grumpy. And I have an irrational fear of hospitals."

"Not irrational," I whispered, sensing his sadness. "After what happened to your sister Bernie."

"Either way, if we had a kiddo, what would I do if they got seriously ill?"

"You would overcome your fear and be with them. You did that for my father when he was shot."

Now it was his turn to become red as a beet. "But your da, he's…"

"Family. Just like our kid would be."

Neither of us spoke for a while. We just gazed into each other's eyes. We'd been a couple for six years, not taking into account the time he was gone. Married just over a year.

But my love for him was like a drug. One look into those eyes felt like an injection of pure joy to the point of overflowing. And maybe that was it. I had so much love for him, I wanted to share it with a child as well. Baby fever, I'd heard it called.

"This is silly. How would we even have a kid?"

"Dunno. But if that's what ya want, I'm sure we'll find a way."

My alarm started beeping. "Ugh. Time to go to work."

A few hours later, I walked out of the house to begin my working day. Mike Ripley's car was where it had been the night before.

With Taser in hand, I approached it cautiously. He was asleep and snoring loud enough for me to hear him outside of the car. I didn't really care. Rayna and Leia were safely away. If he wanted to stake out my house, let him. And if he got violent, he would quickly learn that was a mistake.

I left him to sleep off his bender and drove to Assurity Bail Bonds with the body receipts for Milano and Cooper.

Sadie remained silent after I sat down, barely acknowledging my presence.

"You heard what happened to Krueger, I take it," I said.

She was busy typing something on her computer. "I did."

"Wasn't like I killed him. Hell, I never even met the man until we found him dead in his own cooler."

"I know." She continued typing, not bothering to look in my direction.

"But I did find Milano. And Cooper." I slid the body receipt an inch closer to her. "Damn near risked our lives doing it, but we got him."

She stayed silent.

"You're not blaming me for Krueger's death, are you? I mean, the man was seriously dark and twisted. You should have seen his house, not to mention some things in that cooler." Like the human meat puzzle. "Not surprised he offed himself."

She finally stopped typing. "No, I do not blame you. Per se. But maybe if you had picked him up sooner."

"Sooner? How was I supposed to know he'd blow his brains out?"

"It's not good for my reputation to have a client turn up dead. I rely on referrals for business."

"You think Leroy Drake would've found him any sooner? Fat chance."

Sadie was always threatening to fire me and hire Drake for fugitives I had trouble finding. On the rare occasions she did that, she often hired me back when Drake turned up goose eggs. The man couldn't find his way out of a hat.

She looked at me and sighed heavily. "Probably not. As I said, I don't blame you. It's just frustrating. I am allowed to feel frustrated."

Wow, a rare glimpse into Sadie Levinson's humanity. "I get that. I'll try not to make a habit of having your clients end up dead. So, you got any more wayward defendants?"

"Currently, no. I'll have the bounties for Milano and Cooper transferred to your bank account by Friday."

That was the way it was. Sometimes there were more bail jumpers than I could handle. Other times, there was nothing. Feast or famine, as they say. At least I got paid for Milano and Cooper.

"All right. Have a nice day."

She barely acknowledged me as I left.

On my way back to the parking garage, my phone rang.

"Jinx Ballou," I said, not recognizing the caller ID.

"Ms. Ballou, I need your help." The voice was familiar, a bit choked with emotion, but I couldn't place it.

"Who is this?"

"Nancy Turner."

Nancy the necro. Fuck me. "What do you want, Ms. Turner?"

"The police are saying Donnie killed himself."

"Yeah, they tend to say that when someone blows their own brains out." I considered hanging up on her. I should have, but I didn't.

"He didn't shoot himself, Ms. Ballou. He wouldn't. He's Catholic."

"My mother's Catholic. Some may believe suicide is a sin, but trust me, when the walls start closing in, religion can go right out the window." Hell, I had been there a time or two myself.

"Not Donnie. He wasn't depressed. And he didn't own a gun."

"Look, your boss was a weird little man who was facing jail time, possibly prison. Maybe he couldn't handle it. Especially after losing his medical license. It's enough to make even a devout Catholic do the unthinkable."

"But the FBI was offering him an immunity deal."

"A deal for what? What else was he involved in?" After my previous dustup with the feds, I was curious.

"I don't know. He wouldn't tell me."

"So why bother me about it? Tell it to the cops. That detective… What was his name? Montana. He seemed like a good sort. Tell him."

"I did. He's convinced Donnie's death was a suicide."

"Then talk to the feds."

"They won't talk to me. Someone murdered him, and no one cares. Maybe you did it. Killed him out of spite."

"You kidding me? I lost out on a sizable bounty thanks to him being dead. I'd much rather he be alive."

"I thought you people got paid either way. Bring 'em back dead or alive. Isn't that what they say?"

"Not these days."

"Well, somebody killed him." A long silence followed. "I want to hire you to find the murderer. Maybe then the police will do something."

"Not interested."

"Please, Ms. Ballou. Whoever killed him may come after me next." She paused for a moment. "I can't pay you anything right now, but if I can find a buyer for New Life Medical Resources…"

"Even if I was interested, which I'm not, I don't work for free. Or IOUs or credit. Or exposure. I'm not a charity. I require a retainer of two grand for starters. My advice is to forget about Krueger and start looking for a new job."

I hung up, hiked up the stairs to the third floor of the Arizona Center parking garage, and climbed into my truck.

I sent out a text to the team, letting them know we didn't have any new jobs but that I'd be checking in with other bail bond agencies. Caden, Rodeo, and Zahara were all on salary, so it was like an unplanned vacation.

As I drove to the Hub, I couldn't get Krueger out of my mind. Turner's notion that Catholics never committed suicide was bogus. When life, depression, and despair got enough of a grip on you, it didn't matter what you professed to believe.

What did suggest someone staged his suicide was this alleged deal Krueger had with the FBI. If he had immunity, his world might not be collapsing around him. So why take the bullet train into the afterlife?

At the same time, whoever he was flipping on certainly had a motive to kill him. So who did he have dirt on?

If anyone knew besides the tight-lipped feds, I would have thought that Nancy Turner would. But if she was begging me to find his killer, wouldn't she have told me everything she knew? Did Krueger have something going on that his office manager didn't know about?

All of that was just speculation at this point. And I certainly wasn't taking the case. Turner had no money.

I was going to check in with Second Chance or Pima Bail Bonds and see if they had any work for me. If not, Conor and I could take Diana up to the mountains and enjoy the fall colors. Even play in the early-season snow up at Hannagan Meadow in the White Mountains.

But even though I was no-way-no-how looking into Krueger's death, it still haunted me. Murder was funny that way.

CHAPTER 26
KRUEGER'S DAUGHTER

WHEN I WENT to the Hub, Becca was already there. She looked up at me expectantly, and I realized I had promised to stop at Tres Leches. I'd been so preoccupied with this Krueger mess that I'd totally spaced on it.

"Sorry," I told her. "I'll go grab us some coffees."

She shook her head. "Don't worry about it. I'll have some of the coffee from the break room."

"That sludge that Troy Reid makes?" He was a game developer who worked a few tables over. "That stuff will rot your kidneys."

"Not if I put in enough cream and sugar."

"There's some fine biochemical rationalization," I said, chuckling. "Really, I promised I'd bring the coffee. I can run down the street and be back in a flash."

"No, sit."

I did and brought her up to speed about Rayna and Leia staying with Avery's dad. Then I told her about Krueger's death and Turner's plea for help.

"You going to do it?"

"Work for Nancy the necro? I don't think so. For starters, she's got no money to hire me. And secondly, I have no interest in helping her. Whatever happened to that creepy man is not my concerned."

"And yet something in your voice says you're desperate to know how he died."

Damn, she knew me too well. That was hardly surprising, since we'd been besties since the sixth grade.

"Am I a little curious whether he really offed himself? Sure, maybe. But if he didn't, he really pissed someone off. Someone with the smarts and the means, motive, and opportunity to kill someone and cover their tracks well. I got enough problems chasing after fugitives. Like my father said, don't go chasing trouble."

"Except you don't have any cases at the moment."

"Not with Sadie. But Second Chance or Pima Bail Bonds might have something. And if not, maybe I'll take the rest of the week off. Enjoy a little downtime for once."

She grinned at me but said nothing.

The questions surrounding Krueger's death nagged me, even as I called the other bail bond agencies I worked with. None of them had anything for me, so I texted the team to tell them to enjoy a long Halloween weekend.

It was only Thursday. The Phoenix Gender Alliance was having a costume party on Saturday night, even though Halloween itself wasn't until Monday. Conor and I could spend Friday and part of Saturday up in the high country and be back in time for me to show off my new Captain Marvel costume. Yeah, I was a bounty hunter who did cosplay. So what?

WinterCon, a local comic book convention, was a month away, and now would be a good time to work out the kinks in my costume. Some of the final touches needed work. Didn't want to risk a major costume fail. Plus, I was still deciding whether to wear a short blond Carol Danvers wig or the Captain Marvel space helmet I'd made with glowing monofilament, or say "to hell with authenticity" and go with my long dark hair.

Since I was already at the Hub, I decided to get caught up on my bookkeeping before heading home to relax.

I was in the middle of filing my quarterly sales taxes when Leia called on the burner I'd given Rayna.

"Hey, kiddo," I said. "How's the new digs?"

"Nice, though I wish I were back home."

"Yeah, I hear ya. No place like home. How's Mr. Jeong?"

"He's really nice. And he's got a General Leia tattoo on one of his arms. I asked Mom if I could get one, but she said not until I'm eighteen."

"Probably a good idea. You have a lot of growing to do."

"Do you have any tattoos?"

I blushed. "A couple. In some private places."

"Oh."

"Is there a reason you called?"

"I wanted to go to the Phoenix Gender Alliance costume party. But Mom won't let me go. I was hoping you could talk to her and change her mind. Are you going?"

"Maybe, but it's a grownup kind of party. You'd probably be bored out of your mind."

"I don't care. I'd still have fun. Mom won't let me go because DCS wants to take me away."

"Yeah, that is a bigger issue. You wouldn't want them to force you to live with your dad or some stranger."

"But they won't have to know I'm there. I'd be in costume with a mask and everything."

"Like I said, the party's more for grownups. Is the Hatchling group having a party this year?"

"They canceled it because of the stupid new law. They're just going to do a Zoom call. Meh. I want a party."

"Look, you've got many, many years ahead of you. Maybe you and your mom and Bobby J. can do something fun. Like have your own *Star Wars*-themed party."

"He and Avery are just going to be passing out candy to trick-or-treaters. Borrrinnnggg."

"I'm sorry, Leia. Hopefully, Kirsten and Lambda Legal can stop this new law, and you can go back to your normal life soon."

"Why's it gotta be like this? Why do people have to be so mean?"

"I dunno, kid. Being trans is hard. It was hard for me. And I know it's hard for you too. But people like you and me, we're tough. Like superhero tough. We're resilient. You know that word *resilient*?"

"Duh! I'm not stupid. I do read. It means we can get through stuff."

"Exactly. Princess Leia, or rather General Leia—she had to go through a lot of hard stuff too. She got captured by Darth Vader. Then her entire planet got blown up. Her friends and family, all gone. But she stuck it out and eventually the Rebellion won, right?"

"Yeah, but that's just a bunch of movies."

"True. We just got to stick it out like she did. And you're not alone. You've got your mom, your grandma, Avery, Bobby J., Kirsten, me, Conor, and even your new friends in the Hatchlings. We're all working together to keep you safe."

"I know."

"And many years from now, young trans kids will be saying, 'That Leia girl, she's such an inspiration to me. She gave me the courage to come out and be my true self.'"

"Yeah, right."

"I'm serious, Leia. I never thought people would say that to me, but you did. When *Phoenix Living* outed me a few years back, it cost me my job, and it's been a pain in my butt since then. But it also gave people like you and your mom the courage to do what you needed to do. There's an old saying, 'We stand on the shoulders of giants.' You know what that means?"

"No."

"It means the people who came before us, who demonstrated courage or shared their knowledge—they've helped us get where we are. And we will do the same for those who come after us. So in time, you will become someone else's giant."

"Never thoughta that."

"I've also learned something else. Something my dad taught me."

"What's that?"

"Don't postpone your happiness wishing for things you don't have. Be happy now. Enjoy being with people who care about you. Enjoy the good things in your life, even when a lot of things aren't perfect."

"You sound like my mom."

"Your mom's a smart lady."

"Yeah."

"Look, I'm sorry you can't go to a party, but have fun with Bobby J., Avery, and your mom. Okay?"

"I will. Thanks."

"I'll talk to you soon."

"Oh, almost forgot. My mom says there's going to be a protest at the State Capitol on Saturday morning. We can't go, obviously, but Mom says it's important for as many trans people as possible to be there."

"Okay, I'll look into it." An incoming call beeped on the line. "I have to take this call. Take care, Leia."

"You too."

I clicked over to the new call. "Jinx Ballou."

"Ms. Ballou, I need your help."

She wasn't Nancy Turner, but I recognized the voice. "Amy Krueger? How can I help you?"

"The police are wrong. My father did not... would not kill himself. Someone murdered him and made it look like a suicide."

I took a breath. First Nancy the necro. Now Krueger's daughter. "Ms. Krueger, I'm sorry for your father's death. Truly, I am. But if the police are saying it's a suicide, it probably is."

"He wouldn't hurt himself. Not like that."

"How do you know? You said you rarely spoke with him."

"He'd been staying with me since getting out on bail."

"You said you didn't know where he was." Anger crept into my voice. I had to remind myself this woman was grieving her father's death.

"I'm sorry I lied. His lawyer was negotiating a deal with the FBI. They were going to give him immunity. No prison time, and he'd be able to continue his work. So he had no reason to hurt himself."

"Why were the feds giving him immunity? Who was he flipping on? What was he involved in?"

"I don't know."

"Well, you have a good day, Ms. Krueger. And again, sorry for your loss."

"No, please don't hang up. I need your help."

"Ms. Krueger, Amy, what are you asking me to do?"

"I spoke with Sadie Levinson, Dad's bail bond agent. She said, in addition to being a bounty hunter, you were also a licensed private investigator. I want to hire you to find out who murdered my father."

"Like I told Ms. Turner, even if I were interested in taking the case—which I'm not—I don't work for free."

"I can pay you."

That was certainly better than Nancy the necro's eternal gratitude, but still. "I don't know."

"Please, Ms. Ballou, I need answers. You said Great Harvest had helped your friends. I'm asking you now to help me. Please."

I hated when people begged. As much as I tried not to be,

I was a sucker for desperate people. I knew what it felt like to have nowhere to turn.

"I require a two-thousand-dollar retainer up front and charge a hundred dollars an hour plus expenses. No guarantee on results. It may turn out he really took his own life. Or if someone did kill him, I may be unable to determine who did. You pay either way. Is that understood?"

"Yes. I understand. Someone did this to him. They must be held accountable."

"Also, if someone did kill him or I otherwise find evidence of a serious crime, I turn my findings over to the police, and what they do with that information is up to them. They may do nothing. I'm not a cop. I'm not a vigilante. No murder for hire. Are we clear?"

"Yes."

I considered this agreement some more. I'd rather go see the autumn leaves along the Mogollon Rim. The town of Strawberry was having a fall festival.

"Please, Jinx. I need this."

"Before I say yes, you gotta come clean with me. What illegal activity was your father involved with?"

"I don't know, and that's the truth. He kept me out of it to protect me. All he told me was that he was involved with something online. My father was a good person. He didn't deserve to die like this."

I still didn't know whether to believe her. "Fine! I'll send you the contract. Sign it and pay the retainer, and I will try to get to the bottom of things."

"Thank you so much, Jinx."

CHAPTER 27

A LIST OF SUSPECTS

I HAD little experience investigating murders. I'd been a patrol officer for only a year when I quit to join Conor's bounty hunter team. But between my short stint in patrol and several years chasing fugitives, I had learned a few things.

First, people who took their own lives didn't always leave notes. When they were in that awful emotional swamp, they weren't thinking about anyone else. They just wanted the pain to stop.

And as I told both Turner and Krueger, when life pushed a person beyond their limits with no hope of life getting better, religious beliefs didn't mean shit. When life already felt like hell, people didn't care what happened next.

On the other hand, suicides could be staged, and some were more convincing than others.

As a patrol officer, I'd been called to several scenes in which the victim had allegedly died of a self-inflicted gunshot wound. I found one victim with a gun in his dominant left hand, but the entrance wound was behind his right ear. Not even a contortionist could pull off a shot like that.

Another victim was allegedly discovered by her husband with the gun nearby and both hands clasped around a rosary. But she would have died instantly from the GSW. No grabbing the rosary at that point.

Sometimes, it was impossible to know one way or the other, and the detective made a judgment call or chalked up the manner of death as undetermined. Especially if they already had a sizable caseload. Case triage.

In Krueger's case, I'd had neither the time nor the inclination to study the crime scene when I was in that cooler of the dead. If anything was there to contraindicate a suicide, I hadn't seen it. Apparently, neither had Detective Montana.

In ninety percent of homicides, the killer knew the victim. Usually, the culprit was a family member or a jilted lover. Sometimes a disgruntled neighbor, a coworker, or business associate. For someone like Krueger, that made a long list.

His questionable business decisions had left at least one family bitterly angry. And if Krueger was dropping the dime on someone that the feds were investigating, that certainly put them high on the list of suspects.

I had no idea about Krueger's love life, if he even had one. He was currently unmarried. But that didn't mean anything. For all I knew, he and Nancy the necro could have been getting it on. I tried hard not to think about that.

"Going off to play PI, are we?" Becca asked with a gleam in her eye.

"Krueger's daughter is convinced someone murdered him, even though Peoria PD is ruling the death a suicide."

"So she wants to hire you to tilt at windmills?"

"Presumably. I don't know this Detective Montana all that well, but he seemed competent. I'll poke around, learn what I can, but unless something pops up in the next few days suggesting homicide, I'll collect my fee and call this case closed."

"It seems strange that he would call you only to shoot himself in the head."

"Yeah, well, he was a strange little guy. The man had a Frankenstein-style monster made from multiple bodies in his cooler. That was after he sold the body of someone's mother to get blown to smithereens. Maybe the guilt or the madness eventually got to him."

"Maybe."

When I received a confirmation that Amy Krueger had paid the invoice for the deposit and signed the contract I'd sent, it was time to get to work.

I called her, and we agreed to meet again at her office.

When I arrived, I asked her, "Who do you think killed your father?" The ten-thousand-dollar question.

The woman sitting before me was not the composed executive I'd met two days earlier. Her face was puffy from crying. Her hair was mussed, and her earrings didn't match. She clung to a wadded tissue in one hand.

"I honestly don't know. He told me several families were unhappy about where he'd sold their loved ones' remains."

"Not just the one he sold to the defense contractor?"

"No. Once news of that case broke, other families began inquiring what happened to their loved ones."

"And what did happen?"

"Most were sold to organizations in the medical field—med schools, tissue labs, and instrument companies demonstrating new tools and techniques. What most people think of when they hear the phrase 'donated to science.'"

"But not all?"

"He sold three to a car manufacturer that used them as crash test dummies. Sold five to Life Revealed. They do those traveling exhibits of cadavers that are preserved through plastination and partially dissected to reveal the body's different systems."

I'd gone to one such exhibit with my mother, who worked as a trauma nurse in the E.R. She found it endlessly fascinating. I found it creepy as fuck.

"Didn't Life Revealed used to use the bodies of executed Chinese prisoners?" I asked.

"They did. New laws forced the company to switch to bodies that were acquired under more humanitarian means."

"Any other controversial sales?"

"He sold two to the body farm near Wittmann."

"A body farm? What the hell is that?" I wasn't entirely sure I wanted to know the answer.

"It's a joint venture between the Phoenix crime lab and Central Arizona University's medical school. They place cadavers in a variety of environments and study the decomposition process under the different conditions."

"Right." I could feel my lunch threatening to come up on me.

"Most body farms are located in temperate environments. This is the only one in the desert. Technically, it is for science, but some families objected when they learned their loved ones were, as one relative put it, 'just rotting in the sun or left for the coyotes and the maggots.'"

"I can see how they might be upset. I'll need the names of all the family members who were objecting to how their loved ones' remains were disposed."

"Dad's office manager, Ms. Turner, can provide that information. My father never mentioned any names to me."

"Are you and Ms. Turner close?" From the way Ms. Krueger spoke her name, I gathered they weren't.

"I... I know about her past court case. Not really sure what to think. Are we close? No, but she worked for my father, not me. That was his business."

"What about this immunity deal with the FBI? Can you tell me anything about what he would tell them? Did it have to do with him selling corpses? Or something else?"

She shook her head. "As I said, he refused to tell me. His

way of protecting me. His attorney, Tiffany de Grassi, would know."

"Was it drugs? Human trafficking? Money laundering?"

"I don't know. My father was a strange man, Ms. Ballou, but he was ultimately a good man. Whatever he was involved with, his part in it was motivated by a desire to do good. Of that, I have no doubt."

"Anything else you can tell me that could help me find out who killed him?"

"No."

"Were he and Ms. Turner…"

"Intimate? Not as far as I know. They were just colleagues."

Another idea popped into my head. "Who was the transplant surgeon who did your kidney surgery?"

"Dr. Kaur? Such an amazing woman. Great surgeon. Never had any complications. She and my dad went to med school together."

"How can I get in touch with her?"

Krueger looked sad. "You can't, I'm afraid. She died last March."

"She's dead too?" That was interesting.

"According to the news reports, Dr. Kaur rear-ended a semi while coming home from a shift. Died on impact. It broke my heart. She saved my life."

"What was her full name?"

"Jaswinder Kaur. Why? You think there's a connection to my father's death?"

"Just trying to learn all that I can." I wrote the surgeon's name in my notes. "I will investigate your father's death, but as I said, it may turn out he did in fact take his own life. Or I may not come up with anything conclusive one way or the other. But I will look."

"Thank you, Jinx. I truly appreciate it. People think my father was a creepy little monster. And he was certainly…

different. But he was also my dad. And he was committed to helping further the study of science and the preservation of human life."

"Yeah." That was all I could say. I shook her hand and left.

This investigation gave me several possible directions to take. Top of my list of people to interview was Detective Montana, to learn what his investigation turned up that led him to conclude Krueger's death was a suicide.

Then I'd speak with Krueger's lawyer, Tiffany de Grassi, to find out what Krueger was going to tell the feds.

CHAPTER 28
JINX TALKS TO MONTANA

I DROVE to the Peoria Police Department and had to wait in their lobby for an hour before Detective Montana saw me.

"Ms. Ballou, how can I help you?" he asked.

"I need to speak with you about the Donnie Krueger case."

"No need, Ms. Ballou. You're off the hook on this one. We've ruled it a suicide."

"His daughter isn't so convinced."

He sighed dramatically and extended his hands. "Not unexpected, to be honest. No one wants to believe a family member took their own life."

"She said he didn't even own a gun."

"He bought it a few months ago, shortly before he was arrested. We confirmed it with a gun shop in north Phoenix. Guess he didn't bother telling his daughter about it."

"And yet both his daughter and his office manager are convinced someone else killed him and made it look like a suicide."

"Ms. Ballou, with all due respect, I've been on the job for seventeen years and a homicide cop for the past six. I know a suicide when I see one."

"Detective, I'm not trying to tell you how to do your job."

I stopped. This conversation wasn't going the direction I intended. "Can you at least tell me the time of death?"

He hesitated. Cops hated to give out information to anyone not wearing a badge, especially private investigators. In this case, though, I felt we had a connection.

"According to the M.E.'s preliminary report, the extreme cold of the cooler made it difficult to determine the exact TOD. Best estimate was that it occurred sometime between midnight and 0400 yesterday morning."

"That's interesting. Someone claiming to be Krueger called me at eight forty-five yesterday morning. Krueger would have already been dead for at least four and a half hours. You don't consider that suspicious?"

"Like I said, the extreme temperature in the cooler made it difficult to determine an exact TOD."

"How did Peoria PD know to show up shortly after we did?"

"Peoria Emergency Services received a call stating that people were entering the New Life Medical Resources building armed with assault rifles. The caller did not ID themselves. Patrol was dispatched to investigate. That was when we found your team there."

"And you don't think it suspicious that someone posing as Krueger called me when he was already dead? And then Peoria PD got a call about armed gunmen? Like maybe the same person made these calls?"

His expression told me his patience was wearing thin. "Ms. Ballou, I have plenty of actual murders to solve. I don't need some ex-rookie-turned-vigilante playing armchair detective and telling me how to do my job. If you need any further info on this case, I suggest you speak with our PIO or file a FOIA request. Good day, ma'am."

I chafed at the vigilante remark. Clearly, I wasn't getting anywhere with him. Unless I came up with something conclusive, he wouldn't reopen the case.

"Thank you for your time, Detective." I left and called Tiffany de Grassi.

"Law offices of Farber and Nelson. Ms. de Grassi speaking."

I introduced myself. "Mr. Krueger's daughter hired me to look into his untimely death. I'd like to know about this immunity deal he had with the FBI. What was he going to tell them?"

"I'm sorry, Ms. Ballou, but that information is privileged."

"But Krueger's dead."

"Still privileged. And part of an ongoing federal investigation, I'm afraid."

"An investigation into what, exactly?"

"As I said, I am not at liberty to discuss the matter."

"But his daughter believes he was murdered. Don't you owe it to your client to find out what really happened?

"Mr. Krueger was my client. The only thing I owe him at this point is my silence. Last I checked, Peoria PD classified his death as a suicide. And I'm still owed my fee. So you can tell his daughter once I get paid, maybe I will have some information to share. Until then, my lips are sealed."

"Always about the money with you lawyers, isn't it?"

"Do you work for free? Of course not. Mr. Krueger told me you were threatening to drag him back to jail so you could collect a big fat bounty over nothing more than a miscommunication about his court date. And now you're working as a PI for the daughter? All pro bono, I'm sure. Have a good day, Ms. Ballou."

And that was the end of that conversation. I considered reaching out to Agent Velasco but didn't figure I'd have any better luck. The feds were less talkative than cops and lawyers combined. With their star witness to their investigation now in the morgue, Velasco and Gleeson could try to nail me for interfering in a federal case. Best not to poke the bear if I could avoid it.

So where did that leave me?

For starters, I knew Krueger hadn't called me to turn himself in. Whoever had called me probably also called 911, perhaps to frame me for his murder in case the staged suicide didn't hold up. That meant they held a grudge against Krueger but were meticulous enough to make sure the blame didn't fall back on them. So most likely not a crime of passion. So no jilted lover or cuckolded lover's husband.

That still left a lot of people with a motive to kill Krueger.

My gut told me that the culprit was most likely tied to this federal investigation Krueger was helping with. He was involved with something. But what? Something illegal but that somehow helped people if his daughter was to be believed. But I couldn't find anyone who knew anything who was also willing to talk to me.

And then there were the unhappy family members whose loved ones were sold as crash test dummies or for target practice or left outside to rot. Death brought out a lot of potent feelings in people. When a loved one was treated with such obvious disrespect, that added fuel to the fire. Clearly a motive. But would they know I was looking to return Krueger to custody? Seemed like a stretch.

Then again, for all I knew, maybe one of his neighbors hated his over-the-top Halloween decorations so much that they took the law into their own hands. People killed for the most ridiculous reasons these days. But again, how would the murderer know to call me?

And I couldn't rule out Nancy the necrophiliac. She knew how to reach me and knew I was looking for Krueger. She had access to the building and held a grudge against me for arresting her the year before. But why kill him?

Maybe she and her boss had a falling out. Maybe he

caught her getting all freaky with a cadaver. But if she'd killed Krueger, why hire me? Why stage a suicide but then cry murder? That didn't fit.

As much as I hated it, I needed to have another talk with Nancy Turner to learn about everyone who might have a motive to kill Krueger. Especially the unhappy families.

I called her, unsure whether she was at the office or at home, polishing the old résumé.

"Hello?"

"Ms. Turner, it's Jinx Ballou. I agreed to look into your boss's death, after all."

"How much is it going to cost me?"

"Nothing. I'm working for his daughter, Amy. She said several families were angry over what Krueger did with their loved ones. I need a list of everyone who's complained about situations like this in the past six months. Starting with the family of the woman he sold to that defense contractor. I need names, phone numbers, any contact information you have."

"That will take some time."

"Good thing you don't have to go in to work, then."

"Not true. I have to deal with other body brokers to liquidate our assets and close the business. And then there's the matter of looking for a new job. That's a full-time job in itself."

"And by liquidate assets, you mean selling off dead bodies?"

"Human remains. Yes."

"Wow, we really are just so much meat to you people, huh?"

"But not without value. Our bodies can still contribute to society."

"And there are other body brokers here in town?"

"Not locally but across the state and elsewhere."

"Well, if you really want me to find out who killed your

boss, then make compiling that list of suspects a priority. Unless you're the one who killed him, and this whole thing is a smokescreen."

"What? I would never. He was one of the few who actually respected me."

"Then get me that list."

I hung up and drove back to the Hub. This time, I remembered to pick up a regular latte for myself and a pumpkin spice latte for Becca.

"How goes the sleuthing side gig, Nancy Drew?" she teased.

"Slow." I filled her in on my lack of progress.

"You'll figure it out, Jinxie. You always do."

"I'd prefer to be slapping the cuffs on a fugitive. There was a time I dreamed of being a homicide detective, but honestly, being a bounty hunter is more fun. Usually."

A check of my email showed the Phoenix Gender Alliance had sent a message announcing the details of the Saturday protest at the State Capitol Grounds. I wasn't sure what good it would do but gave Becca a heads-up.

"I heard about that," she said. "Easton and I will be there. Even if it doesn't change anyone's mind, it's important to be seen taking a stand. Who knows? This could be the Stonewall of a new generation."

"Yeah. Just what we need. Three days of rioting in the streets with police. I'll be sure to bring some bricks with me."

"We have to do something. Can't just sit on our hands and hope things will get better on their own."

I'd never seen her so animated. She wasn't even trans, although her partner, Easton, was nonbinary. They both took this fight personally.

"You're right. I was hoping to go up to the mountains, but maybe it's better if I show up at the protest."

I opened my file on Krueger and located the original

police report from several months earlier, which included the names of the family members that Krueger had gotten in a scuffle with.

It wasn't clear who had actually thrown the first punch, but Krueger was the one the police charged. Maybe because of what he'd done to the cadaver in question.

Dr. Rashaad Wilson had filed the assault charge. He was the son of Charise Wilson, whose body Krueger had sold to the military contractor. He worked as a dentist in Phoenix's Biltmore neighborhood.

A search on SkipTrakkr turned up the numbers for his office and his cell. I called the latter, not wanting to run the gauntlet of dealing with a receptionist or any other gate-keepers.

"This is Dr. Wilson. How may I help you?"

"Dr. Wilson, my name is Jinx Ballou. I was hired to apprehend Donnie Krueger after he jumped bail and could use your help. Would you be able to meet me for a few questions?" I hoped he hadn't heard that Krueger was dead.

"Ms. Ballou, I think you're a little late to the party. That worthless excuse of a man finally did the world a favor and put a bullet through his skull. I don't normally speak ill of the dead, but in his case, I'm willing to make an exception."

"I understand. What he did with your mother's remains was reprehensible. But there appears to be more going on. I think you can help me get to the bottom of it."

"What do you mean? That piece of garbage rid the world of his sorry ass. Problem solved. End of story. What more do you need to know?"

"Difficult to say over the phone. Could we meet? I'd greatly appreciate it."

He didn't answer right away, which made me wonder if maybe he was involved. "There's a coffee shop at Biltmore Fashion Park. The Java Jolt. You know it?"

"Sure." I didn't, but I could find it. "I can be there in half an hour."

"That will be fine. I'll be wearing a royal blue polo shirt."

I looked down and saw I was wearing a faded Pink Trinkets concert T-shirt. "I'll be the one in the body armor with the words Bail Enforcement on the front."

Just in case the good doctor turned out to be the killer, it never hurt to be prepared.

CHAPTER 29

BITTER COFFEE

THE CAFE WAS at a third capacity when I walked in—a fair number of young mothers with their broods in strollers, people of all stripes typing away on laptops, and a few high-schoolers laughing and chatting, done with class for the day.

Dr. Wilson sported a full beard and, unsurprisingly, a brilliant, perfect set of teeth. He wore a teal Kangol wool cap on his head, and I got the impression he was coming from or going to a game of golf.

"Ms. Ballou," he said when I sat across from him. "What is it you need to know? What's really going on?"

"I'm investigating Donnie Krueger's death."

His gaze narrowed into a laser-like focus. "You a cop?"

"No. I'm a bail enforcement agent. I was originally hired to apprehend Krueger and take him back to jail after he didn't show up to court."

"But the man's dead. So why'd you want to talk to me?"

"Evidence has come to light that someone may have had a hand in his death."

"Police say the man committed suicide."

"The police may have missed some things."

"Hold on, lady. Are you accusing me of murdering the

man? Sounds like you are. Because naturally, if someone killed that son of a bitch, it must be the Black man, right?"

I could appreciate his indignation, having been falsely accused of horrific crimes myself. But just because he was pissed didn't make him innocent.

"I'm not saying you had anything to do with his death. I'm just trying to find out who all might have had a motive and opportunity to kill the man."

"A lot of people. Just ask the lawyer who was organizing the class action suit. Benton Cambridge is his name."

"Someone's filed a class action suit against him?" This was the first I'd heard of it.

"It was in process. He wronged dozens of families, treating their loved ones' remains like they were just so much meat. Of course, with him dead, who knows what will happen? His estate will probably get tied up in probate until nothing is left."

"Have you spoken with the other families involved?"

"No. I only talked with Mr. Cambridge and his paralegal. And now they're not returning my calls. Just sent us an email yesterday stating that everything was on hold while they reassessed."

"Let me ask you, where were you early Wednesday morning?"

"Are you seriously asking me that?"

I waited, holding his gaze.

"Doesn't matter where I was. My mother's remains were mutilated and riddled with shrapnel so that man could put a few more pieces of silver in his pocket. Was I pissed? Sure as hell was. But, lady, you got a lot of damn gall asking me a question like that after what we've been through. Whoever killed that man deserves a medal. To hell with you and your investigation."

I half expected him to throw his coffee in my face. Probably would have done the same if I'd been in his shoes.

Instead, he stood, glaring at me, and tossed his cup in a nearby trash can.

"I'm sorry, Dr. Wilson. But there is a killer out there. Justice needs to be served."

"Sounds to me like justice was served already. You have a good day, ma'am."

All eyes were on me after he marched out of the cafe.

Okay, so Dr. Rashaad Wilson felt Krueger deserved to die. Didn't provide an alibi. Motive, possible opportunity. But did he have the means? If Krueger was shot with his own gun, that meant someone had to get it away from him. Or maybe threaten him in such a way that it coerced Krueger into shooting himself.

Wilson certainly looked in shape. And he was a dentist, so he was intelligent. But his SkipTrakkr report showed no criminal record for him or his siblings. Nothing stood out to suggest Wilson was a murderer other than his animus toward Krueger. He was still a suspect, but my gut told me he wasn't the shooter.

As I sat there, pondering my next move, my phone rang. The caller ID said it was Becca.

"Hey, girl, what's up?" I asked, not bothering to hide the annoyance in my voice. A small boy a few tables over taunted his infant sister in a stroller while his mother ignored them, too busy chatting with someone on her phone.

"I may have found something on your guy, Krueger."

"Yeah, what's that?"

The little girl in the stroller was reaching for something— probably a toy—that her brother held out of reach above her. He'd lower it so that it was almost within her grasp, then pull it away again.

"Remember how I told you he was into cryptocurrency?"

"Yeah?"

The little girl emitted a piercing squeal of frustration.

Their mother continued to pay them no mind, even as everyone else in the café glared daggers at her.

"I connected him to someone else who was also using crypto. A guy who made payments to Krueger."

"Who?"

"Thomas Remmert, MD. He's a nephrologist."

"What the hell's a nephrologist? Wait, is that someone who predicts people's futures by reading the bumps on their head?"

The mother finally snatched the toy out of the boy's hand and gave it back to the baby. Now he started wailing.

"No, payasa. That's a phrenologist. A nephrologist is a kidney doctor."

My attention switched fully back to Becca. "A kidney doctor? Krueger's daughter received a kidney a while back. Suggested it was a miracle. A gift from a good Samaritan. Maybe Krueger made a deal under the table, paying Remmert with crypto."

"Except Remmert was the one paying Krueger."

I considered that. Why would Remmert pay Krueger in cryptocurrency? Was Krueger selling Remmert kidneys from cadavers? If so, why the cloak and dagger of using cryptocurrency? Maybe this was what the feds were investigating.

"Any idea what Remmert was paying for?"

"No. But they both had connections to a site on the dark web called Red Market."

"What's that?"

"My guess is it's a marketplace for some type of contraband. I haven't been able to get in yet. You need a referral code from someone else who is already a member just to create an account. And the level of encryption and security is impressive. Could be selling any number of things. Drugs. Human trafficking. Weapons. All the above."

"Considering Krueger was a body broker and Remmert

is a nephrologist, my money's on his involvement in black-market organ harvesting. Maybe Remmert learned Krueger was going to spill the beans to the FBI."

"Certainly possible. Also Remmert was receiving large crypto payments, too, but I haven't yet determined from whom. Multiple sources, it looks like."

"Maybe Krueger was supplying Remmert with kidneys who would then sell them to his patients, helping them jump the donation waiting list."

"But by the time Krueger gets a body, is the kidney even viable?" Becca asked.

"Hell if I know," I conceded. "I'm not a doctor. Maybe he has a supplier that gets them to him immediately after death. But what else could it be?"

"Don't ask me. You're the super sleuth."

"Yeah. Suddenly, I feel out of my depth. Maybe I should call Amy Krueger back and tell her to hire a full-time PI. Not sure I'm the right person for the job."

"Bullshit! You're exactly the right person for the job. You're smart and resourceful, and you care about justice."

"Just talked with someone who felt Krueger got the justice he deserved. I'm not convinced he's wrong."

"Maybe. But if someone murdered him, they could kill again. Especially if they're involved in some black-market organ-trafficking ring. There could be a lot of innocent people being hurt."

I had to admit she could be right. But wasn't the FBI already looking into it? Or maybe they weren't. Maybe their case was something else entirely, which meant no one was investigating this one.

"Okay, thanks for the info on Remmert. Maybe I'll pay him a visit."

"Happy to help, compa."

I hung up and ran a search for Remmert on the mobile app version of SkipTrakkr.

I discovered he worked out of a clinic in the Deer Valley area, close to the airport. No criminal record, but financially, he appeared to be leveraged up to his eyeballs. Six maxed-out credit cards. Also, a seven-figure mortgage, a boat on Lake Pleasant, child support, alimony. What I didn't find on SkipTrakkr was a cellphone number. No home number, either. I would have to go through his office to reach him.

I tossed my empty cup in the trash, hopped in my truck, and took the Piestewa Freeway north to the Loop 101. Then I headed west to Seventh Avenue and eventually turned onto Deer Valley Parkway.

I'd been in this part of town a year earlier, searching for a fugitive who ended up shooting my father. I hoped this visit would be a little less fraught with bad juju.

CHAPTER 30
WHO IS THOMAS K. REMMERT?

PATIENTS PACKED the office of Deer Valley Nephrology Associates despite it being late afternoon.

The receptionist who slid open the frosted glass window looked frazzled. Her face was flushed, eyelids drooping, and hair escaping what appeared to have started as a neat bun. Someone was clearly having a bad day.

I smiled, if for no other reason than to let her know I sensed her frustration, whatever the cause, and could empathize.

"May I help you?"

"I'm here to see Thomas Remmert."

"I'm sorry, but Dr. Remmert didn't make it in today. We're rescheduling all of his appointments. The soonest we have…" She typed on her keyboard. "Looks like three weeks from now. Sorry."

"I'm not a patient. This is a personal matter."

"Concerning?"

"A criminal investigation."

Her eyes dropped to the bold yellow letters on my body armor. BAIL ENFORCEMENT AGENT. No points for being observant, but it finally dawned on her. "As I said, Dr. Remmert isn't in today."

"Is he at home?"

"I'm not allowed to give out that information."

"It's very important I speak with him. Privately. I would hate for Dr. Remmert's patients to learn about the illegal activities he's been involved with." I said this last part loud enough to attract the attention of the people in the waiting room.

She glared up at me. "Look, ma'am, I don't know what so-called illegal activity you're talking about, but Dr. Remmert is a good man. He's not a criminal. We were expecting him in today. But he didn't show. He's probably at home with the flu or something and unable to come to the phone. Now, if you don't mind, I'm trying to reschedule his patients."

Whether she had any connection to whatever happened between the good Dr. Remmert and Krueger, I had no idea. But it didn't seem productive to press the issue.

"Okay, thank you for your time."

I walked back out to the Green Dragon. Krueger turned up dead, and a day later, his partner in crime blew off work? Couldn't be a coincidence. Maybe he was already in the wind. Or maybe he was at home packing. A voice in the back of my head told me I was on the right track.

I pulled up Remmert's home address on SkipTrakkr. He didn't live far from the office. Lucky for him. And now lucky for me. I was there in ten minutes.

His was a two-story house in a pricy neighborhood. No gaudy Halloween decorations like at his buddy Krueger's place. Just the morning newspaper still in his drive. Probably too busy packing to worry about the daily headlines.

I parked on the street and rang his doorbell. After a few minutes with no response, I pressed it again. Then I pounded on the door. Still nothing. Garage was shut, so no way to know if his car—a 2021 Audi, according to SkipTrakkr—was inside. He could be long gone by now.

On a whim, I donned a latex glove and tried the door-knob. It was unlocked. Interesting.

Walking into someone's house uninvited wasn't breaking and entering if the door was unlocked, was it? It was just entering. Well, and maybe trespassing if push came to shove. And I couldn't claim hearing someone screaming as a defense, the way we could at Krueger's.

But I had reason to be concerned for Dr. Remmert's safety. After all, an associate of his had recently been killed. Remmert hadn't shown up to work. Wasn't answering his cell. Basically, this was a wellness check, right? Something his medical staff was too busy to do. I was such a humanitarian.

"Dr. Remmert?" I called when I stepped inside. "Anybody home? Trick or treat."

The security panel on the wall in the entryway had a small green light. Green was good. No alarms. No cops showing up. Though I had to wonder if Remmert had left without setting the alarm. Seemed unlikely. If he was here, though, why wasn't he answering? Something was very wrong.

Maybe he couldn't hear me. The house was big, after all. Each of the two stories was about two thousand square feet. Maybe more. And a nice place like this probably had good insulation between the walls, so sound didn't carry. So I started nosing around, hoping to find the wayward nephrologist.

Everything in the home was pristine, aside from a couple of flies buzzing around. No dirty dishes in the sink. There was a load of clothes in the dryer, but who didn't have that?

Then I caught a scent no one wanted to smell. Ever. I covered my nose with a bandana I kept in my pocket, and followed the odor upstairs, where it grew much stronger. Three bedrooms led off of the main hallway. Guest bedrooms empty. Guest bath empty. Master bedroom empty. Master bath… not empty.

Flies buzzed with maddening intensity around the body of a heavyset white guy in a tub of blood. Dr. Remmert, I presumed. Someone had done him the discourtesy of slicing open the left side of his throat. Arterial spray decorated one wall. Defensive wounds marked both arms, and a scalpel lay on the tile floor next to the toilet.

"Guess you're not running after all, huh?" I said to Remmert.

He didn't reply, fortunately.

I should have left right away and called 911 from one of my prepaid cell phones. That would have been the smart thing to do.

But I figured since I was here, I might as well snoop around a bit. Possibly discover what Remmert and Krueger were up to that involved large crypto payments and maybe get a lead on who was tying up the loose ends.

One of the guest bedrooms doubled as a home office. On top of a modern desk sat a small laser printer, an empty rectangular basket labeled To Be Filed, a monitor, a laptop stand, a Bluetooth keyboard, and an external hard drive.

What I didn't see was an actual computer of any kind. Just several USB cords leading to where it had once been. Whoever killed Remmert must've taken it. Shit!

The desk drawers were all locked. I was about to pull out my lockpicks when the wail of a distant police siren broke the dead silence. I froze. Had I set off an alarm after all?

I slipped the external hard drive into my pocket, hoping Remmert had been using it as a backup to his laptop, and decided it was time to vamoose.

As I turned to leave, a crumpled piece of green paper in the wastebasket caught my eye. It was the same money-green color that I used for my reward posters because people saw the reward offer began imagining more green in their wallets. Or so some marketing guru once told me.

I uncrumpled paper and cursed. Sure enough, it was one of my reward flyers for Krueger. Why did Remmert have this? And did whoever kill him see it? Did they know I was looking into the matter? Would they come after me next?

I hustled back downstairs and peeked out the living room window to the street. No cops. The sirens had faded. They were probably responding to another call. I was in the clear.

I opened the door and spotted someone walking a dog along the sidewalk, headed this direction. The last thing I needed was to be seen coming out of a house dressed in full gear where a dead man would eventually be found. I slipped back inside until the dog walker had passed. Then I walked as casually as possible to the Green Dragon. *Nothing to see here, good neighbors.*

I drove down Deer Valley Road to a fast-food joint near the Black Canyon Highway. There, I pulled out an old burner phone I kept in the glove box. I popped in a SIM card I'd taped to the outside, then dialed 911.

"There's been a murder," I muttered to the emergency dispatcher in a deep, raspy voice. I rattled off the address, then hung up and pulled out the SIM card.

There. I'd done my duty of reporting the crime. I only hoped the police wouldn't find any evidence I'd been there.

On the drive home, I called Becca on my regular phone.

"I've got news," I muttered, though I wasn't all that enthused about sharing my recent discovery.

"Me too," she replied. "I identified another one of Krueger's crypto buddies."

"Yeah? Who?"

"Dr. Matthew Stromberg. He's a trauma surgeon at Hohokam Regional Medical Center in Mesa. Works in the emergency department."

"You're kidding. That's where my mom works."

My mother was a trauma nurse. No doubt she had seen a lot of nasty shit on the job. Probably what made her worry so much about me in my current profession. She knew what a life of catching bad guys could cost people.

"I figured she might know him," Becca said.

"How is Stromberg connected to Krueger and Remmert? Has he been making payments to Krueger as well?"

"Just the opposite. Krueger's been paying Stromberg. An average of twenty grand with each payment, several times a month."

I considered that for a moment. "Any money changing hands between Stromberg and Remmert?"

"Not as far as I can see."

"So Remmert was paying Krueger, and Krueger was paying Stromberg. Two doctors and one former doctor."

"Also, I got into Red Market."

"How?"

"Krueger's backup server in the cloud. Generated myself a referral code. Used that to get in."

"Bold. So what kind of site is it?"

"As you suspected, it's a clearinghouse for body parts of all kinds. Skeletons and skulls from India. Viable hearts, lungs, kidneys, and livers from all over the world—Asia and South America, mostly but also Eastern Europe and the States. People post what body parts they're looking for, while others share what they're selling. It's like Craigslist but with lab reports talking about alleles, blood types and a whole litany of TLAs."

"TLAs?"

"Three-letter acronyms. Medical jargon. I figured out some and guessed at others, and quite a few I had to look up. And let me tell you, these organs don't come cheap. Especially with the associated medical costs in the US. But if you need an organ and you're too sick to travel overseas, this could be a matter of life and death."

"Must be how Amy Krueger got her kidney a few years ago. I wonder if she knows?"

"Dunno."

"Have you found any connection to a Dr. Jaswinder Kaur? It would have to have been over six months ago. She died in March."

"Kaur? No mention of her name so far. Who is she?"

"Transplant surgeon who did Amy Krueger's kidney surgery two years ago."

"And she's dead too?"

"Yeah, and she's not the only one. Found Remmert at home in the tub, dead as Dickens's proverbial doornail."

"¡Madre Diosa! Someone shot him too?"

"No. Slit his throat. Bathroom was a study in scarlet."

"Nice Sherlock Holmes reference."

"Thanks. Three dead doctors is starting to look like a pattern. Not good."

"You think Stromberg is behind them all?" Becca asked.

"No idea. Even if Stromberg killed Krueger to keep him from talking, why kill Remmert or Kaur? Unless the feds were trying to flip them too. The whole transplant industry is shrouded in secrecy, according to my mom. She's seen her share of patients in the ER that didn't make it. Donors' and recipients' identities are kept confidential. Nice for protecting someone's privacy but also opens the door to black-market operations."

"Like an elaborate terrorist organization where sleeper cells are kept separated. If one person gets busted, they don't know enough to bring down the whole organization. I thought those stories of people getting roofied and waking up in a tub of ice minus a kidney were just urban legends."

I laughed nervously. This situation was creeping me out. "They are, as far as I know. But I've seen reports about people in poor communities being pressured to donate a kidney as a way of escaping poverty. Only it never works out as promised. And because of the illegal nature of the deal, there's no recourse."

"Capitalism at its finest," Becca replied. "Exploit the vulnerable to benefit the privileged. What are you going to do?"

"I should talk to my mom."

"You don't think she's involved, do you?"

"No, but she might give me insight into Stromberg. Help me understand what kind of guy he is."

"And Remmert?"

"I called 911 from a burner. And may have purloined a backup drive for his laptop."

"Sweet. You bringing it to me?" She loved nosing around other people's computer files.

"I'm heading home for now. But if I need your expertise, I'll bring it to the Hub in the morning."

"Fine. Be that way."

"Thanks for the tip on Stromberg. I'll be in touch. See you tomorrow or at the protest on Saturday."

"Take care, bestie."

CHAPTER 31

TALKING WITH MOM

CONOR WASN'T HOME when I arrived. I grabbed Diana's leash and texted him as I took her for an evening walk.

Outside, the autumn air was deliciously cool. I smirked when I caught sight of Mike Ripley's car still parked a couple of houses down. Diana and I walked in the other direction.

If he was still hanging around, he didn't have a clue where Rayna and Leia really were. If he wanted to waste his time sitting on his ass and staring at my house, let him. And if he got belligerent again, I had a small pistol tucked in a pancake holster at the small of my back.

Just as I made the turn to come back home, Conor called and informed me he and his team were tracking down a fugitive porch pirate. He wasn't sure when he'd be home. I wished him good hunting.

I thought again about combining our two bounty-hunting companies. We'd be able to spend more time together and save a bundle on overhead costs. His current office manager, Meredith Ashley, could probably handle the additional load.

I had only left his team after we started dating, and I was

afraid my dating the boss might lead to tension in the ranks. But now we were married. It could work. Unless it didn't.

As Diana and I grew closer to home, Ripley's headlights flashed on. He cruised my way slowly. Diana must have picked up on my tension because she slowed her trot, keeping her eyes trained on the vehicle. I switched Diana's leash to my left hand and drew the pistol, keeping it down at my side.

The car stopped next to me and the window rolled down with a hum.

"I demand to talk with my wife and son." He looked like hammered shit and smelled worse.

"Last time I checked, you have neither a wife nor a son. Can't help you, buddy. Sorry, not sorry."

"You damn well know what I mean."

"Calling Rayna your wife instead of your ex doesn't change her wanting nothing to do with you. And calling Leia your son just makes you a toxic father and a bigoted piece of shit. Besides, they're not here."

"Bullshit! I saw them drive here."

"And then you fell asleep. They're gone."

His blotchy face turned a uniform scarlet. "Where the fuck are they?"

"Sorry, dude. Can't help you."

"You're going to regret this. I have rights."

"You do. For starters, you have the right to remain silent. Also, the right to an attorney. Because if you do anything to hurt them, you'll spend the rest of your miserable existence behind bars. I'll make sure of it."

"I have parental rights. Rayna refuses to let me see him."

"Leia wants nothing to do with you. She has a say in this matter. Maybe if you weren't such a pathetic, hateful, bigoted piece of shit, she'd change her mind. Besides, a little birdie told me you're behind on your child support. She's well within her rights to refuse you visitation."

"This ain't over, bitch. I swear I'll..."

Diana jumped up and started barking, leaning her head in the window.

"Quiet, girl," I instructed, and her barking became a low, primal growl.

"Don't threaten me, Mr. Ripley. I've taken down Chechen mobsters, Latino gangbangers, and an entire horde of right-wing nut jobs like yourself. They all regretted it. Those that lived long enough to do so. My advice, back off. Maybe educate yourself on what it means to be the parent of a trans child. And for fuck's sake, pay your damn child support."

Diana jumped away as Ripley rolled up his window. The car sped off down the street. I had a feeling that wouldn't be the last I'd see of him. Not that I was worried.

Back inside, I fed Diana and called my mother.

"Hey, Mom. How are things?"

"Your father's glad to be back at work. I think he's settling into the routine finally."

"That's good to hear."

"You're not calling to cancel for Sunday, are you?"

Family Sunday brunch was a tradition in our family. Not showing up was considered a mortal sin unless you were sick or had some other very legitimate reason not to be there.

When my life had spiraled into the toilet after Conor disappeared, I had blown brunch off for months, despite pleas from my family. It was not my best moment. I had missed it terribly, but I couldn't bring myself to show up again until I pulled my life back together.

"I'll be there, Mom. I promise. But I need to ask you something."

"What's that, dear?"

"You know a Dr. Matthew Stromberg?"

"Of course. I've worked with him for many years.

Brilliant doctor, very kind. He volunteers at a community clinic down in Rio Rico a few times a month. Why?"

"You don't think he'd be mixed up in anything… criminal, do you?"

"Jenna Christina Ballou, why would you ask such a question?"

Her tone of voice told me I'd stepped on an emotional landmine. She made no bones about how some doctors she worked with were arrogant pricks who considered themselves gods.

But there were a few she admired, either for their skills or their dedication to their patients. Apparently, Stromberg fell into both categories.

"I'm sorry, Mom. I didn't mean to upset you. It's just that his name came up as part of an investigation."

"What kind of investigation?" she demanded.

"You ever met a man named Donald Krueger?"

"Hmmm, the name rings a bell. I've heard it recently."

"He was found dead a few days ago."

"Oh dear, I do remember him. He had lost his license years ago after burning his initials into a transplanted liver. The hubris of that man. I never knew him personally, but I heard stories."

"Such as?" I wasn't so much concerned about Krueger's checkered past, just fishing for a new lead.

"He was a talented surgeon. In fact, I've heard Dr. Stromberg speak of him once, but long ago. Said it was a shame a talent such as his was going to waste for what he described as an adolescent prank. Never mind that Dr. Krueger was in his thirties, at the time. But what's this got to do with you and your investigation?"

"Do you know a Dr. Thomas Remmert? He's a kidney doctor."

She paused briefly. "No, doesn't ring a bell. Now, Jenna, what this is all about?"

"I was hired to look into Krueger's death."

"Shouldn't the police be doing that?"

"The police have chalked it up as a suicide. But I'm not so sure."

"And you think Dr. Stromberg's somehow involved with Krueger's death? That's absurd. They were colleagues. Even if Krueger was involved with something illegal, I can assure you Dr. Stromberg would never be. He's dedicated all of his time and energy to saving lives. His mission is his life now."

"Okay. I believe you." I didn't, really. Stromberg was connected somehow. I could feel it. I just wasn't sure whether he was the murderer or another potential victim. Someone was killing doctors connected to the Red Market website. I intended to find out who.

"Have you heard what the Department of Child Safety is doing to trans children and their families?" my mom asked.

"I heard." I didn't mention Rayna and Leia. "Phoenix Gender Alliance is planning a protest on Saturday."

"PFLAG called, asking us to go." I heard her sigh. "Honestly, sweetheart, I don't think your father and I are up for it. After what happened at your wedding…"

"It's okay, Mom. No need to explain. You and Dad have always been there for me when I needed you. Not every trans kid is so lucky."

"It's a shame what this world is coming to. Punishing parents and doctors for supporting trans kids. I just don't know anymore."

"Yeah, me either."

"Are you going to the protest?"

"Not sure what good it will do, but Conor and I will probably be there. Gotta do something, right?"

"Please, please, please, Jenna. Be careful. Those crazies with the assault rifles and hate in their hearts. If they show up to counterprotest, it could get ugly."

"Trust me, Mom. I can handle myself. If anything happens, I can help keep the others safe."

"That's probably a good thing, I suppose. Okay, then, I'll see you Sunday. I love you."

"Love you too, Mom."

I hung up.

CHAPTER 32

ARRESTS AND PROTEST PLANS

I GOT another text from Conor that he'd made the arrest and would arrive home within the hour, with takeout from Grumpy's Bar and Grill. While I waited, I plugged Remmert's external hard drive into my laptop. To my delight, it wasn't encrypted, and I began exploring.

Most of the contents held little interest. The majority of the files were tied to his work as a nephrologist. Patient files, research, business admin stuff. I located an email library, but again, much of it had to do with his patients and their care or other matters related to the medical practice.

On the personal side, I found a section on his taxes and a vast directory of photos of him traveling the world with what I assumed was his family. There was also a directory of porn but nothing kinky or illegal. No disgusting child smut or anything.

I doubled back to the work-related directories. Nested deep into some otherwise benign content was a directory labeled RM. Red Market, perhaps? I dove deeper. Patient histories, lab reports, a separate set of financials, and a Word document listing his passwords for his various cryptocurrency accounts, of which he had several. Had this guy never heard of a password manager?

Remmert had been hired by wealthy patients desperate for a variety of organ transplants. I recognized a few of the names. A former US senator and lifelong smoker had received a lung transplant. The son of a well-known real estate developer was now the proud owner of a new liver. A former chief of staff to a Republican ex-president had a new lease on life, his heart problems a thing of the past now that he had a new ticker. There was even a file on Amy Krueger. So that was how she jumped the line and got a new kidney.

I didn't begrudge these people the gift of life they had received. But what about the people on the waiting list who lacked the money or connections these wealthy recipients had? And where exactly did these organs come from? Becca had mentioned impoverished people donating kidneys in hopes of securing new lives for themselves and their families —and how it rarely worked out as promised. But what about the hearts and lungs and livers?

In a country where decent healthcare was insanely expensive, who lived and who died all too often depended on wealth and privilege. Too many people had to forgo medicines and procedures that would improve their quality of life because they couldn't afford it, or their insurance wouldn't approve it.

What would it mean if I disrupted this organ trafficking black market by tracking down Krueger's and possibly Remmert's and Kaur's killer? Would some rich person die? Would a poor person be saved? Or would everything continue as normal?

I had a sinking feeling it would be the latter. Black-market industries were remarkably resilient. Trying to stop them was like playing Whac-A-Mole. You brought down one little guy and his criminal gang. But plenty more always popped up to take their place. Where there was a need and the greed, there would always be a black market. Especially when the stakes were life and death.

Feeling exhausted from digging into Remmert's hard drive, I switched gears and began researching Dr. Kaur—specifically, her death. There wasn't much. Only a couple of local news stories that said little other than "Local surgeon dies in fiery crash. Loop 101 shut down for hours." Nothing suggested a police investigation of the incident.

"Anybody home?" Conor called from the front of the house.

"In here."

I met him in the kitchen and kissed him with all the passion of a half-drunk teenager on prom night. Before I knew it, we were in the bedroom, tearing off each other's clothes. All of this mess about transplants and murder triggered a primal urge to celebrate life in the most carnal of ways.

After we were both sated and exhausted, he served dinner while I filled him in on my investigation of Krueger's death.

Before I could ask about his day, Rayna called on the burner I had given her.

"Hey, how's it going?" I asked hopefully.

"Police have arrested five sets of parents and put their kids in the system."

"Shit. Families with trans kids?"

"Yes. They've also arrested two pediatricians, including Leia's."

I wanted to reassure her that the courts would overturn the law and that life would soon return to normal. But things hadn't been normal in this country for a long time, and with so many fascists in key positions of power, the situation only looked grimmer by the day.

"Are you two still safe at Bobby J.'s?" I asked.

"We're here. I fear we're putting him at risk. If DCS or the cops find out we're here…"

"Bobby's a smart man. He understands the risks. The

important thing is that Leia's safe, and she has you. We all stand together."

"I've spoken with Chelsea Quiñones, one of the organizers of Saturday's protest. She's figured out a way for us to be there, sort of."

"Rayna, I know you want to be there, but…"

"It will be virtual. A Zoom call. They'll have a screen and a projector. Chelsea said she's got it all arranged. Assuming we don't run into technical glitches. I feel it's important our voices are heard. That people can put human faces to the story and see we're simply a loving family and not some pervy cult."

"I can't argue with that." Still, I worried the police might trace the connection somehow. "You can count on Conor and me being there. In person."

"Thank you, Jinx, for all that you've done. You're a true hero."

"I'm just doing what I have to do. Give Leia my love."

"Will do."

She hung up, and I filled Conor in on what she told me.

"Fecking bastards," Conor growled. "I left Ireland to get away from this kind of madness."

"I know. Not sure what good the protest will do, but I can't sit idly by."

"Aye, ya can count on me there too, love."

"How was your day?" I asked, desperately needing to change the subject.

He offered a weak smile. "Caught the bloody porch pirates, all three of them. First nicked the one, who then turned on his mates. Wankers had a bedroom stacked floor to ceiling full of boxes they'd pinched. Three fugitives in one go. Not a bad day's catch."

"I'm glad."

He gripped my hand. "Hey, love. I know this anti-trans bollocks is bad. But if there's one thing I've learned from you, it's that the members of the trans community are bloody tough as steel. No matter what those bastards try, you all keep coming back with courage, beauty, and grace. I don't know what will happen in the future, but I'd like to think that justice will eventually triumph."

"We can hope."

"Aye, that we can."

That night, I debated what to do regarding the Krueger investigation. Someone was killing doctors connected to the Red Market. I couldn't go to the police with what little I had. And I didn't dare go to the feds, even if they were probably already looking into it. They'd no doubt lock me up for interfering in their investigation.

The only thing I could do was try to warn Dr. Stromberg.

CHAPTER 33
JINX ASKS MOM FOR HELP

EARLY THE NEXT MORNING, I called my mother again.

"Mom, I need you to get me a meeting with Dr. Stromberg."

"Why?" she asked defensively.

"I know you think he's a great guy. And maybe he is, but I have reason to believe he's mixed up in something not so great. His life could be in danger."

"Jenna, if he's in danger, then you need to go to the police."

"I can't. I'm not even sure what all's going on. And the police already ruled Krueger's death a suicide. But other doctors have been killed, and they were all connected to Krueger."

"Whatever is going on, I don't like that you're involved. I think you need to drop this and turn over what you have to the police, who have the resources to investigate." She sounded like Velasco and Gleeson.

"I can't. Not yet, at least. I just need a few minutes alone with Dr. Stromberg. If nothing else, at least to warn him."

"Punkin, I love you, but whatever you think Dr. Stromberg is involved with, you're wrong."

"I hope I am, Mom. Truly, I do. But if I'm right, and someone is planning to kill Dr. Stromberg, doesn't he deserve to know? Just ask him to meet with me."

"I'd be happy to pass along a message."

"That won't work. I need to speak with him ASAP. And privately."

"Fine. I will talk to him. We're both scheduled for first shift today. I will ask if he will meet with you. But please, sweetie, do not make me regret this."

"I won't. I promise."

I could tell she wasn't happy with me interfering with her professional life. But if it saved his life, she would be glad I did.

After I hung up, Conor eyed me warily. "Oi! You getting your mum involved in this?"

"Just asking her to make an introduction. Trying to save a man's life."

He didn't look convinced, but he said nothing.

"And if he knows who may have killed Krueger, Kaur, and Remmert, well, so much the better."

"Aye, there it is. Just watch your back on this one, love."

"Always."

My mother called back an hour later, saying that Stromberg had agreed to meet with me provided he wasn't otherwise occupied saving a life. Considering he was a trauma surgeon in an ER, I figured it was the best I could hope for.

I decided the situation was getting complicated enough that I needed some backup, so I reached out to my team.

Rodeo was out hiking in the White Tank Mountains with his daughter Gwyneth and my brother Jake. Zahara didn't answer her phone. Fortunately, Caden was at home and chomping at the bit to be useful. I brought him up to speed on the Krueger investigation. We agreed to meet at the hospital.

When we met outside the ER entrance, Caden asked, "You really think someone is targeting doctors involved with this Red Market website?"

Neither of us wore our gear this morning, just polo shirts with the Ballou Fugitive Recovery logo on the front pocket. I figured a low-key approach might work best in this situation. Especially when we brought up the Red Market.

"I'm not sure what to think. Hoping Stromberg can give us some answers."

The emergency department waiting room was remarkably quiet, with only a smattering of people in need of urgent medical care. The morning news programs played from wall-mounted televisions.

"May I help you?" asked the woman at the check-in desk.

"We're here to see Dr. Stromberg. He's expecting us. I'm Jinx Ballou. This is my associate, Caden Morrow."

She narrowed her eyes as if trying to place me. "Ballou? You're Gianna's daughter."

I smiled in acknowledgement. "Yes, I am."

"And you're here to meet with Dr. Stromberg?"

"Yes. Like I said, he's expecting us."

"Just a moment." She made a phone call. When she hung up, she said, "Dr. Stromberg is currently in surgery, I'm afraid."

Shit. "Do you know how long he'll be?"

"I'm sorry. I don't. You're free to wait."

I considered my options. I needed to speak to him and had no other pressing needs. Turning to Caden, I said, "I guess we wait."

And wait we did. For hours.

"You think Stromberg's the killer?" Caden whispered while *The Price Is Right* played quietly on a nearby television. Drew Carey announced that a woman on the screen had won a new car, and she looked like she was having a heart attack.

"Hard to say. The way my mother talks, the man practically walks on water. Dedicated his entire life to helping people. Even volunteers a few times a month at a clinic down by the border. If it were up to my mom, the Catholic Church would canonize him as a living saint."

A string of commercials for pharmaceuticals and a Medicare supplemental insurance plan played on the TV now.

"What if they're not related?" Caden asked. "The one who staged Krueger's death, the one who killed Kaur, and the one who killed Remmert. Could be three different murderers."

I had wondered the same thing. Krueger had been shot and his murder staged to look like a suicide. Someone had cut Remmert's throat with a scalpel. Doubtful any cop would consider that a suicide. Kaur had presumably died in a traffic accident. Such different MOs could suggest different killers. Or one killer who liked to change things up to hide the pattern.

"I don't know. Could be different murderers for hire but the same person pulling the strings. It takes some planning and finesse to stage a suicide. And then to call us in. Maybe Krueger's death was carefully planned, but Remmert's appeared spur-of-the-moment. I didn't see any signs of a break-in at Remmert's. Suggests he knew the killer. Maybe the killer showed up at the good doctor's house to discuss the Red Market but things went sideways. Maybe Remmert was going to talk to the feds, and the killer eliminated him as well."

My mother was fond of the saying, "Speak of the devil and he appears." No sooner did I mention the feds than my phone rang. Who was on the other end? None other than Special Agent Velasco of the good old Federal Bureau of Interrogation.

"Hello, Agent Velasco. Enjoying the lovely morning?

Aren't these cool autumn days wonderful? Are you dressing up for Halloween? Trick or—"

"Cut the nonsense, Ballou. We need to talk."

"About?"

"About something we should discuss here at FBI headquarters."

"I did not kill Krueger. Suicide, remember? That was the official report by Detective Montana."

"I'm aware of the official manner of death in the Krueger case, Ms. Ballou. I understand you're working for the daughter as a private investigator."

How the hell did she know that? "Sorry, Velasco. I can't discuss my cases with you. Confidentiality and all that. You understand."

"No, I do not understand. You need to leave this matter alone."

"Why?"

She didn't answer.

On the TV, two contestants were bidding on the final showcase. One was a vacation to Aspen, Colorado. The other was an RV with all kinds of amenities. I couldn't help wonder how these people paid the income taxes on these winnings. The IRS was always hungry for its cut of the prize money.

"Your investigation into Krueger's death ends now."

"Velasco, while I respect the important work you do, I have the right to investigate cases for which I'm hired. So unless you want to show me your cards, don't expect me to show you mine. Have a nice day, and happy Halloween." I hung up.

"The feds again?" Caden asked. "What do they want?"

"Apparently, they are not happy we're investigating Krueger's death."

A man in surgical scrubs approached us. I guessed he

was in his late forties. Not tall but fit for his age. Sandy blond hair with a trim graying beard. Gentle eyes. Slim.

"You must be Gianna's daughter, Jenna." He clasped my hand in both of his. "She's told me so much about you. Such a pleasure to meet you in person after all these years. I'm Dr. Matthew Stromberg."

Caden and I stood. "Morning, Dr. Stromberg. A pleasure to meet you as well. This is my associate, Caden Morrow."

They shook hands. "I apologize for the delay. We had a patient come in with a serious knife wound."

"You're here to save lives," I replied. "We understand."

"So, to what do I owe the pleasure of this visit?"

"Could we talk privately?" I asked.

"Of course. Follow me."

STROMBERG LED us to a room a little way down the hall and closed the door behind us. It was like a small waiting room. A quiet room, no doubt, for grieving families who'd lost a loved one.

"Gianna tells me you're a bounty hunter," he said with glee in his voice. "How exciting that must be!"

"It can be."

"Well, I can't imagine how I could be of help in any of your cases. I don't know anyone who's jumped bail. That is what you do, isn't it?"

"Normally. In this case, a private party hired us to investigate a suspicious death."

"Really? Whose?"

"Donnie Krueger," Caden said.

With that, Stromberg's excited visage faded a bit. "Ah, yes. I heard about Dr. Krueger's death on the news. Very tragic. I thought the police had determined he'd taken his own life. But you believe someone murdered him?"

"There are some details that don't add up. How well did you know Krueger?" I couldn't bring myself to call him Doctor.

"We interned together at Phoenix Baptist Hospital. Of

course, that was a long time ago, but we stayed in touch. Occasionally played a round of golf. He was a talented surgeon, if a bit eccentric. Saved countless lives. Unfortunately, some men in my profession develop a certain hubris. Especially the highly gifted ones, of which Dr. Krueger was one. He made a mistake, and it cost him. I dare say the medical community suffered a loss when his medical license was revoked. I didn't much keep in touch with him after that, I'm afraid."

"No? Not even through the Red Market?" Caden asked.

Caden had adopted the role of bad cop, though that hadn't been part of the plan. With Stromberg being such a close associate of my mother's, I didn't want to rock the boat too much. At least not directly, and not until I was sure of the extent to which he was involved. But I didn't mind if Caden pushed a little harder.

Stromberg looked genuinely confused. "Red Market? I'm sorry, but I'm not familiar with it. Is that a new supermarket chain? I have my groceries delivered through a service, since my free time is extremely limited."

"The Red Market is a site on the dark web," I explained. "Human organ trafficking."

"And we know you're involved," Caden added.

I shot him a glance that told him to ease up. Direct accusations like that could shut down an interview, especially when we had no authority to arrest or detain someone.

"What my associate means to say," I said, "is that we have discovered a connection between this website, Krueger, and other physicians in the Valley. More concerning is that it appears someone connected to the site is killing local doctors."

"Killing doctors? Others have died?"

"You know a Dr. Remmert?" Caden's tone was less accusatory this time.

"Not personally, but I recognize the name. Nephrologist, right?"

"Yes, the police found him dead yesterday. Murdered. Both Krueger and Remmert were involved with the Red Market. We've connected cryptocurrency transactions that showed Remmert was making large payments to Krueger."

"Whatever for?"

"We believe Krueger was acting as a middleman, providing human organs for transplant to other doctors such as Dr. Remmert."

"Oh my." Stromberg looked concerned. "You don't think they'd target me as well, do you?"

"Are you connected with the Red Market?" Caden asked, not bothering to disguise the triumph in his voice.

Stromberg gave a deep sigh. "Are you recording this?"

"No," I lied. My phone was in my shirt pocket. And it was recording everything. "Just between us."

"You've met Amy, I take it," he said. "Dr. Krueger's daughter."

"Yes," I admitted.

"Sweet girl. Very bright. But she was… not doing well. She had developed hemolytic uremic syndrome from an E. coli infection. Clots had formed in her kidneys, leading to renal failure. Dialysis was keeping her alive—but barely. Donnie… Dr. Krueger, rather, reached out to me, since we had been colleagues at one time. He was desperate to save his girl and asked if I knew someone who might consider becoming a donor. He'd already been tested and wasn't a suitable match. Amy's mother was no longer in the picture. I agreed to do a little testing on the side. That was it. I didn't expect much. Finding a suitable unrelated donor is like finding a needle in a haystack."

"And what happened?" I pressed.

"By some miracle, I found a woman who was indeed a suitable match. Matched on all six alleles. It was like winning the lottery, statistically speaking. I explained the situation to this woman. And, though it was technically illegal, I promised her compensation. Seemed only fair. She was saving a life and risking her own. Everyone else involved would be paid for their contributions. Why shouldn't the genuine hero of the story receive some reward as well? And so we made arrangements through this site called the Red Market."

"Of course, you did," Caden remarked with more venom than I would have liked.

"You have to understand, it's not a black market for organ trafficking. It's more a clearinghouse for professionals who believe that donors should be compensated for their gifts of life. And I was only there to help Amy. And if you've met her, you know she is doing good work, helping to feed the hungry. Work made possible only by the courage of others, particularly my patient."

"Who was this patient?" I pressed.

"I'm not at liberty to say. Even among the Red Market, confidentiality is key for everyone's safety."

"What about a Dr. Jaswinder Kaur?" I asked. "Did you know her?"

"We were acquainted. She was a talented transplant surgeon. Tragic about her death."

"Indeed. You knew she was the one who transplanted Amy Krueger's new kidney."

"I didn't know that, but it wouldn't surprise me. As I said, I only facilitated helping the Kruegers find a donor. Was she involved with Red Market?"

I stared deeply into his eyes. "You tell me."

I could see the wheels turning in his mind. "Are you suggesting someone is murdering doctors connected to this organization? You think someone will come after me next? I was only involved the one time."

I didn't answer, preferring to let the fear and silence pressure him into saying more.

"This is all very disturbing," he said, "but I don't know what you expect me to say."

"How is it all these doctors died under mysterious circumstances?" I asked. "Who runs the Red Market? Are they local?"

"I don't know. Honestly, I don't. After Dr. Krueger's daughter's case, I had nothing to do with any of it. The focus of my life is my patients here and at a clinic in southern Arizona."

He was holding something back. I could tell. He may have been a talented surgeon, but he was a lousy liar.

"You can talk to me, or you can talk to the FBI. I hear they're looking into this as well. Or you could end up dead like your associates."

He shook his head vigorously. "No, I can't. The Red Market is saving a lot of lives. It may be illegal, but it's important work. I won't interfere with it. And honestly, it sounds like someone killed Dr. Krueger because he was talking to the FBI. Better for everyone if I keep what little I know to myself."

"That may not be enough to keep you safe."

"Nevertheless, I'm not saying any more about it. The lives that the Red Market is saving take precedence. I took an oath to protect life."

I had to admit his selflessness surprised me, assuming he was being truthful. Maybe he really was the man my mother described. And she had worked with him for years, so I guessed she'd know. And yet something niggled in the back of my mind that I was missing a critical piece of the puzzle.

"I hate to ask you this, but where were you early Wednesday morning? Say, between midnight and six o'clock."

"Are you accusing me of something, Ms. Ballou?" His tone sharpened.

"I'm trying to eliminate you as a suspect so I can focus on the actual killer."

"If you must know, I was sleeping. I woke at five, as I do every morning, and was here at the hospital at seven."

"Can anyone verify that?"

"I live alone, so no."

"And you were here at the hospital all day? What about Wednesday evening?"

"I was here until six o'clock, then went home. I had a shower and an early dinner, and I attended a chamber music concert at the Phoenix Convention Center from eight until about eleven. And from there, I returned home. Is that sufficient?"

"Yes, thank you."

Very little of that information was verifiable. But the questions were worth asking.

"Good. I would hate for Gianna's daughter to think me a murderer."

"If someone is after you, I could have Caden or one of my other team members provide protection until whoever is responsible can be brought to justice." *Or keep an eye on you until you incriminate yourself further*, I thought.

He put a gentle hand on mine. "Thank you for the offer, Ms. Ballou, but that won't be necessary. There's no reason for anyone to hurt me."

I wasn't convinced. If he was the killer, he was very much a threat. And if he wasn't, the real killer might still consider him a liability.

"Thank you for your time, Doctor. I will do what I can to find whoever's responsible and bring them to justice."

"I wish you the best of luck. Your mother speaks highly of you, though she worries terribly for your safety."

"I know she does."

When Caden and I walked back into the parking lot, he turned and said, "I used to be a corrections officer. As a matter of survival, you develop a sense for when people are lying. That guy's holding something back."

"You felt it too, huh?"

"He seems sincere in his concern for his patients and for saving lives. But there's something he's not saying."

"Could just be something embarrassing," I admitted. "When I was a cop, suspects lied about their alibis because they didn't want people finding out they were having affairs or were hanging out at gay bars or BDSM dungeons."

"Didn't exactly strike me as the BDSM type."

"You'd be surprised," I said with a smirk.

Caden raised an eyebrow. "You?"

"No, though some members of Phoenix Gender Alliance have confided in me that's their kink."

"Really? Who? Spill, girl."

"Sorry, but they spoke to me in confidence, so I can't say."

"Party pooper. So what's the plan now?"

"I'm going to research Stromberg and Remmert further. Call logs, bank transactions, anything that will point me toward who killed Krueger. I may reach out to the detective investigating Remmert's murder. See if I can get anything out of them."

"Yeah, good luck with that."

"I'll let you know if I need you for anything else."

"I've got no plans other than the protest tomorrow morning and the Phoenix Gender Alliance party that night. So call me if you need me."

"Will do, Caden. I know you've been trying to prove yourself now that you're back on the team. But you don't have to. I wouldn't have rehired you if I didn't think you could handle the job."

"Thanks, Jinx. I appreciate that."

On the drive back to the Hub, I noticed someone tailing me on Country Club Drive—a black Ford Explorer. To confirm, I made a broad loop, turning east on McKellips, south on Mesa Drive, west on Brown, and then back north again on Country Club. The black Explorer stayed a few cars back the entire way.

I suspected it was the feds, most likely Velasco or Gleeson. But for all I knew, it could be Krueger's killer.

Fine, I thought. *Let the games begin.*

CHAPTER 35
A CHAT WITH THE FEDS

CATCHING someone tailing me was always unsettling. It was never for something good, like "Hey, I was following you because you were so beautiful I wanted to give you these flowers" or "You just won a lifetime supply of Ghirardelli chocolate" or "I absolutely love your fake soccer-mom SUV."

So who was it this time? The feds? Maybe the cops? Annoying but probably not the end of the world. Aside from my taking Remmert's backup drive, I had broken no laws. And they most likely didn't know about the hard drive. I just had to remember not to mention it over the phone in case they were listening in on my conversations.

Or had Mike Ripley changed vehicles or hired someone to keep tabs on me in hopes I'd lead them back to his family? If that was the case, things could get a little dicey. Guys like him got their rocks off controlling people to compensate for their own feelings of inadequacy. And when people like me took away that control, they resorted to violence.

There was another possibility. My shadow could be involved in the Red Market. Possibly whoever killed Krueger and Remmert. If that was the case, I might have already led them to Stromberg. How long had they been tailing me? On the drive to the hospital, my mind had been so preoccupied with the upcoming protest that I hadn't been paying as close attention as I normally did.

I debated my options for losing the tail. If it was the feds, they already knew where I lived and worked. And I was already planning to head back to the Hub, so there was no reason to lose them. Trying to do so could get me into more trouble.

If it was someone with nefarious motives, the best course of action was to be ready in case they tried something. They may or may not know where I worked or lived. So I didn't want to risk leading them back there.

As I approached a Burger King, I saw an opportunity. I pulled into the lot and parked. My pursuer parked several spaces away. I swiftly pulled on my body armor and slipped out of the truck, my Ruger held down at my side.

Keeping low and using a nearby work truck for cover, I hustled toward the idling Explorer. Government plates. Feds.

I holstered my pistol and approached the driver's side of the Explorer. The tinted window lowered. Agent Velasco glared at me. Gleeson sat in the shadows on the passenger side.

I flashed a fake smile. "Wow! Imagine running into you two here. What are the odds?"

"Get in," she muttered.

"Excuse me?"

"Get in the truck. Now."

I took a step back. "Are you arresting me?"

"Should we?"

"Look, I got nothing to talk with you about. I'm simply a private citizen stopping to pick up some lunch. Either of you care for a Whopper and fries? My treat."

She stared at me impassively. "Why were you at the hospital?"

"My mother works there. What do you think?" Not technically a lie. "Am I no longer allowed to spend time with my own family? I don't recall anything along those lines in the new transphobic law."

"Just get in the damn truck, Ballou," Gleeson said. "Or we will detain you for as long as we deem necessary."

I wanted to tell them to go to hell. They had no grounds to detain me. But that didn't mean they wouldn't. "Whatever."

I climbed into the back seat but left the door open a crack, just in case I decided our conversation was over. Didn't need to get trapped with those childproof locks.

"What do you want to talk about?" I demanded. "I have work to do."

"Why were you at Dr. Remmert's home?" Gleeson asked.

So it was going to be one of those conversations. I didn't respond and considered calling Kirsten. The air in the truck grew stale despite the AC and the slight breeze coming through my partially ajar door.

"Answer the question, Ms. Ballou," Velasco pressed.

"Sorry, I don't know a Dr. Remmert."

"A witness saw someone matching your description leaving his home yesterday about the time the police received an anonymous call reporting he'd been murdered."

"A witness saw someone matching my description? What? A woman with long dark hair? Do you know how many people fit that description? This is Arizona. Maybe they saw you, Velasco. You fit that description."

"Driving a green SUV like yours and wearing body armor," she added. "Why were you there?"

"I should call my attorney."

Gleeson glared at me. "Answer the damn question, or we'll put you somewhere your attorney can't find you."

"Fine, I was there. I showed up to ask him a few questions. Found his door open and was concerned for his safety, especially since he hadn't shown up to work and wasn't answering his phone. I found him dead in the tub and called it in. I didn't kill him, if that's what you're thinking. I needed to talk to him."

Velasco asked, "About what?"

"A case I'm working."

"The Krueger case?" she replied. "You need to drop it."

"You can't tell me to drop it. I was hired to investigate a suspicious death that, despite what Peoria PD thinks, was not a suicide."

"You are interfering in a federal investigation."

"Like hell I am. Look, I'm guessing you're investigating this Red Market organ-trafficking thing. Fine. We have parallel investigations. No law against that. You want to know what I know? It appears Krueger was supplying Remmert's patients with kidneys and possibly other organs. And now they're both dead within days of each other. But I do not know who killed them or why unless they found out that Krueger was talking to you people."

"How did you know Krueger and Remmert were involved in the Red Market?" Velasco pressed.

"I'm an investigator. I investigate."

Neither Velasco nor Gleeson looked impressed with my snarky answer. I sure as hell would not give up Becca. I'd sooner go to prison than flip on her.

"We know about your little hacker friend," Gleeson said with a sneer.

"What hacker friend?"

"Rebecca Maria Alvarez."

"She's not a hacker. She's an IT security consultant. If she were a hacker and you could prove it, you would've charged her by now."

"Ms. Ballou," Velasco said, her tone suddenly less confrontational, "innocent people are being harmed by this organization. So if you really care about justice, you will share everything you know so we can bring down this organization."

"I have."

"Where was Krueger procuring these organs?" she asked. "Was he working alone, or did he have help? Were there other medical personnel involved?"

I wasn't yet ready to give up Stromberg, since I wasn't sure how deeply he was involved. Was his participation limited to helping Amy Krueger a few years ago? Or had it continued? "I have no idea who Krueger's supplier was. Somebody else on the Red Market. It could have had multiple sources on there."

"Is your mother involved?" Gleeson asked. "Was that why you were meeting with her?"

Shit! My protecting Stromberg was now implicating my mother. "What? Hell no! My mother would never be involved in anything like that."

"And if she was, you wouldn't tell us anyway."

I wanted to smack the sneer off his face. But I wasn't willing to go to prison for the privilege.

I ignored him and spoke directly to Velasco. "My objective is to discover who killed Krueger. But if I learn who is sourcing these organs, I will let you know. All right? I've had enough of these ridiculous threats and accusations. I'm on the level."

"Very well. But I expect you to live up to your end of the bargain," she replied.

"Can I go now?"

"For now."

I stepped out of the truck.

"Hey!" I heard Gleeson call. "What about lunch?"

CHAPTER 36

THREAT ASSESSMENT

I ARRIVED BACK at the Hub without incident but fumed the whole way. One of these days, that smug prick Gleeson would push someone too far. I only wished I'd be there to see it.

When I sat down at my workstation, I filled Becca in on my adventures. She was horrified at Gleeson's threat of knowing about her questionably legal activities.

"¡Hijo de puta! What if they arrest me?" she asked, clearly shaken.

"They won't. He was fishing. But from now on, might be best if we keep everything legitimate. This app you used for deciphering crypto transactions…"

"CryptoTracer? Totally legal, at least for now. I'm sure the feds aren't happy about it being out there, but a buddy of mine developed it and left it open source. The blockchain is in the public domain, distributed across multiple networks. The app simply finds patterns in the dizzying number of transactions."

"I still don't understand how you crack the anonymity."

"When someone uses a cryptocurrency to buy something shipped to them, they have to use their name, or at the very least, their address. That links the account and the transaction to their personal data. From there, the app can make other connections. The whole anonymity aspect of crypto collapses like a house of cards."

"Any more luck on who else may have been supplying Krueger with organs for transplant?"

"Other than Stromberg?"

"He claims he was only involved with helping Krueger's daughter."

Becca did a double take. "If he told you that, he's a pinche mentiroso. Krueger may have first got him involved to help his daughter, but he's been active on the Red Market ever since. Not just with Krueger, either. He's made deals with another broker. Some puto who goes by the handle Portman. Stromberg received a payment from them just yesterday."

"Are you serious? Shit. I was hoping Stromberg really was one of the good guys."

"Maybe he thinks he is. Providing organs to those who need them. But these black-market organ traffickers are screwing over donors. Es muy malo, chica. Sometimes, these donors vanish altogether. I'm wondering if that's what's been happening to some of those missing and murdered indigenous women."

The thought sent a shiver down my spine. "So if Krueger was talking to the feds, that would put a crimp in Stromberg's side hustle and give him a motive for murder. But he didn't strike me as a killer. And why kill Remmert? Or Kaur, if her accident was staged?"

"No se."

"Any idea who this Portman person really is?"

"Not yet. They're good at covering their tracks. I ran a search for doctors with the last name Portman, but…"

"No hits?"

"Just the opposite. Too many hits. There were several in Arizona alone. Psychologists, dermatologists, internists, even a couple of surgeons. And for all we know, Portman may not even be in the state or may not be a licensed doctor. A harvested kidney can be viable for up to thirty-six hours. Portman could be anywhere or anyone."

"Send me what you gleaned from Stromberg's crypto accounts. Also, you can finally dig into this." I handed her the hard drive I'd taken from Remmert's house. "Maybe you can find something I missed. Something that connects Stromberg directly to Remmert."

"With pleasure." She looked like a toddler opening Christmas presents.

Meanwhile, I ran Stromberg through the skip-tracing app. In the report, he looked like any other successful doctor. He had a home in Fountain Hills and a summer house in Colorado. He employed a personal chef and a housekeeper. Rarely dined out, but when he did, he went to the finest restaurants in the Valley. He had a subscription to several medical journals and was fond of literary fiction hardcovers.

He was originally from Virginia and had graduated from Yale School of Medicine. Did an internship at Phoenix Baptist, as he had told me.

He traveled a few times a month down to Rio Rico, presumably where he volunteered at a community clinic. Was that where he found prospective donors?

I studied his phone logs. The guy still had a landline as well as a cell. Plenty of calls to the hospital and other physicians throughout the Valley. Also, occasional calls back and forth with the Clínica Comunitaria Rio Rico. Nothing that really stuck out.

No guns registered in his name. No criminal record other than a few speeding tickets over the years, all paid. He had a few social media accounts but wasn't active on any of them.

Nothing I could find pointed at him being anything other than a workaholic doctor. Of course, I knew that wasn't the complete story.

When Becca sent me the information she'd put together on Stromberg's crypto activity, I got a fuller picture of this man's life. Several times a month, he received crypto payments in the five- to six-figure range, all via the Red Market site, where he went by the handle Stormbringer.

He converted some of these payments to cash through a broker, but most he kept in his crypto wallet. He also made purchases directly from merchants who took this type of currency as payment, including a travel agency called BitJet. In her notes, Becca explained these transactions were how she identified Stromberg as the owner of the accounts.

Over the past two years, our little organ-harvesting doctor had been jet-setting to France, Germany, and Poland, as well as Pakistan, India, and Thailand. What was the purpose of these visits? Tourism? Humanitarian medical care? Or something more nefarious? Maybe all the above.

Around five, I packed up my stuff to head home.

"Find anything interesting on the hard drive?" I asked Becca before I left.

"A lot on Remmert and the transplants he was doing under the table. I'll be honest. I was surprised that the surgeries took place at major hospitals across the state. Would have figured they'd use some back-alley facilities."

"The power of confidentiality," I replied. "Everything is compartmentalized. By design, the right hand doesn't know what the left hand is doing. Anything pointing at Stromberg as the source?"

She shook her head, looking disappointed. "No mention of him or this Portman person anywhere in the drive. They covered their tracks well."

"Damn. Anything suggesting he received threats or about Krueger talking to the feds?"

"Nope. Nothing like that either."

"Shit. Okay. Thanks for looking. Guess I'll see you at the protest tomorrow." I hugged her.

"You can count on it. We'll show those pendejos they can't get away with stripping the trans community of its civil rights."

On the short drive home, I let my mind wander about the Krueger case. Three dead doctors. A fourth who seemed like a nice guy but was deeply involved with the Red Market. Was he the killer? Or a future victim?

Still, I couldn't rule out any of Krueger's unhappy customers. If he'd done some of those things with my parents' remains, I'd sure be pissed as hell. And people in this country killed others for the stupidest reasons these days.

As much as I didn't like to chalk things up to coincidence, that was entirely possible. That someone unrelated to Krueger had murdered Remmert. And that Kaur's death truly was accidental. But my gut told me the Red Market was the key to finding Krueger's killer.

I passed Conor walking Diana when I arrived home. By the time they returned, I was sautéing ground pork, chiles, and onions for tacos.

"Hello, love." He kissed me. A bruise on his cheekbone was darkening. "Something smells good."

Diana leaned against me, nearly knocking me over. Damn, she was getting big.

"What happened to you?"

"Eh, some cheeky bastard wanted to have a go after we cornered him. Got in one good lick before I snapped on the cuffs. All in a good day's work. How about you? Are ya any closer to finding who knocked off that Krueger bloke?"

"Maybe. That doctor my mom works with is involved in black-market organ harvesting. He seems like a nice guy. But when I confronted him about it, he lied and said he'd just done it the one time to help Krueger's daughter. But his Red Market account shows he's still doing it and making bank."

"You think he did in Krueger and made it look like a suicide?"

"So far, I've got nothing to prove or disprove it either way."

I turned off the stove and served the tacos with a premade salad.

Conor sat in his usual seat, then jumped up again and handed me something from his back pocket. "Almost forgot. This was delivered with the day's post. It's addressed to you."

The envelope he handed me had no stamp or address on the outside. Opening the envelope revealed a folded piece of plain paper. I unfolded it and a lump formed in my throat when I read it.

"Well, I'm clearly getting to someone."

I handed it back to him, and he read it aloud.

"'Back off bitch or your next.' Nice penmanship but no points for punctuation or spelling. And whoever wrote this doesn't know ya very well, do they? Telling you to back off? Might as well have said 'Come get me' for all the good it will do them."

He was right about the penmanship. Block letters. But if I was honest, it did make me a bit nervous. After my father nearly died from a gunshot wound after a mob of bigots crashed my wedding, I didn't take such threats as lightly as I used to.

"Doesn't look like a doctor's scrawl," I said. "But I imagine there are doctors with excellent penmanship, especially if they don't want it to look like their normal handwriting."

"Think it's this Stromberg bloke?"

"Not sure. I'm not ruling him out." I pulled up the video feed from our security cameras. Around eleven, someone drove up in a dark sedan, either black or dark blue. A person wearing a hoodie, shades, and a balaclava stepped out and put the envelope in the mailbox. Male, most likely, based on body shape. But nothing identifiable beyond that. I replayed the footage for Conor.

"What do you think?" I asked. "Looks like a guy, but beyond that, nothing recognizable."

"Aye, definitely acts like a pro. No license plate visible when they drove away either."

"Couldn't be Stromberg. I was talking with him when this guy was here."

"So maybe he's not your culprit."

"Guess not."

My phone rang. "Geez, can't a girl just eat?"

I wasn't going to answer it, but the ringtone was Journey's "Don't Stop Believing," my mother's favorite tune.

"Hey, Mom. We're in the middle of dinner. Can I call you back?"

"You accused Dr. Stromberg of murder? Jenna Christina Ballou, how could you embarrass me like that?" She sounded like she was in tears.

"Mom, I didn't accuse him of murder. I simply asked for an alibi. And he gave me one." Sort of. "Thing is, he really is into some bad shi—stuff."

"Oh, really? Such as?"

"Black-market organ trafficking."

"Jenna, that's absurd. He would never…"

"Mom, I have proof. And he admitted it to me."

"I don't believe it for one second. Not Dr. Stromberg."

"Why? Because you think you know him? I wouldn't make something like this up, Mom. You know I wouldn't make such accusations unless I was sure."

She didn't answer right away. I could hear her breathing. "It has to be a mistake, a misunderstanding. He's such a generous soul."

"I really wish I were wrong about this, Mom. I'm sorry. Maybe he thinks he's doing the right thing."

"What do you intend to do with this information? Ruin an otherwise good doctor's career?"

"Honestly, I don't know. I'm primarily interested in whether he killed Donnie Krueger. If he didn't, then he may be at risk too. But the feds are already investigating this organ-trafficking ring. Just a matter of time before they look at him as well, if they aren't already."

"I find it hard to believe Dr. Stromberg would get involved with something like this."

I didn't know what to say to her.

"I'm sorry for yelling at you, punkin. But you've put me in an awkward position at work."

"I understand. I'm sorry. I know you have a lot of respect for him."

"Do you really think he murdered those other doctors?"

"I don't know. But he lied to me about some things. Doesn't make him a murderer, but it makes him look suspicious." I decided not to tell her about the threatening note. She worried too much about me already.

"I understand. Do what you feel is right. I trust you."

"Thanks, Mom. That means a lot."

"On a different subject, are you still planning to attend the protest tomorrow morning?"

"I am."

"Be careful, dear. There's already talk of counterprotesters showing up with assault rifles. Those Oath Breakers or whatever they call themselves."

I knew who she was talking about. "I promise I'll be careful, Mom."

"Sorry for interrupting your dinner."

"I'll see you Sunday at brunch."

CHAPTER 37
THE PROTEST

ON SATURDAY MORNING, Conor drove us downtown for the protest rally. He parked in the garage on Adams, a few blocks east of the Capitol. Pedestrians dressed in Pride colors were everywhere, heading en masse toward the protest as if attending a sporting event at the stadium where pastel pink and blue accented with rainbows were the home team colors.

Chelsea and Phoenix Gender Alliance must have really gotten the word out to all our members and allies.

"Ya okay, love?" Conor took my hand, entwining his fingers with mine as we walked. "Yer awfully quiet."

He was right. Despite the beautiful blue sky above and the cool, clean air, I'd barely said anything all morning. Dark memories threatened to drag me back down into the emotional hole I'd barely escaped from a few years ago.

"Last time we were downtown for a protest, a bomb killed a bunch of people."

"Aye, but we took down those responsible. They won't be here."

I envied his optimism, but the rise in violence over the last few years had left me wary.

"The members of White Nation may be rotting in prison,

but there's been no shortage of others taking their place. Proud Boys, Oath Keepers, the Patriots of Liberty Caucus. Even Womyn Born Womyn. Remember how they ruined our wedding?"

"Trust me, love. I haven't forgotten. But no matter what those bastards do, you and me and the trans community, we will overcome. Despite everything, despite the bloody bombings, despite our wrecked wedding, you and I are still together. Our love is more powerful than their hate."

I hugged him, clinging to his sense of hope. Despite all that he'd been through in Ireland, in Afghanistan, and here, he still believed in a better future.

I could hear the crowd before I could see them. Chants, drums, shouts, cheers, voices amplified by megaphones. Conor and I turned a corner, and the mass of humanity came into view. It stretched from the Arizona Capitol Museum across Seventeenth Street into Wesley Bolin Plaza and into the surrounding parking lots. Every queer person in the state seemed to have shown up. It was like the Pride Festival multiplied.

Rainbow and trans flags fluttered in the cool breeze. Signs waved with slogans like Trans Lives Matter, I Love My Trans Child, and Gender-Affirming Care Saves Lives. Many people wore shirts with similar messages. Members of the Sisterhood of Perpetual Indulgence, identifiable by their over-the-top nun costumes and outrageous makeup, passed out flyers. I recognized many familiar faces from the community. Good to be among my tribe.

But I couldn't relax completely. Cops in full riot gear stood at the perimeter, presumably to keep order. But the queer community and law enforcement had a long and troubled history. On my last day as a cop, I'd endured transphobic taunts from my fellow officers. If shit went sideways, I had no idea whose side they'd land on.

Making matters worse, a small contingent of counterprotesters held their own little rally. Their signs bore phrases like Keep Men Out of Women's Spaces, Stop Grooming Children, Trannies Are Predators, and others suggesting that gender-affirming care was child abuse. Among their throng of hate were some people dressed in military-style gear and holding assault rifles. At first glance, I mistook them for police, but a closer look revealed they were like the wackos who attacked the US Capitol during the January 6 insurrection.

A small stage had been set up in front of the Capitol Museum entrance. Moments after our arrival, my friend Chelsea Quiñones stepped up with a microphone in hand. She and her wife, Izzie, were the owners of L Street, a women's bar on Camelback Road. She was also one of the leaders of Phoenix Gender Alliance.

Chelsea stood about six feet tall, with broad shoulders and a prominent brow. Anyone would clock her as trans. But she didn't care. She still looked fabulous with her purple and blue hair, goth-style makeup, leather corset, and multiple facial piercings.

She once told me her life's motto was "I don't do subtle." That was for damn sure. I had a lot of respect for her. No surprise she was organizing the protest.

"Good morning, beautiful people!" she announced.

"Good morning!" the crowd shouted back.

"My name is Chelsea Quiñones, and I am a proud transgender woman." More cheers went up.

"Thank you all for having the courage to show up today and send a message to our government that we will not allow our community to be bullied. Especially the youngest and most vulnerable among us."

A deafening roar of support rose.

"In the Declaration of Independence, Thomas Jefferson wrote, 'We hold these truths to be self-evident, that all men are created equal, that they are endowed by their Creator with certain unalienable Rights, that among these are Life, Liberty and the pursuit of Happiness.' These are the principles upon which this country was founded, despite how flawed those founders were.

"Our First Amendment guarantees us the right to free expression. The Fourth Amendment guarantees us a reasonable expectation of privacy and protection against unreasonable search and seizure. The Fourteenth Amendment affords us all equal protection. HIPAA laws ensure that medical information should be private between doctors and patients. And yet Governor Denton, in the waning days of her disgraceful term in office, has seen fit to deny our community these inalienable rights."

The cheers of support turned to passionate shouts of profanity-laced anger. Presumably toward our embarrassment of a governor and her lackeys in the state legislature.

Behind Chelsea, volunteers set up a large screen and a projector.

"Our pathetic, bigoted governor has turned the Department of Child Safety into a sadistic department of cruelty and bigotry. Tearing frightened trans kids from their loving families while also imprisoning their parents and their doctors. They do this not out of ignorance. They know trans kids thrive in supportive families where gender-affirming care is available. They already understand that trans kids denied this support are several times more likely to take their own lives.

"Denton and her cronies know this, but she signed this bill anyway because the cruelty and suffering is the point. It is the defining principle of white Christian nationalists like Denton and her ilk. They *want* trans kids to suffer and die. They *want* to hurt caring parents and properly trained physicians. They are bullies who thrive on the suffering of others.

"These are the same cruel people who deny rape victims and people with ectopic pregnancies access to life-saving abortions. The same people who turn a blind eye to lethal police violence against people of color. The same people who'd rather arm teachers than ban assault rifles. The same people who care only for protecting the whims and privilege of powerful white cis-het men while the rest of us suffer and die under their bootheels."

From the cluster of counterprotesters, a man in an expensive black suit began chanting loudly into a megaphone. "Groomers! Groomers! Perverts! Perverts! Molesters! Molesters!"

I recognized him as Josiah Faulkner, the head of the Patriots of Liberty Caucus.

Chelsea turned to them. "Oh, how rude of me. I forgot to welcome our dear friends from the Patriots of Liberty. Do you really believe in liberty, Josiah? Or are you just interested in control and cruelty? Because if you really believed in liberty, you'd join us in this fight against oppression."

The right-wing nuts continued their inane chants.

The rest of us booed them. The energy in our crowd shifted from defiant solidarity to primal hostility.

"What a sad little group you are," Chelsea taunted. "You must feel very insecure about your beliefs. Why else would you feel the need to force them onto us? But I got news for you, and I want all of your people to hear me. The hate in your hearts is eating you up like a cancer. Your leaders are petty little tyrants who eschew logic and accountability. And like all the petty little tyrants in history, their days are limited. Remember Hitler? Dead in a bunker. Napoleon? Exiled for life. The Confederacy? Failed. Soviet Union? Collapsed."

That got a rise out of the counterprotesters. Shouts of "Fuck you, faggot!" rose above their hate- filled chants.

"Your leaders know they offer nothing of value, but they're desperate to remain in power. So they feed you lies and convince you that everyone else is the problem. Ask yourself what will happen to you when they are finally held accountable. Did Trump pardon the insurrectionists when they were arrested? No. They're in prison while he remains free. I encourage you to walk away while you can. Join us in restoring freedom and liberty for all."

The haters continued but with less enthusiasm than before.

Chelsea waved them off as if they were annoying flies. But the shift in the crowd's energy concerned me. The cauldron was coming to a boil.

A wash of blue lit the screen behind Chelsea, followed by the Zoom app logo, and finally a girl's larger-than-life smiling face. Leia Ripley. Next to her sat Rayna.

Chelsea pointed toward the screen. "My dear friend, Rayna, and her daughter, Leia, have joined us via the miracle of modern technology. They wanted to be here in person, but the risk that our state-sponsored stormtroopers might arrest them made that impossible. Welcome, Rayna and Leia."

Cheers of joy erupted from our supportive community. The level of tension in the crowd abated somewhat. But I remained wary. The counterprotesters continued their chants, slurs, and jeers.

"You want to go first?" Rayna asked her daughter.

Leia nodded. "My name is Leia Ripley. I am a transgender girl."

My ears rang from the deafening shouts of joy and support. Conor put an arm around my shoulder and squeezed.

"I knew I was a girl when I was three, even though I had a boy body. I kept it a secret until a couple of years ago. I was very sad. When I told my parents, they argued a lot."

Her face flushed with emotion. "My mom was very supportive. But my dad got angry and mean. He called me a faggot. After they divorced, I still had to go to his house twice a month. I hated it because he wouldn't let me wear dresses. He even cut off my hair with electric clippers once. I cried for a week."

I felt myself tearing up in empathy.

"So I stopped going. And my doctor helped me get medicine so that my body would change the right way in puberty. It makes me very happy. I like being a girl. I got lots of friends at school.

"Then they passed the new law. I couldn't see my friends anymore. We had to go into hiding. I'm not allowed to say where I am. I feel a little like Anne Frank, the Jewish girl who hid from the Nazis. There are people out there who want to kill me just for being trans. They want to lock up my mom. They already arrested my doctor."

She started openly crying. "Why do they do these mean things?"

Leia disappeared from camera view. Her mother offered her whispered words of comfort before turning back to the camera.

"I love my daughter," Rayna said, motherly concern hardening her expression. "I didn't know what to think at first when she came out to me. But I'd rather support and love my transgender daughter than bury a dead child. The people who passed this vicious, cruel law—they would rather she be dead. They would rather she suffer. I will not let them do that to her or any others. Trans kids have a right to exist. They have a right to healthcare that helps them thrive and enjoy life."

"Fuck you, bitch!"

A nearby shout jolted me out of listening to Rayna's story. Ten feet from me, Mike Ripley stood with a large semi-automatic pistol in his hand. The crowd around him backed away.

"You stole my son from me! I will make you sorry!"

I charged toward him even as he raised his weapon and fired several shots toward the stage. We collided and hit the ground. As I wrestled for the gun, he pulled off a few more random gunshots. I slammed his hand hard against the concrete, forcing him to drop the pistol.

He caught me with a punch to the jaw, powerful enough to make me see stars. I blocked the next blow and twisted his arm, causing him to cry out in pain. Conor appeared next to me and flipped him onto his belly, holding him down with a half nelson. I stumbled away and snatched up his pistol before anyone else picked it up.

"Drop the weapon. Do it now!" Two police officers appeared out of the crowd with their service weapons pointed at me.

CHAPTER 38
HOLDING

"EASY, OFFICERS," I said as calmly as I could. Ripley's pistol dangled from my thumb in the trigger guard. "We stopped the shooter. It's over."

"Drop the gun and get on the ground, bitch!" one of the cops demanded. He looked all of eighteen years old and as jittery as a cat in a kennel full of hungry Rottweilers. "Do it before I blow your fucking head off."

So that's how it is, I thought as I carefully lowered the gun to the ground, raised both my hands, and got down on my knees. "The threat has been neutralized, Officer," I told the kid. "Just relax. It's cool."

"Leave her alone!" someone in the crowd said.

Another protestor yelled, "She didn't do it!"

"Fucking fascist pigs!"

When the kid approached me, the crowd pressed in around him and his partner, a woman with some years on her. She had a heart-shaped face, hair in a tight bun, and a glare that could cut hardened steel.

This situation was turning into a nightmare. Bad enough to have one angry shooter. Now, the air crackled with the need for violence against a state that dared weaponize the law against us. It was a need for bloodshed and revenge for decades of harassment.

"You people back off, or I will arrest you," the female officer ordered, waving her weapon at the stern-faced mob, who backed away.

The kid stayed focused on me. "Get on your belly. Hands behind your head. Fingers laced."

I complied. "Officer, I'm not the one…"

"No talking."

Cuffs pinched my wrists. I couldn't see what was going on, but a cacophony of voices rose with increasing violence.

"You can't arrest her!"

"We won't let you!"

"Let her go!"

"Goddamn cops!"

More gunshots shook the air, followed by screams and cries of pain. As an acrid scent filled the air, my eyes burned. I started choking. *Tear gas! Fuck!*

The kid and his partner jerked me to my feet and dragged me through the agitated crowd. They'd both donned masks. I struggled to see through the pain and my watering eyes, but I caught glimpses of cops and civilians going at it. What the hell was happening?

"Can't see. Can't breathe," I wheezed.

The cops ignored me.

After stumbling along for what felt like miles, they tossed me into the back of a squad car. At least the air was fresher in there. My eyeballs stung as if I'd rubbed them after chopping chiles. I coughed and wheezed and struggled to relax enough to prevent mucus from filling my lungs.

Where was Conor? Who'd been shot? And why the hell were the cops arresting me? I'd disarmed the gunman, for the love of pizza!

Eventually, the cops deposited me in a closet-sized interrogation room and left me alone once again. By this time, mucus and phlegm covered the front of my shirt. My eyes were swollen and gritty, like I had a nasty case of pinkeye. My hands were still cuffed behind me, my fingers long-since numb.

I'd had enough of this shit. I located the cuff key I kept on a bracelet. Uncuffing oneself wasn't as easy as it looked. Especially when the key was attached to a bracelet. But I had practiced for hours a while back, and it paid off. In a matter of minutes, I was free. Sort of. I was still locked in an interrogation room. I chucked the cuffs into the far corner of the room and rubbed at my face. God, it hurt!

After what felt like a few hours, a man in a suit walked in.

"Well, well, well, Jinx Ballou. We meet again."

The voice was familiar, but I couldn't place him. My eyes were so swollen I wouldn't have recognized my own mother if she were sitting in front of me.

"Who the hell are you?"

"Really, Ms. Ballou, I'm hurt you don't remember me after all our quality time together."

I stayed silent.

"Detective O'Reilly. Garza's former partner. We had a nice chat about you breaking into people's homes without permission."

Fuck me. "What do you want, O'Reilly? This isn't your precinct. And I didn't break any laws, certainly didn't break into anywhere."

"I was called in after the mob downtown turned into a riot. Seems you are in a heap of trouble, as are your merry band of tranny protestors. You're being charged with aggravated assault, kidnapping, and interference in a child-safety investigation."

"What the hell are you talking about? I disarmed the shooter. I acted in self-defense and the defense of everyone in the crowd."

"That wasn't what the officers saw. You're also being charged with criminal gang activity."

"Criminal gang activity? What the fuck are you talking about? That's absurd. I'm not part of any gang."

"I beg to differ. I have proof that you are and have been for some time."

"Oh really? And what gang would that be?"

"Phoenix Gender Alliance."

I laughed at the ridiculousness of the situation. "You are a special kind of stupid, O'Reilly. The Phoenix Gender Alliance isn't a gang. We're a transgender support group."

"Who is obstructing multiple child abuse investigations. You, in particular, have been accused of kidnapping and interfering in a child-safety investigation of one Luke Ripley."

"Accused by the man who opened fire onto a crowd during a peaceful protest a few hours ago. And the child's name is Leia, you bigoted ass."

"Charges also include unlawful assembly."

"We had a right to be there and protest. We had permits and everything." At least I assumed Chelsea had taken care of that.

"The permit did not include a sound stage or projection equipment. Thus the permit is void. The assembly was illegal. And your group has been classified as a criminal gang. Though if you tell me where Luke Ripley and his mother are hiding, we might cut you a deal to lessen prison time."

This was all bullshit posturing. And I sure as hell wasn't falling for it.

"I want my lawyer."

"Fine." He slid my phone over to me. "But you're going down for this one, Ballou. I'll make sure of it."

I could barely see out of my swollen eyes, but somehow, I called Kirsten. When she didn't pickup after the third ring, I worried that maybe she'd been arrested too. I'd caught a glimpse of her in the crowd. But she finally answered in the middle of the fourth ring.

"Oh, thank God. Kirsten, the fucking cops arrested me. I'm at the downtown precinct."

"Okay, Jinx. Stay quiet. You know the drill. I'll be there as soon as I can."

I hung up and turned back to O'Reilly. "I need to wash my face. The tear gas is still burning my eyes. And I want some water to drink."

"Yeah, we'll see about that." He got up, picked up the cuffs from the corner where I'd thrown them, and shot me a glare before leaving the room. At least he didn't slap the cuffs back on me. And the worst effects from the tear gas were wearing off. Small mercies.

I called Conor while I waited but got no answer. I left a message telling him where I was and what I was being charged with.

When the door opened again a while later, my body tensed, automatically going into defensive mode. I relaxed when I saw Kirsten standing there. Her usual flawless makeup was gone, and her face was a little red, but she looked otherwise her normal professional self.

"Oh, Jinx, you look awful."

"Thanks," I muttered. "Nice to see you too."

"Have they let you rinse off your face?"

I shook my head.

"Bastards." It was the first time I remembered hearing her curse.

She handed me some wipes out of her purse, which I used to clean my face. My skin felt raw and puffy, but the wipes cool and soothing.

"Any idea what happened to Conor?" I asked. "I called, but he didn't pick up."

"I don't know. It was so chaotic. Chelsea's..." she paused,

choking on emotion. "She's dead, Jinx. Several others were shot too. Police arrested a lot of us."

"Fuck!" My worst fear was losing Conor all over again. If Ripley shot him, I was going to toss that fucker into an abandoned mineshaft and set him on fire. Tears once again burned my eyes.

"What are they charging you with?"

"Aggravated assault, presumably for disarming Leia's dad. He was the one shooting at the stage. I stopped him. Also, they're charging me with criminal gang activity. They think Phoenix Gender Alliance is a gang. How can they do that?"

"The county attorney is no friend to the community, unfortunately," Kirsten said. "She's a vigorous supporter of the new law. They probably suspect members of the group have been hiding trans kids and their families from DCS. Unfortunately, the Nazis are running the show right now."

"Talk about theater of the absurd. What do we do?"

"The best we can. I'll bring in the detective, see if I can't get him to drop the charges against you."

"Good luck with that. He seems to have a hard-on for me. Same guy from earlier this week that wanted to bust me for trying to apprehend Tod Cooper at his buddy's house."

"Be that as it may, I'll do everything I can to get the charges dismissed."

Detective O'Reilly walked in minutes later, a smug grin on his face. "Ready to confess?"

"Seriously, Detective, this is beneath you," Kirsten said. "This isn't even your department. You're what? In the burglary division?"

"Yes, I am, counselor. And your client has been tied to a string of burglaries and was caught breaking into a home earlier this week, as you recall. I should have charged her then. Clearly, she has a complete disregard for the law."

"You didn't charge her earlier this week because you

knew the county attorney wouldn't prosecute such a ridiculous case."

"Maybe not, but she'll prosecute this one. Turning the State Capitol grounds into a bloodbath?"

"She did no such thing. She subdued the man who fired on the crowd and acted in defense of herself and others. Your aggravated assault charges are completely bogus."

"Let's talk about this man, Michael Ripley." O'Reilly turned to me. "He claims you kidnapped his child and wife."

"What a load of shit!" I blurted out.

"We're getting warrants now to search your home."

Good luck with that, I thought. "Search away, Detective. I didn't kidnap anyone, nor are Rayna and Leia at my home. You've got nothing."

"Seriously, Detective," Kirsten added. "You have no case against my client. Not for the assault, the kidnapping, nothing. As for these ridiculous criminal gang activity charges, the media will have a field day with this. If you pursue this case, you and the county attorney will only embarrass yourself, not to mention open yourself up to a major lawsuit. You could lose your shield."

"Last chance to help yourself and confess," O'Reilly replied.

"I have nothing to confess."

"Suit yourself." He stood, opened the door, and signaled to someone. "Jenna Ballou, you are under arrest…"

I tuned him out as he rattled off the bogus charges.

"I will get you bailed out," Kirsten whispered to me.

"Find Conor first. Make sure he's okay."

"I will. Hang in there."

Two patrol officers cuffed me and transported me to the Fourth Avenue Jail. But not to the women's section.

"Hey!" I protested as they opened the door to the men's

part of the facility. "You can't stick me in here. I'm a woman, for fuck's sake!"

"Not what I'm told," said one of the officers. He had a shaved head and lifeless eyes. "O'Reilly says you're a man. You get put in with the men. Them's the rules."

"Motherfuckers! You can't do this." I tried to pull away, and the CO slammed my face against the cement-block wall.

"Keep resisting and you'll get worse, faggot."

CHAPTER 39
FREEDOM

I WANTED to fight the COs who were frog-marching me to the men's holding facility. But the effort would have been futile. My best hope was that Kirsten bailed me out before anything worse happened.

A cell door clanged open, and the COs shoved me inside. After the door was closed again, they removed the cuffs.

I studied my surroundings. Three cellmates. Two white guys and one Latino sat on benches lining the far side of the cell.

One of the white guys looked like he was sleeping off a bender. The other eyed me like a hungry wolf staring down a prey. He bore facial tats that were probably gang related. The Latino guy had dark skin and long hair, with a side shave. I got a gang vibe from him, too, but he had no visible ink. Just something about his wife-beater tank and the hardness in his stare.

"Well, well," said the white gangbanger. "No one said nothing about gettin' a conjugal. You lost, little girl? Come here and sit on your daddy's lap."

I didn't respond. I was exhausted and wanted nothing more than to take a long shower and sleep. But I dared not take a nap while locked in a cage with these guys.

"Don't be shy, baby. You sure have a purty mouth. Let's see you smile."

I turned partially away from him, leaning against the bars but keeping him in my peripheral.

"What? You won't smile for me? Your whore of a mama teach you to be so rude?"

I continued to ignore his attempts to bait me, focusing instead on my breathing. My throat was still raw from the tear gas, but it was better than it had been.

When the gangbanger's ongoing lurid taunts didn't get a response from me, he stood. "Don't like being ignored. Certainly not by some cunt like you."

I faced him but said nothing.

"This is your lucky day, little girl. I'm gonna make a woman outta you. And you'll thank me. I promise you that. Feeling my cock in your pussy. Less you ain't got no pussy? You one of them faggots, likes to play dress-up? That why they stuck you in here with us?"

He approached me slowly.

"I can fuck you up the ass. Don't make no nevermind to me. Either way, you're getting fucked."

His hand shot out, reaching for my throat. He missed.

Despite my exhaustion and discomfort, my body thrummed with adrenaline. With lightning speed, I twisted his arm around and slammed him into the bars. Before he could react, I had him in a choke hold. Not easy to do to someone several inches taller than me, but I managed, thanks to my training and many years taking down assholes like him.

He slapped the bars for a few seconds, eyes wild with fear. But I held my grip. When his body slumped, I held it a little longer then released him. Reluctantly. I would have felt no guilt in relieving the world of his ugly presence, but murdering a fellow inmate might impact getting the charges against me dismissed.

"Now who's fucked, asshole?" I kicked him and turned to my dark-skinned cellmate, giving him a warning glare. "You wanna be next, ese?"

Throughout the confrontation, he hadn't moved or said a word. He chuckled quietly but remained silent. Figured he got the message. I wasn't a wilting violet. Sure as hell wouldn't be some rapist's plaything.

I moved to a corner of the cell where I could keep an eye on my cellmates. The perv eventually groaned to consciousness again, rubbing his head. "What the fuck just happened?"

He raised himself to his hands and knees, turned his head, and spotted me in the corner. His glare was pure violence, but he said nothing. Instead, he stumbled back to his original seat.

An hour later, a CO walked up to the cell. Not one of the ones who had put me in here. "Jenna Ballou?" he asked.

"Yeah?"

"Bail's been posted."

After I was released, Conor and Kirsten both met me in the waiting area. I rushed into his arms, so grateful to hold him, to smell him, even if he was still redolent of the bitter scent of tear gas. Or maybe it was just me. I cried.

"It's okay, love," he soothed. "You're safe now."

"They put me… in men's holding," I choked out between sobs.

I wasn't normally this emotional, even in the face of injustice, but between the protest turning violent, the effects of the tear gas, facing the trumped-up charges, and defending myself in a men's jail cell, I'd hit my limit.

"Bloody pricks. Come on, love. Let's get ya outta here."

When we got to the parking garage, I thanked Kirsten for her help.

"We've still got a lot of work ahead of us to deal with

these charges, but I think in the end, we will prevail," she assured me. "Justice is on our side."

I wasn't so certain. "I hope you're right."

On the drive home, Conor said, "Kirsten filled me in about Chelsea getting killed. I'm so sorry."

"Yeah, me too. Poor Izzie. They were such a cute couple. If I had been one second faster…"

"Don't beat yourself up over it, love. Not your fault that fecking wanker did what he did. You're not Wonder Woman."

"I know. Any word on who else was shot?"

"I don't know. News reports are saying three other people were hit but no idea who or how badly."

At home, I took a long shower then put the clothes I'd been wearing in the trash. They reeked of tear gas. I didn't know if I could ever get that awful stench out no matter how many times I washed them. My body still seemed to stink of it, but maybe it was just a scent memory.

Afterward, I crawled into bed. It was only four in the afternoon, but I was exhausted from the day's chaos.

Hours later, Conor woke me. He'd made dinner. I wasn't hungry, even though I'd gone without lunch. He pushed me to drink more water to help flush my system. I did that, at least.

I had been looking forward to attending the Phoenix Gender Alliance Halloween masquerade, but it had probably been canceled after the tragic events at the protest. Even if it wasn't, I was in no mood for a party.

When Conor came to bed, we made love. Feeling his muscular body next to me and inside me helped a lot, even though it took what little energy I had left.

I slept fitfully, the thunder of gunshots echoing in my dreams. Blood was everywhere. I was searching for something, but I couldn't remember what it was when I woke on Sunday morning.

Physically, I felt better than I had. Emotionally, it was as if someone had blown a cannonball-sized hole through my soul. I kept thinking of Izzie, Chelsea's wife, and what she must be going through. Conor was still asleep when I climbed out of bed.

I slipped into the kitchen and made a phone call. It rang three times and rolled over to voicemail.

"Izzie, it's Jinx. I'm…" Emotion tightened around my throat like a boa constrictor. "So sorry about Chelsea. I know what it's like to lose the one you love. Even though… I don't know what I'm saying. Call me when you can. Let me know how I can help. Even if it's just to be there for you. You've always been there for me. I love you, sister."

I hung up. The message I'd left was so pathetic. But I couldn't think of anything else to say.

I had several messages of my own to respond to. From my mother, Jake, and Caden. But I wasn't up to talking to anyone else at the moment. I'd see my mother and Jake soon enough at Sunday brunch. Caden could wait until later.

Conor walked in, bleary-eyed, and poured us both a cup of coffee. "Morning, love. How're ya feeling?"

I shrugged. "Numb, mostly."

"We going to your mum's for Sunday brunch?"

"Yeah. I need some serious family time."

"Aye, sounds like a good idea. Police released the names of the other people Ripley shot yesterday."

"Who?" I braced myself for the bad news.

"Rosalyn Jefferson, Chad Irwin, and Sadie Levinson. All reported in stable condition."

"Shit." I knew all of them. Rosalyn was a friend from Phoenix Gender Alliance. Chad and his boyfriend, Mace, had let me stay with them for a while after I left an ex-boyfriend many years ago. And Sadie…

"What the hell was Sadie doing there?" I asked. "I never mentioned the protest to her."

"Must've heard about it somewhere else. Probably showed because of her friendship with you."

I felt bad that she'd shown up as an ally only to get shot. If only I had disarmed Ripley sooner and more efficiently. So many people around me ended up getting hurt. My father was shot at my own wedding. Caden had been shot while working with me a few years ago. My mentor, Juanita Valdez, and several of her employees had been shot, some of them killed, at a queer fundraiser by members of White Nation I'd been after but hadn't yet caught. The same organization had set off bombs at Wesley Bolin Plaza and on the Piestewa Freeway, killing dozens and injuring hundreds. Nearly killing Conor.

That gnawing depression and sense of worthlessness crept back into my mind—my trauma demons whispering that the world would be better off without me.

I took a long, slow breath. No, I told my demons. I will not crawl back into that dark hole of despair. Even superheroes made mistakes. Even Wonder Woman and Captain Marvel and Xena had their limits and their demons. And they were comic-book superheroes.

It was one thing to grieve and another to take on the guilt of someone else's violence.

"I know it's not my fault," I told Conor. "I just wish I could have done more."

"Aye, we all feel that way. Let's get dressed and head over to your folks' place."

CHAPTER 40
A CHANGE IN PLANS

ON THE DRIVE to my parent's home in Mesa, my phone rang. It was Becca. She had left several messages the day before, but I'd been too miserable and exhausted to call back.

"Thank Goddess you're okay," she said. "I was so worried. I saw you fighting with that gunman. Then the tear gas. It was crazy. And then when I couldn't get ahold of you, I feared the worst."

"I'm okay. But I was arrested." I told her the story.

"¡Pinches putos! How can they do that to you? You stopped the shooter and saved who knows how many lives. And they wanted to arrest you?"

I had no answer to her question. "How are you and Easton?"

"My chronic fatigue's kicking my ass today. No surprise after yesterday's locura. Easton is shaken but fine. They're taking care of me."

"I'm glad they're there for you."

"I've been digging further into Stromberg. I hacked into a private chat on the Red Market site between Stromberg and this Portman person."

I was worried that she was telling me this over the

phone. What if the feds were listening? But at this point, I needed a win.

"What'd you find out?"

"Portman has been acting as the middleman for Stromberg and doctors with patients needing organ transplants. He's local and killed Krueger, Remmert, and Kaur. Stromberg said he wanted out of it, but Portman wouldn't let him."

"Who is this guy?"

"No se. But he seems to have connections with law enforcement, somehow keeping the Red Market off their radar. I haven't been able to nail down where he works. Could be a cop, someone in the county attorney's office, a powerful politician. I don't know. But he manipulated Peoria PD to rule Krueger's death a suicide and Kaur's death an accident. I pulled up the police report on her case. Both the brakes and airbags failed. Clearly sabotage. But the case was closed, chalked up as an accident. Portman knew all about Krueger agreeing to talk to the feds. Took him out before he could. And Jinx, they know you're involved."

"Shit."

"Also, I've confirmed that Stromberg works down at that clinic in Rio Rico a few weekends a month."

"Yeah, I've been thinking about that too," I replied. "If he's still supplying organs through Red Market, he may be getting them from his patients down there."

"Exactly. Rio Rico's a minority-majority community with a lot of immigrants from Latin America. A portion of them are probably undocumented. If they disappeared, how hard would the law enforcement look for them?"

"And didn't he just receive a payment from Portman?"

"He did," she acknowledged. "According to the message board, he found a match for someone who needed both a kidney and a liver. Portman is supposed to pick them up for transport at two. A person can live with only one kidney, but a liver is a different story. Stromberg is going to kill someone and harvest their organs."

"Shit." I would not let that happen. I did the mental math. "Do we know when Stromberg's planning his next trip down there?"

"Today, according to his texts."

"Okay, thanks for the information. I'll do what I can to stop him."

"Watch your six, Jinxie. These people have already killed three doctors and Goddess knows how many innocent people."

"Yeah, but they weren't me. And I've got Conor with me."

"Good hunting, bestie."

"Thanks."

I hung up. "Change of plans, babe," I told Conor.

"I heard. Where are we going?"

"Rio Rico. Down near the border."

"Your mum's going to rage over you canceling at the last minute."

"I know, but someone's life is on the line. I think Stromberg is going to murder someone to harvest their organs."

"We definitely can't let that happen."

"Drive us back home so we can gear up. Meanwhile, I'll make some calls and see if I can't round up some backup."

I called Rodeo, but my brother answered. "Jake?" I asked. "Why are you answering Rodeo's phone?"

"We're at the hospital."

Panic gripped my chest. "Oh, my god? Did something happen to Rodeo? Was he shot?" I hadn't even known they'd be at the protest.

"No, it was the tear gas… He had a bad reaction to it. Doctors say he has chemical burns in his throat. He was right next to one of the canisters. They have him sedated and on a ventilator right now."

"Shit. Jake, I'm so sorry. Do Mom and Dad know?"

"They do. They picked up Gwyneth. How are you doing, sis? You didn't get shot, did you?"

"No, just arrested. I tackled the shooter, but then the cops arrested me, along with a bunch of the other protestors. Calling us a criminal gang."

"That's so messed up. I should have been there, but we were up against a deadline on renovating a house. We'd already scheduled for a new A/C system to be installed, and I had to be there."

"I'm glad you weren't. Something bad might've happened to you too. What's Rodeo's prognosis?"

"The doctors are cautiously optimistic. But he could have long-term respiratory problems because of the exposure."

"I'm pulling for him."

"Thanks. Give Mom and Dad my love at brunch."

"I won't be there either."

"Why not? You're not still in jail, are you?"

"No. It's a work thing. I gotta go. Give Rodeo my love."

I hung up and called Zahara. After the phone rang several times, she answered sleepily. "Hello?"

"Morning. You available for a job?"

"Sorry, Jinxie. Julie and I are in Colorado. We'll be back on Tuesday. You should see the snow here. So white and peaceful."

"Sounds nice."

"How'd things go at the protest yesterday?"

"Not well. But you enjoy the rest of your extended weekend. I'll see you Tuesday."

I was zero for two. I called Caden.

"Jinx, are you okay? I left you a message after I saw the cops grabbed you. I've been worried."

"I'm okay. But I need your help. You up for a job?"

"I am this afternoon. I'm out hiking with some friends up near Tonto Natural Bridge. But I can bail if you need me. Just tell me where and when."

I gave him the address of the Rio Rico community clinic. "Conor and I are headed there now. Meet us there when you can."

"Will do. I should get there around one or so."

I made one last call.

"Jenna, punkin. Why didn't you call me back yesterday? Are you okay?" My mom's voice shook with maternal worry.

"I'm sorry. I wasn't feeling well yesterday." I told her about the arrest. "Jake told me about Rodeo. Sounds bad. How's Gwyneth doing?"

"Worried. You're still coming this morning, right?"

"Well, that's what I'm calling about. Someone's in trouble."

"Who?"

"One of Stromberg's patients down at the clinic in Rio Rico. I think he's going to murder them to harvest their organs and…"

"Jenna, you are wrong. Dr. Stromberg is not a murderer. He cares about people."

"Mom, I'm sure about this. Stromberg may care about people, but the truth is he's been sacrificing innocent lives from vulnerable communities to save people from wealthy families. He's been doing it for a few years now. And he's in league with the person who murdered three other doctors involved in this black-market organ trafficking ring."

"If you're so convinced, call the cops. Let them handle it."

"Because this other person has ties to law enforcement. Maybe a cop. Maybe something higher up. I don't know. They covered up Krueger's death as a suicide and another doctor's death as a car accident."

"You aren't going down there alone, are you?"

"Conor's with me. And Caden's going to meet us there."

"Just the three of you?"

"I'll be okay. I'm sorry about missing brunch, but…"

"I understand. You have a life to save. I trust you, and I love you. Please come home safe."

"Thanks, Mom. I will. I love you too."

When Conor and I arrived home, we rushed inside and armored up. No Tasers this time. I was armed to kill. As we headed toward the door, Diana whined when we wouldn't let her come with us.

"Sorry, girl," I said. "We'll be home soon. I promise."

We took the Green Dragon. Despite its larger size, it still got better mileage than Conor's restored '68 Charger. But I let him drive while I made some phone calls.

Sadie Levinson was the first. She was home. The bullet had grazed her thigh. Her wound was superficial.

"I'm glad you're all right, Sadie. I'm sorry you were hurt for showing up to defend my community."

"I saw what you did, Jinx. Taking down the gunman. It was… it was very brave. Honestly, in all these years of working together, I never truly appreciated what it must be like for you, apprehending my defendants, some of whom refuse to surrender without a fight. And to do so as a woman…"

I was frankly flabbergasted at her level of empathy. Must have been the pain meds she was on. But still, I felt she had an honesty that she normally hid behind a mask of professionalism. In Valium veritas, perhaps.

"Thanks, Sadie. I appreciate that."

"Be at my office tomorrow morning. We have a few clients who failed to appear last Friday. I probably won't be in for a week. But see Rena. She'll have the details."

"I'll do that. You get better."

Then I called my friend Chad. His boyfriend, Mace, answered.

"How is he?" I asked, worried.

"Sleeping. I was so afraid I'd lost him, Jinx."

"Yeah, I hear you. But he's going to be okay?"

"So the doctor says. Would love to see you. We're at Banner UMC on McDowell. They're going to move him from the ICU to a regular room soon. I can text you when I know."

"It might be closer to tonight before I can be there. Something I have to take care of this morning."

"Catching bad guys?"

"Something like that. Give Chad my love when he wakes. I'll be there when I can."

"Thanks, sweetie."

I called my friend Rosalyn, but she didn't answer. I left her a message, letting her know I was thinking of her. She and I weren't exceptionally close, but as a fellow trans woman, she was still family.

I still hadn't heard back from Izzie. I didn't want to imagine what she was going through right now, grieving her wife Chelsea's murder. Even after a few years, the trauma of believing Conor was dead was still fresh in my mind. The dark emotions flooded into me again, settling into my body like a poison.

"Chad and Sadie doing okay?" Conor asked.

"Seem to be. Rosalyn didn't answer. I should have stopped Ripley sooner."

"Stop battering yourself over this. Ya couldn't have done any more than ya did."

"I know you're right. But I can't help feeling the disappointment and the guilt."

"I tortured myself for years over Bernie's death. All the fecking what-ifs. If I'd not let my da get me involved with the IRA. If I hadn't made that phone call with the bad intel.

But all the wishing in the world won't bring my sister back. Even hating my da for his part in things didn't help. Eventually, I realized all that hate and guilt were bollocks, a bloody cancer eating away at my soul. Had to let it go, or I'd drive myself mad."

"You ever visit him in prison?"

"Who? My da? Couldn't or the police woulda locked me up, too, then. My ma did for a while. But she stopped. Every time she walked into that prison, she pictured Bernie's broken body. It did her in."

"Yeah, I can appreciate that. Think you'd visit him the next time we visit your mom in Dublin?"

"Can't say I haven't thought about it. He was a good father up till that point. Ya woulda liked him. And he woulda loved you too. Still, I don't know. We'll see. Forgiving him is one thing. Not sure I'm ready to see him again. Don't even know what I'd say, to be honest. Not sure I want to hear what he'd have to say, either."

"I get that." I clasped his hand and stared out at the vast scrub desert before us.

CHAPTER 41
DOWN SOUTH

SINCE WE HADN'T EATEN any breakfast, we grabbed a few burritos at a drive-thru taco stand in Tucson. It was nearly noon by the time we reached Rio Rico.

The area was much greener than I thought it'd be. Lots of trees. Mostly ironwood, cottonwood, and mesquite, but it still felt like an oasis compared with the vast stretches of desert we'd driven through, where there was nothing but rock, sand, cactus, and scrub.

Clínica Comunitaria Rio Rico was in a strip mall on the frontage road west of I-19. The parking lot was near full. Popular place.

We cruised through the lot and spotted Stromberg's car, a black Lexus sedan.

"Well, he's still here," I said, as much to myself as to Conor.

"Aye, now what's the plan?"

"I want to go in there and wring his neck. Get him to confess and tell me who Portman is. Becca said Portman is supposed to pick up the kidneys and liver at two. The clinic closes at one. So when the last patient leaves, we move in."

"Ya think he'd do it here? Do they have the facilities for such a thing? It's just a community clinic."

"The nearest hospital is Nogales, about fifteen minutes south of here. But he couldn't harvest multiple organs from a living donor at a hospital."

"Unless he made it look like the donor was already dying from natural causes," Conor suggested.

That sent a chill right through me. "Possible, I suppose." I considered our options. "Once Caden gets here, we move in."

We waited for the better part of an hour. The parking lot emptied as patients and their loved ones left.

At a quarter to one, Conor started fidgeting. He wasn't usually the restless type, even when crazy shit was about to go down.

"You okay?" I asked.

"Don't think that burrito I had's agreeing with me. My belly feels like it's gonna explode out my arse."

"Caden should be here any minute now. The clinic closes in about fifteen minutes. Run over to the QT and use their restroom."

He checked his watch. "All right. Be right back, love."

"Feel better." I kissed him, and he raced across the parking lot to the convenience store like a man on a mission. Nothing more miserable than diarrhea on a stakeout.

No sooner had Conor dashed into the store than I spotted Stromberg walking out of the clinic with two women, one white and wearing lavender scrubs, the other Latinx and dressed in normal street clothes.

They approached Stromberg's Lexus. The woman in street clothes, who I figured for a patient, seemed unsteady on her feet. The nurse helped her as they climbed into the vehicle. I did not know where they were headed, but I had a pretty good idea what would happen if no one intervened.

I considered trying to block them in, but it would be hard to do with no backup. Caden still hadn't arrived.

I glanced toward the convenience store but saw no sign of Conor. "Come on, come on, come on."

When the Lexus hummed to life, I realized I had no choice. I hated to leave Conor behind, but I couldn't afford to lose Stromberg and allow his patient to die.

I followed the Lexus out of the parking lot, keeping a hundred feet back so as not to tip them off. The timing was good because we passed a church just as services were letting out. I allowed a couple of cars to get between us.

Stromberg turned south onto the interstate, then left onto Ruby Road and left again onto the Frontage Road heading north. He passed several industrial buildings before finally pulling up to a gate at a fenced lot surrounding a plain aluminum-sided building. A sign read Nogales Medical Supplies. The gate opened electronically.

I continued on the frontage road, watching the Lexus drive toward the building. The gate closed automatically.

After parking at a nearby industrial office park, I grabbed a pair of wire cutters from the back of the Green Dragon and ran back toward the fence encircling the medical supply warehouse.

As I cut through the fence, I saw Stromberg park next to a dark sedan in front of the building. He and the nurse dragged the Latina woman out of the Lexus.

"No, I changed my mind," the woman yelled frantically in Spanish. She tried to pull away from her captors. "Please, I don't want to do it. Just take me back." Then her body sagged as if she'd been drugged.

Stromberg opened the door of the building and, with the nurse's help, forced the frightened woman inside.

I needed to let Conor know where I was, but there wasn't time. I had to get in there and stop this before that poor woman got chopped up into so many spare parts.

Once I'd cut a big enough hole in the fence, I tossed aside the wire cutters and raced to the door. I found it unlocked and was relieved I didn't have to waste another few minutes trying to pick it. I drew my Ruger and slipped inside.

I expected the cavernous interior of a warehouse, but it more closely resembled a small hospital, right down to the chilly temperature and the smell of antiseptic. The overhead lighting was off, reminding me of those horror movies set in hospital wings that were under construction. All that was missing was a creepy soundtrack.

I moved cautiously past an empty reception area and began clearing a series of examination rooms.

Come out, come out, wherever you are, I thought as I checked one room after another.

The sixth room along the corridor was a surgical suite. But it, too, was dark and empty.

The muffled sound of voices caught my attention. I followed the voices to a corner on the far side of the building. When I rounded the corner, light glowed through the windows of a pair of double doors. My pulse quickened. *Gotcha!*

I was fifty feet from the doors when I felt a sharp sting in my neck. Without warning, a wave of drowsiness hit me like a tsunami. The world melted into oblivion.

CHAPTER 42
TABLE TALK

I CAME to with a scorcher of a headache. I tried to rub my temple only to find my hand wouldn't reach. When I dared open my eyes, the glare of overhead lights intensified my pain. I was in a surgical suite. Shit! And I was naked. Double shit!

My wrists were handcuffed to the rails on either side of the metal table I was on.

"Fuck, fuck, fuck, no!" Panic enveloped me, even as my head swam from whatever drug they'd dosed me with. I yanked uselessly at the cuffs. They didn't give. I tried to slip them, but they were already biting into my wrists. Next to me was a smaller table covered with a cloth. I tried not to imagine the scalpels and other surgical instruments that lay underneath.

Distorted voices drifted in from nearby. Stromberg and another man. I strained to hear what they were saying, but the sound was too muffled. Arguing. I could tell they were arguing.

I took a deep breath and tried to focus. I had to get out of here and save that woman. The handcuff key dangled like a charm from my bracelet. But with each hand cuffed to opposite sides of the table, freeing myself would take the skills of Harry Houdini.

"It breaks my heart that your mother will be losing her only daughter." Stromberg appeared in the doorway, now wearing a surgical gown, gloves, and a cap, as if prepped to operate. He held up his hands, wary not to touch anything and contaminate his gloves. "But you shouldn't have interfered, my dear."

"You're a fucking murderer," I growled. "How can you live with yourself? You took a fucking oath!"

"Honestly, it comes down to numbers. Sacrificing the insignificant to save those who can do much good in the world. You, for instance, will save multiple lives. You have O negative blood. The universal donor. We're still cross-matching your tissue type, but I imagine you'll help several needy people. Those are numbers I can live with. The one for good of the many."

"Monster! Goddamn motherfucking monster!"

"Hardly. Consider Miss Velasquez in the other room. As an illegal immigrant, what kind of future would she have? Probably marry some gangbanger or at best, a migrant farm worker, squeeze out half a dozen kids or more, and end up a drain on society."

"You racist piece of shit!"

"But as an organ donor, her contribution to the world is magnified many times over. Her heart will go to the daughter of a U.S. senator in Wyoming. Her liver to a real estate developer in Chicago. He's really been doing great things in some of the poorer neighborhoods despite his illness. I'm sure he'll do many more once he's feeling better. Her kidneys? One to a police officer in Tempe who was recently shot during a traffic stop. Another to the son of the U.S. ambassador to a country in central Asia. One of the 'Stans, I believe—Uzbekistan or Turkmenistan. Her sacrifice truly is for the greater good."

"That is not for you to decide! She has a right to live, and you have no right to take it."

"And yet this is going to happen. Might as well make your peace with it."

"You won't get away with this. People know I'm here. My husband. The feds. They'll be busting in here any minute to arrest you. But you kill me or the other woman and they'll fucking blow your head off."

A figure appeared in the hallway behind Stromberg. I caught a glimpse of a bald head. Special Agent Gleeson stepped into the room. "The feds are already here."

I'd never been so relieved to hear that dickhead's Mainer accent.

"Thank God! Get me loose. Stromberg's about to murder me and another woman."

But Gleeson didn't move. And Stromberg didn't look worried. What the fuck?

"Aren't ya cunning to track us all the way down here near the border?" Gleeson asked. "Very clever. And if you'll forgive my forwardness, I gotta say there, Ballou, looking wicked hot in ya birthday suit. Made me a believer that trans women are indeed women. All the right parts in all the right places."

"Uncuff me, Gleeson. Now!"

"I tried to warn ya off, but ya just wouldn't listen. Had to go and be a vigilante. Bureau hates vigilantes."

And then I made the connection—Gleeson was Portman. "You sick fuck! Anybody ever tell you that you look like a walking penis?"

"Don't be rude, Ms. Ballou. Let's keep this civilized."

"Civilized? You people are fucking murderers."

"Collateral damage for the greater good," Stromberg said.

"You will not get away with this. People know I'm here," I repeated.

"Ya such a terrible liar, Ballou," Gleeson replied. "No one knows ya here. You drove up alone. Saw ya on the security feed. As for my career, hasn't hurt me so far." He winked at me. "Helps when I can steer the investigations any way I want."

"So you and Special Agent Velasco were in on it?"

"Velasco? Hah! That bitch hadn't a clue. So sure she'd bring down the Red Market. And here I was, operating right under her nose."

"You people are fucking insane."

"Yeah, but we make a lot of money and do a lot of good," Gleeson said, sneering. "Now shut the fuck up, or I'll make your last few hours so miserable you'll beg us to kill you. Doc's got work to do, and he doesn't need ya making a lotta racket."

They both disappeared back out the double doors, leaving me alone. I wanted to scream. I wanted to hulk out. I wanted to be anywhere but where I was.

Why the fuck hadn't I called Conor when I had the chance? Even if Caden arrived to pick him up, he'd have no idea where the hell I was.

I took a steadying breath. "Work the solution. Don't panic about the problem."

I remembered the key on my bracelet. Again, trying to get it into the cuff's keyhole felt impossible. I twisted and squeezed. It'd come so close, but it wouldn't go in or would slip out of my numbing fingers. Felt as if the universe was conspiring against me.

Just as I was ready to give up hope, the key slid in. I twisted it. The cuffs dug deeper into my wrist and pressed hard enough to fracture bone. "Fuck, this is never gonna work."

And then, with a quick ratcheting sound, the cuff opened. In a euphoric rush of adrenaline, I unlocked the cuff securing my other wrist. In a heartbeat, I was free and off the table.

My clothes lay in a heap in the corner. I searched frantically for my weapons, but they were gone. Taken by Gleeson, no doubt. Shit, shit, shit!

I pulled on my shirt, body armor, and jeans, then tore off the cloth covering the medical instruments. There I found a couple of scalpels. They would have to do. What was that saying about bringing a knife to a gunfight?

As I padded into the corridor, Gleeson emerged from a second surgical suite about thirty feet away.

"Stupid bitch. I warned ya." He raised a pistol and fired two shots. They hit me in the chest like a pickaxe. I fell, cracking the back of my skull on the linoleum.

I pressed a hand to my chest and laughed despite the pain when I felt two hot lumps embedded in the Kevlar padding of my body armor. I was alive!

Raised voices echoed in the corridor caught my attention, followed by more gunshots.

"Shoot my wife, will ya? Fecking bastard!"

Conor! Thank God!

I managed to sit up, and the world turned into a Tilt-a-Whirl. That burrito I'd had for lunch threatened to come up.

Conor and Caden appeared beside me.

"Ya okay, love?" Conor asked.

"Just peachy. We gotta save the woman." I struggled to focus on the task at hand.

Caden raised an eyebrow. "What woman?"

"In there!" I pointed toward the other surgical suite. "Help me up."

They lifted me to my feet. I snatched up the scalpel I'd dropped, and we rushed past Gleeson's bleeding body into the other surgical suite.

A masked Stromberg stood over Ms. Velasquez, who lay unconscious on the operating table. He'd made an incision in her abdomen, but the bleeding currently appeared minimal. The nurse stood nearby watching a vitals monitor. Velasquez was still alive.

Conor and Caden trained their pistols on Stromberg and the nurse.

"Get away from her, you monsters," I growled, holding the scalpel out like a switchblade. A wave of dizziness and nausea hit me. I steadied myself by leaning against the double-doors.

"You people are contaminating a sterile environment," Stromberg whined, his voice muffled by his surgical mask.

"Back away, mate, or I'll swear to bloody Christ you're gonna be the one needing a surgeon."

"Or a coroner," Caden added.

The door I was leaning against gave way, replaced by the cold, hard steel of a gun barrel pressed against the back of my head.

"Drop your weapons or I blow the bitch's head off."

Gleeson. Fuck! Must've been playing possum.

I pivoted out of the line of fire and slashed at my attacker's neck with the scalpel. A fountain of scarlet blinded me. Gunshots thundered in the room.

My ears were ringing, further disorienting me. I clung to something mounted on the wall to keep myself upright. When my head cleared, I saw Gleeson on the floor with a look of horror on his face. Blood sprayed from the gash in his neck.

"Now who's the bitch?"

Stromberg shouted from inside the surgical suite. His frantic voice sounded as if we were all underwater. I found Stromberg kneeling over his nurse, who lay on the floor bleeding from a gunshot wound to the chest. Gleeson must have hit her by mistake.

I focused on the woman on the operating table and

pressed a wad of gauze against the incision in her abdomen. "Somebody call 911."

Conor put a hand on my shoulder and said something, but the ringing in my ears made it impossible to make out.

"What?"

He repeated his words and pointed at me, then gave me an "okay" gesture with a questioning look on his face.

"Can't hear. Ears ringing. A little woozy but okay otherwise." I wanted to know how he found me. That would have to wait.

Caden kept his weapon trained on Stromberg whiled talking on the phone, presumably calling 911.

We'd done it. I'd brought Krueger's killer to justice. Better still, we didn't have to worry about him escaping justice. He may have survived getting shot by Conor, but I'd sliced open his carotid, ending his career as a serial killer.

On top of that, we stopped Stromberg from killing another innocent victim. Maybe, just maybe, Velasco could get him to flip and take down the Red Market once and for all.

CHAPTER 43

TRICK OR TREAT

DEPUTIES FROM SANTA CRUZ COUNTY SHERIFF'S DEPARTMENT showed up at the scene within minutes and arrested Stromberg. Ms. Velasquez and the nurse were carted off to Holy Cross Hospital in Nogales. Gleeson was presumably carried off in a body bag, though I was sitting in the back of a squad car at the time.

I immediately put in a call to Kirsten, who reached out to Deborah Walker, a colleague of hers in Tucson.

By the time Walker showed up at the sheriff's substation an hour and a half later, the dizziness and nausea had passed. I hoped that meant I didn't have a concussion.

I filled Walker in on the situation, and with her at my side, explained to a Detective Juan Molina that we had tracked Stromberg to Rio Rico and confirmed our suspicions that he was part of the black market organ trafficking ring. We also confirmed that Agent Gleeson was part of the conspiracy and responsible for the deaths of three doctors. Finally, I had to explain that Gleeson's death was an act of self-defense.

After that, I was left alone in the room for hours while Walker left to act as counsel for Conor and Caden during their interrogation.

By the time the door opened again, I'd fallen asleep.

"Good news," Walker said with a gleam in her eye. "Stromberg confessed. You're in the clear."

I thanked her and she gave us a ride back to our vehicles.

"How'd you find me?" I asked Conor on the drive home.

"A little app called FamFinder."

"Shit, of course." It hadn't occurred to me, but then I'd been focused on tailing Stromberg, at the time. "I love being married to a brilliant man."

"Aye. Just lucky Caden arrived when he did after I came outside and found ya gone."

"Good timing on his part," I said. "How's your digestive system?"

"Better. A little bit of Pepto fixed me up right as rain."

We were halfway home when Special Agent Velasco called. She was not pleased to learn her own partner had been sandbagging the organ-trafficking investigation the whole time, but the evidence was overwhelming. And Stromberg's confession had put it over the top. She insisted I stop by the headquarters in Phoenix to give a statement on Monday. I told her I'd think about it.

Did she thank me for breaking the case? She did not. That was gratitude for you.

Amy Krueger, on the other hand, did thank me when I called her.

She was horrified to learn how she acquired the kidney. Her father had told her it was legit. But deep down, I had a feeling she had known.

"The donor," she said. "You think they're alive?"

"You'd have to ask Stromberg," I told her.

"Thank you for proving that my father didn't kill himself."

When Conor and I returned to the Valley, we stopped by the hospital where Rodeo was recovering. My whole family was there. Jake informed us that Rodeo was showing positive signs and would most likely be off the ventilator in the next day or so.

I finally got ahold of my friend and mentor, Juanita Valdez, who gave me the skinny on Rosalyn Jefferson. She was recovering, but in police custody. The cops had the nerve to charge her with criminal gang activity as well. They had handcuffed her to her hospital bed and had posted a guard outside her room.

I was tempted to sneak in and rescue her. But she needed the medical care as she recovered from her gunshot wound.

The next morning, I was at Assurity Bail Bonds and met with Rena Hoffman, one of Sadie Levinson's bail bond agents. She gave me the files for the new jobs.

"How's Sadie doing?" I asked.

"Sore, bitchy, but otherwise fine," she said, smirking.

"Sounds like our Sadie."

On the drive over to the Hub, I stopped at Tres Leches and picked up a jumbo pumpkin spice latte for Becca and a regular latte for myself.

Becca looked so excited, I thought she would explode. "Can you believe it?"

"What? What'd I miss?"

"A judge is enforcing an injunction against the law banning gender-affirming care. He ordered DCS to cease all investigations into trans families."

"Oh, thank goodness. Rayna and Leia will be so relieved they can finally go home. Now if the Maricopa County Attorney's Office will drop this bullshit about Phoenix Gender Alliance being a criminal gang..."

"Funny you should mention that. I was doing a little digging. It seems our esteemed county attorney, Kellie Turnbull, has some strong financial ties to the Patriots of Liberty Caucus. In fact, she was a paid speaker at one of their recent rallies."

"No shit."

"But also, she recently took a trip to Costa Rica, via Cryptravel."

I didn't follow. "What does that have to do with anything?"

"I checked her crypto wallet and discovered her sister was the recipient of a pancreas transplant about a year and a half ago. Kellie paid a Dr. Thomas Remmert to jump the waiting list and get the much-needed gland."

"Now, that is interesting. I'm sure *Phoenix Living* would have a field day with that information."

Becca beamed. "You are correct. I had a lovely chat with one of *Phoenix Living*'s editors. They're running the story in this Thursday's edition. Along with one about Josiah Faulkner."

"Why Faulkner?"

"Seems the holier-than-thou director of the Patriots of Liberty Caucus has been arrested for online solicitation of a minor."

"Fuck yeah. Funny how they call us groomers and perverts, but they're the ones always getting busted for shit like this."

"The irony is almost as delicious as my pumpkin spice latte."

My mother had been pissed over the news about Stromberg's criminal activities, but was glad that I had saved Ms. Velasquez's life. She wanted to wring the good doctor's neck. I hadn't seen her so angry since my father was shot. Hell hath no fury like an Italian mother scorned.

I wondered what would happen to Ms. Velasquez. Would she be deported after all this? I hoped not. At least she was alive.

Much of Monday afternoon was spent researching my newly assigned fugitives.

Zahara wouldn't be back from Colorado until the following day. Rodeo was in the hospital. And I still wasn't my usual self, still recovering from the last of the effects of the tear gas, the damage to my eardrum, and whacking the back of my skull on the hard floor of that fake hospital. I wasn't going to send Caden after our fugitives alone. We'd take a run at them on Tuesday.

Being so short-staffed all of a sudden made me give more thought about joining my company with Conor's. It would certainly help to be able to shift personnel around as needed.

I was about to call it a day when I got an urgent call from Rayna.

"Jinx, please! We need you! He's trying to break in!"

"Who?"

"Mike!"

Shit! "Call the police. I'll be right there."

"Hurry!"

By the time I arrived on the scene dressed in my full gear, police had half the street barricaded off. I spoke with the patrolman guarding the perimeter, a guy whose nameplate read King.

"Officer King, who's in charge of the scene?"

"Who are you?" He looked down at the words printed on my body armor. "Bail Enforcement? That some new division?"

"Jinx Ballou. I used to be Phoenix PD. Now I pursue fugitives. More importantly, I'm a friend of the residents. I think I can help."

"Look, lady, all due respect, but we don't need help from Bail Enforcement."

"All I'm asking is who's in charge here?"

"Sergeant Ortega at the moment."

"Luis Ortega?"

"Yeah."

"How's Lily and the kids doing these days?" I didn't really care. Just needed to establish that I knew the man.

"Hold on." Officer King got on the radio and called for the sergeant.

Moments later, Ortega appeared. "Jinx Ballou," he said when he saw me. "Still chasing bail jumpers, I see. What do you want? I'm kinda busy with a hostage situation."

"I'm here to help. I'm good friends with the residents, Rayna and Leia Ripley. And I know the hostage taker, Mike Ripley. I think I can help."

Judging from his expression, wheels turned in his head. "Right. The whole transgender thing. Suspect's been ranting about how his wife brainwashed their kid into thinking they're trans."

"I've talked to him before. I might be able to get him to surrender."

"You have any experience with hostage negotiation?"

"A few times when I was a cop." A blatant lie. "And I frequently get fugitives to surrender as well." Sort of true.

"I'm sorry, Ballou. I can't send a civilian into something like this."

"Look, just give me a chance. Those are my friends in there."

A uni approached Ortega. "Sergeant, hostage negotiator's stuck in traffic on the 17."

"Shit. Okay, thank you."

"Come on, Ortega. let me try to talk him down. Or at least keep him from hurting any of the hostages until the negotiator arrives."

"No way. You're a civilian. Anything went wrong, it's my ass. We've got this under control."

I knew from his expression there'd be no convincing him. I walked away. But I didn't leave or huddle with the rest of the lookie-loos.

Instead, I walked around to the next street over and

approached the house from the rear. I spotted a couple of unis who were watching the back door. Shit!

Well, when all else fails, improvise. Act like you belong.

I approached one of the uniformed officers. "Ortega instructed me to make entry through the back," I told him. "You two cover me."

"What?" One of the unis looked at me, confused. "I'll need to confirm."

When he reached for his radio, I put my hand on it and shook my head. "Don't. Radio silence. Suspects got the channel monitored. Ortega says sit tight while I go in."

He didn't look convinced.

I lifted my own radio. It wasn't police band, but it looked enough like the real thing to be convincing. "I'll call if I need backup. Just cover my six, okay?"

He nodded, and I hustled to the rear sliding glass door, drawing my semi-auto as I ran. My luck held. The door was unlocked. Slowly, I opened it, slipped inside, and followed the sound of sobbing.

When I reached the living room, Rayna lay unconscious on the floor, bruises already forming on her face. She was still breathing, which was a good thing. Leia knelt over her body, crying.

Mike Ripley stood at the window a few feet away, peaking through the horizontal blinds at the cops gathered out front. How the hell was he out of jail? Had someone posted his bail?

I aimed my pistol at him. "Hi, Mike. Remember me?"

He spun around and aimed a Colt 1911 in my direction. Its .45 caliber barrel looked huge when I stared down it.

"Jinx!" cried Leia with a mixture of fear and hope.

"How the fuck'd you get in here?" Mike growled. "You ain't no cop."

He had another day's growth of beard, wearing the same clothes I'd seen him in at the protest. His eyes were puffy and red-rimmed, like he hadn't had any sleep in days. His body language screamed rage and desperation.

"I might ask you the same question. This is not your home, and I doubt you were invited."

He yanked Leia up by the back of her collar and held her in front of him like a shield, pressing the muzzle of the .45 to her temple. I couldn't get a clean shot, and even if I could, he could pull the trigger. I couldn't take the chance.

"I'll fucking blow his queer brains out if you don't get the fuck outta here."

"Now, Mike. I know you're pissed about a lot of changes going on. But you need to take a breath. Hurting your child isn't going to help you."

"Shut the fuck up, you faggot freak!"

"Sounds like you want to spend some time with your kid. Without your wife meddling. Am I right?"

"What would you know about it?"

"Hey, I get it. The bond between a father and his child is sacred. Can't go fucking that up."

His expression softened just a bit. His free arm wrapped around her throat. Not a chokehold. More like he was trying to desperately hold onto her.

I continued. "What is Luke supposed to think of his dad holding a gun to his head?"

It killed me to misgender and deadname Leia like this, but I was trying to save her life.

"He needs to be able to trust you. To see you as the hero. Not some psycho with a gun. Put down the pistol, and let's talk this out. Show Luke what it means to be a real man. Real men don't shoot their kids."

He lowered the gun so that it was no longer pointed at her head, but he didn't drop it. "Kid needs discipline. No more of this woke, groomer, liberal elitist queer shit."

"I agree. You wouldn't want Leia to bite the hand that

feeds her." I stressed the words *Leia* and *bite*, hoping she'd get the message. She did.

Leia bit her father's arm with the ferocity of a starving bulldog. When Mike howled in pain, she dropped from his grip. When he raised his weapon again to shoot her, I put three rounds into his chest.

I spent a few hours being interviewed by the police, with Kirsten Pasternak by my side. Not only did they decline to charge me for killing Mike Ripley, but Kirsten had convinced the police and county attorney to drop all charges against all the members of Phoenix Gender Alliance, including me. It may have helped that one of *Phoenix Living*'s reporters called the Maricopa County Attorney's Office with questions about the Red Market and affiliations with Patriots of Liberty.

When I was released, I spoke with Rayna over the phone. She was in the hospital, recovering from a concussion, courtesy of her ex. Leia would stay with Bobby J. until Rayna was released.

Leia was more than a little traumatized by the events of the past week. I would have been too. I hated killing her father like that, but better that than the alternative. I suggested to Rayna that she set up a therapy appointment with my father when she got home from the hospital. She agreed to look into it.

Shortly after sundown, Gwyneth joined Conor and me at our house, where we passed out Kinder Bueno bars to the trick-or-treaters. I was dressed as Captain Marvel. Conor was a very sexy pirate, even with an eyepatch covering one of his emerald eyes. Gwyneth was adorable as Mulan. And Diana the Wonder Dog delighted everyone as her usual self. I wasn't one to put my dog in a costume. Sorry.

My neighbor, Adelina, showed up around eight with a plate full of rainbow-colored Rice Krispies Treats.

"I never got to show my appreciation for you saving Teddy last week."

"Thank you! He hasn't gotten out again, has he?"

"No, I don't think he'll be doing that again soon."

"Good to hear it. Have a Bueno bar."

"Gracias. Trick or treat! Have a good night. Don't let the ghosts get you."

"Trick or treat."

AUTHOR'S NOTE

EVERY BOOK I write presents new challenges. New ways to tell stories. New topics to research. But one of the things that made this story particularly challenging was how personal it was to me.

When I first started writing the Jinx Ballou books, I wanted to write stories with a trans protagonist, but which did not dwell on transgender topics like transitioning and coming out.

But over the past year or so, the transgender community has faced unprecedented levels of attacks from the radical right. Laws not only prohibiting trans athletes from competing or banning trans students from using restrooms based on their gender identity, but laws criminalizing gender-affirming care.

Families with trans kids have been terrorized by the very government that's supposed to protect them. That's fucked up. How evil do you have to be to want to hurt innocent kids? To rip them away from their families, arrest their supportive parents, and deny them life-affirming medical treatment?

As a transgender author, and one of the few in the crime fiction genre, my goal was to put a human face to these stories. I don't know how well I accomplished that, but I tried my best.

Recently, the Texas Attorney General's office reached out to the Texas Department of Motor Vehicles division in order to get a list of all people who had changed their gender markers over the past two years. Not just kids. Adults as well.

This is chilling and terrifying, even to those of us who don't live in Texas.

Meanwhile, the Supreme Court of the United States has hinted at trying to revoke the Obergefell decision that granted same-sex couples the right to marry.

All while the violence against us continues to escalate.

I transitioned more than thirty years ago in a small town in Georgia. I remember how bad it was then. And in a lot of ways, things are better than they were. In other ways, they are getting worse.

So this is why I am telling this story.

Red Market is also personal in another way. Back in 1999, I became the first person living in Arizona to donate a kidney to a stranger.

I don't think of myself as a hero. I don't feel like a hero. I'm just someone who was able and willing to help. And the world needs more of that. People helping people just because they can, just because there is a need.

But I've learned there is a dark side to the whole organ transplant/donation world. The confidentiality that protects medical patients can be used to hide illegal organ harvesting. While some lives are being saved, many vulnerable people are being harmed.

I don't know what the solution is to the shortage of human organs. I've spent a lot of time with people in desperate need of organs. It is heartbreaking. I wish more people would be willing to donate, either after they die, or even while they are alive, like me.

Promises of medical science being able to grow organs in a lab sound hopeful, but are always ten, twenty years away.

Okay, enough preaching. I'll step down from my soapbox.

If you enjoyed this book, I really hope you will leave an honest review wherever you bought it. Honest reviews help readers like you find books they enjoy. And they help authors like me continue to tell stories that need to be told.

Also consider becoming an organ donor. Be that person who helps because you can, because there is a need. Together, we can build a more compassionate world.

Lastly, when you hear someone spreading transphobic lies, please speak out. Trans people like me are just trying to live our lives. We aren't trying to convert anyone. And who knows? Some of us could turn out to be heroes.

Peace and love,

Dharma Kelleher

ABOUT THE AUTHOR

Dharma Kelleher writes gritty crime thrillers including the Jinx Ballou Bounty Hunter series and the Shea Stevens Outlaw Biker series.

She is one of the only openly transgender authors in the crime fiction genre. Her action-driven thrillers explore the complexities of social and criminal justice in a world where the legal system favors the privileged.

Dharma is a member of Sisters in Crime, the International Thriller Writers, and the Alliance of Independent Authors.

She lives in Arizona with her wife and a black cat named Mouse. Learn more about Dharma and her work at https:// dharmakelleher.com.

ACKNOWLEDGMENTS

Even in the world of self-publishing, bringing forth a new book into the world is always a team effort.

Let me start by thanking every member of the transgender community. It is not easy for us to live as our true selves. It takes courage, persistence, and deep level of self-trust. But it also takes the generosity of community to reach out and lift each other up. We are stronger together.

For their brilliant editing skills, I want to thank my editors at Red Adept Editing.

For their assistance with research, I want to thank Mary Roach (*Stiff: The Curious Lives of Human Cadavers*), Annie Cheney (*Body Brokers: Inside America's Underground Trade in Human Remains*), Nick Bilton (*American Kingpin: The Epic Hunt for the Criminal Mastermind Behind the Silk Road*), and Scott Carney (*The Red Market: On the Trail of the World's Organ Brokers, Bone Thieves, Blood Farmers, and Child Traffickers*).

Last, but certainly not least, I want to thank all my loyal fans, especially my newsletter subscribers. Enjoy!